GUNS WILL KEEP US TOGETHER

"Langtry's ability to make this lethal and outrageous clan both funny and somewhat endearing is a testament to her style. Who knew the assassination business could produce so many laughs?"

—*Romantic Times BOOKreviews*

"If you need a really good laugh, then get *Guns Will Keep Us Together*. The characters and plot emphasize a funny, even wacky view of life, and a guaranteed happily ever after."

—*Romance Reviews Today*

"This novel is uproariously funny and will have you chuckling until the last page is turned....*Guns Will Keep Us Together* proves to be a definite keeper novel as it one of the funniest romances I have read in a long, long time."

—*Romance Reader at Heart*

"Another wicked blend of action, romance, mystery, and dark humor, *Guns Will Keep Us Together* gives readers bullets, buff guys, and bad boys...I hope the Bombay family continues on with their deadly misadventures."

—*News and Sentinel*

'SCUSE ME WHILE I KILL THIS GUY

"With an irreverent, tell-it-like-it-is, suburban-mom-assassin narrator, Leslie Langtry's *'Scuse Me While I Kill This Guy* delivers wild and wicked fun."

—Julie Kenner, *USA Today* Bestselling Author of *California Demon*

"Darkly funny and wildly over the top, this mystery answers the burning question, 'Do assassin skills and Girl Scout merit badges mix?' One truly original and wacky novel!"

—*Romantic Times BOOKreviews*

"Those who like dark humor will enjoy a look into the deadliest female assassin and PTA mom's life."

—*Parkersburg News*

"The fast-paced romantic suspense chick lit thriller is over the top, but fans will want to follow suit as Leslie Langtry provides a satirical family drama."

—*Midwest Book Reviews*

"Mixing a deadly sense of humor and plenty of sexy sizzle, Leslie Langtry creates a brilliantly original, laughter-rich mix of contemporary romance and suspense in *'Scuse Me While I Kill This Guy.*"

—*Chicago Tribune*

THE HEAT OF THE MOMENT

Lex shook his head. "I don't have it all together like you. Maybe I never will. My biggest goal would probably be just to find happiness. That's all that really seems to matter."

Damn, he had me there. Wasn't that what everyone wanted in life? Sure, some people wanted fame and fortune. But this gorgeous hunk of man just wanted to be happy. How cool was that?

"There is one thing we both seem to be good at." He grinned and leaned toward me.

My lips met his and oooh la la! As Lex's arms slid around me I chastised myself for going all these years without a man. My hands were just sliding up his muscular arms when we heard shouting down the beach.

I wanted to ignore it until I recognized the word, "help" being screamed over and over. Lex and I jumped up and ran down the beach toward camp…to find our shelter in flames.

Other *Making It* titles by Leslie Langtry:

GUNS WILL KEEP US TOGETHER
'SCUSE ME WHILE I KILL THIS GUY

Stand By Your Hitman

Leslie Langtry

NEW YORK CITY

A MAKING IT Book®

September 2008

Published by

Dorchester Publishing Co., Inc.
200 Madison Avenue
New York, NY 10016

ISBN 10: 0-8439-6037-X
ISBN 13: 978-0-8439-6037-2

The name "Making It" is a trademark of Dorchester Publishing Co., Inc.

Printed in the United States of America.

10 9 8 7 6 5 4 3 2 1

Visit us on the web at www.dorchesterpub.com.

This book is dedicated to the memory of Adrienne Alma Boquet Johnson—my grandmother—a talented and very creative woman who had big dreams for me.

I'd like to thank Leah Hultenschmidt and Kristin Nelson for making my life as an author possible. Thanks to Emily and Ava Cummings, Brit and Ali Reschke for helping with my writing time by keeping the kids occupied. To Dad, Uncle Mike, Uncle Steve, Uncle Tim & Aunt Anne for your support. To Bernie and Michelle for loaning me Conor this time for this book. And, as always, thanks to my family; Tom, Margaret and Jack.

A huge thanks to Todd and Lisa Welvaert for twenty years of laughter. Here's hoping for at least twenty more.

Stand By Your Hitman

Chapter One

REX KRAMER: *Do you know what it's like to fall in the mud and get kicked . . . in the head . . . with an iron boot? Of course you don't, no one does. It never happens. It's a dumb question . . . skip it.*

—Airplane!

I stared at the letter in my hand. I was making the same face I'd made a few moments earlier when checking my phone messages. It's not a pretty face. You wouldn't like it.

Dear Ms. Bombay,

Your application has been accepted. We are thrilled to have you as a contestant in the new television program, *Survival*! We received thousands of applications for the show, but quite frankly, your video blew everyone away here at CAB network. I don't think I've ever seen anyone defuse an explosive device so quickly. You are exactly what we are looking for. In a few days, you should receive a complete package in the mail with all of the information you will need. I look forward to meeting you next month.

Sincerely,

Bob Toole

Executive Producer, CAB

1

Well, that wasn't right. I'd never applied to be on *Survivor*. True, it was one of my favorite shows. But I think I'd remember submitting an application. It's not like I go around videotaping myself defusing bombs every day. Okay, there was that once, but I just wanted to see what it looked like in the third person. It was my little egoist guilty pleasure. No one knew I had it. Or at least, I thought no one knew.

So, maybe that's what Bob is talking about. Hmmmm. If I didn't send it in, who did?

"Mom!" The unanimous shout came in unison from my two teenaged sons, Montgomery and Jackson Bombay. My name is Mississippi Bombay, but I prefer Missi.

"In here," I responded suspiciously. Did they do this?

Monty and Jack popped their heads through the doorway simultaneously. Fraternal twins, you'd never look at them and even think they were related. Monty was tall and gangly, with dark hair and green eyes. Jack was short and stocky with a shock of unruly red hair and freckles. In spite of their physical differences, the boys shared one obnoxious personality.

"Do I need to ask?" I waved the letter at them.

Monty snatched it out of my hands and began to read. "Cool! Mom, this rocks!"

Jack grabbed it from his brother and scanned the page. "Ohmygod!" He shouted it as one word. "How cool are you? Why didn't you tell us?"

From the looks on their faces, I surmised they didn't do it.

"So you had nothing to do with this?" I had to ask just to make sure. I haven't survived this long as a single mother of twin boys without confirming everything. Usually twice.

They shook their heads. "We would've if we thought you were interested—" Monty started.

"But we never dreamed you'd want to go on the show!" Jack finished.

I swiped the letter from Jack and put in on the table. "Well, it's obviously just a joke, so we'll forget about it." I now had other ideas. After all, I came from a family of assassins. A prankster or two in the gene pool was to be expected.

You heard me right. Assassins. The Bombay family has had a monopoly on the biz since ancient Greece. Every blooded member of the family begins training at the age of five and works until . . . well, forever. My grandma was just forced into an early retirement or she'd still be taking on contracts. Not that she needed to. She was on the Council. That's the geriatric crew who runs the operations, dishes out assignments, and kills off renegade family members. That's right. This family business isn't exactly optional. And if you screw up or screw over the family, the Council will take you out.

I broke free of my mental meanderings to find the boys gone. Oh well. Where could they go? We live on a small, private island off the coast of South America.

Speaking of mental fragmentation—I've been experiencing that a lot lately. Maybe it has something to do with being forty-five. Or it could be that I haven't had sex in a long, long time. Being widowed will do that to you. Well, that and the isolation of being on an island no one but my immediate family lives on. Or it could be the bizarre nature of my work. Besides killing people for a living, I'm a bit of an inventor. It's my only creative outlet. And it was one more service I could offer the Bombays.

What do I invent? Oh, this and that, really. Hairdryers that can blow your head off, lilies that can suffocate you, explosive jockstraps . . . the usual bric-a-brac, I guess. My mind began to meander again and I started thinking about Pop-Tarts. I LOVE Pop-Tarts. But only the chocolate-fudge ones. I could eat those for every meal.

The Pop-Tarts made me think of Kleenex, which reminded me that I still had a few finishing touches to make on my latest explosive device. I headed for the lab.

Mantisnuts was the secret word I spoke into my security system. The door popped open and I went in thinking it was time to change my password. Maybe something like *bananaface*. Did praying mantises have testicles? I wasn't sure. At least in the figurative sense they did. It takes balls to make love to a woman you know will bite your head off afterward.

On a table in the middle of the room was one of those Wacky WallWalkers. Remember those? Real big in the eighties. I had several back then. Anyway, for those of you who are big hair and shoulder pad challenged, they were these sticky little octopuses (octopi?—what is the plural anyway?) you threw at a wall or sliding glass door (sliding glass doors were also very big in the eighties) and it kind of flopped, ass over, um, tentacles all the way down the wall. You'd think something like that would be a failure, wouldn't you? But the inventors of that stupid little toy (did I mention that I owned several?) made millions. You never know what will hit it big.

It was with that in mind that I decided to work with the gummy little bastards as some sort of explosive device. Remember Tom Cruise as Ethan Hunt in *Mission: Impossible*? The first one—not the crappy sequels. Anyway, he had that stick of gum he just had to fold in half and stick on the aquarium at that restaurant in Prague, and it blew up? Of course, it was ridiculous. Have you ever tried to fold a stick of dry gum in half? It snaps in two, doesn't stick to itself—doesn't stick to anything really, so it wouldn't have worked in real life. But that's okay, cuz I liked the movie.

The trick with the Wacky WallWalkers was to get just the right compound that would ignite as it struck a solid surface and wouldn't affect its inherent gumminess. I didn't want to overdo it, but I wanted something that would do the job. I wasn't sure what the job was yet, but it didn't matter. I loved working in my lab. I could work with whatever I wanted and the family didn't give a damn. Ha.

An hour later found me behind my blast shield as I blew up my fifth piece of glass-coated drywall. I was having a pretty good time too. That is, until the alarm went off. I'd set it to high because I wanted to know if anyone came into my lab unannounced.

"Hello, Mississippi." York Bombay stood in the doorway. I couldn't stand that man. My mom's cousin York was a creepy old dude. Of course, his father, Lou, was much worse. Thank God he's still locked up with Grandma and the other former Council at that maximum-security nursing home in Greenland. I folded my arms across my chest and made up my mind to definitely change my password. How the hell did he get it, anyway?

"What's up, Uncle York?"

He forced a grin and reached over to fondle Charo from my B-list bobblehead collection. I made a mental note to scrub them with Clorox later.

"Well, my dear, the Council requests your presence. Tonight at seven."

Chapter Two

Canada is like living in the upstairs apartment over a really cool party you weren't invited to.
— Jon Stewart, *The Daily Show*

I dug my nails into my arms to keep from reaching for the remote control on my top shelf that could electrocute him. Then I tried not to smile thinking about that.

You see, York's been pissed off at me since I had to deal with his favorite nephew, Richie, one year ago. That's when I minorly electrocuted the old Council too. I'd secretly installed a mechanism in all five members' elbows under the pretense of getting their biometric info. It was kind of a backup plan, but it came in handy when the Council kidnapped my favorite cousin, Gin's daughter, and my generation was locked into a sort of Mexican standoff with the old guys. My little invention took them out and they still don't know why. In fact, the new Council didn't even raise their eyebrows when I injected them with the same device. Of course, they thought I was just giving them malaria shots (never use the same lie twice—it always backfires). I'd say what they don't know won't hurt them, but in this case it actually will.

"Fine. I'll be there." I said stiffly. I watched him walk

out of my lab and did that little full-body shake you do when you walk into a spider web. Then I changed my password to *deaduncleyork*.

"What do you mean, you got me on *Survivor*?" I was in shock from what the Council had just told me.

"I called an old friend of mine," my mother explained. "You were a shoo-in." She smiled like she'd just told me I looked nice in this shirt—which is usually followed up with "why can't you find a man/ woman/dog?" That's right, my mother would rather see me as a lesbian instead of single. "And it's *Survival*, not *Survivor*, dear."

"What?" I asked.

Mom smiled at me now like I was about to get on a special bus to go to a special school. "It's a brand new Canadian show. But it's pretty much the same thing as *Survivor*."

I folded my arms over my chest. "You got me onto a cheap, Canadian knockoff of *Survivor*? Are you nuts?" It was an odd question, considering that most of the time people thought *I* was nuts.

Aunt Carolina nodded. "Of course we are. But it's a good assignment nonetheless."

Huh?

Mom added, "I think it will be good for you. You should get out more, meet people. And you are a bit on the pale side dear. A little sun will make you look healthy."

I rolled my eyes and thought about the remote control in my workshop. No, I had to save that for when I really needed it. And in this family that usually meant when your relatives pointed guns at you.

"Is there really a job, or is this another one of your blind date schemes?" I asked. "Cuz I've got to admit, you really went above and beyond on this one."

Uncle Monty spoke up. "Yes, Mississippi. It really is a job. An important one too. You are the only one who can do it."

I crossed my arms. "Cut the flattery and tell me the truth."

The Council members all looked toward the media booth, where I noticed York was struggling with the A/V equipment. I hated when they tried to do stuff without me. Most of them were still afraid of computers.

"I got it!" York called out.

The big screen came down from the ceiling. Then it stopped midway and went back up again. I threw up my hands and went to the booth to straighten everything out. I have a knack for technology. It's one of the things I really like about myself. Well, that and the ability to hang four spoons off my face at one time. I worked my whole freshman year in college to be able to do that.

"You guys should spare me the drama and just let me do this." I muttered to myself as I pushed the right buttons to make the screen come down and the PowerPoint presentation run. I'm sure York heard me, but wisely chose not to respond.

I rejoined the Council, who acted like I didn't have to bail them out . . . again. On the screen was the photo of a man about my age. Reasonably attractive, with dark hair and a nice smile, this guy must be the Vic (the family's nickname for our victims), I thought.

"Isaac Beckett." Uncle Pete took over. I liked Uncle Pete. He had a neat, rumbly sort of voice that was warm and comfy.

"Our client believes Beckett is an arms dealer who knows the names of several undercover CIA agents and has threatened to reveal his list to some rather unfriendly nations. He went missing a month ago, and through some genius research on Burma's part"—he nodded to his cousin Burma (an Englishman)—"we found that he'd gotten onto this show."

"So why do I have to get on the show? Can't we just take him out before they ship these idiots to wherever?" I didn't want to go on *Survival*, dammit. I wanted to stay at home, making cult toys from the eighties explode.

Mom gave me that look again. "Because we still don't know where he is and won't until he ends up on-site."

"Okay," I shrugged. "I'll just go and take him out after the show wraps."

Monty shook his head. "For one month, he'll be inaccessible to us and have full access to a television crew. We can't risk the fact that he could leak information to millions of people. Information that should be buried with his dead body."

It's funny how my family talks. To someone not

familiar with the Bombays, our conversation might seem a tad threatening.

"And you want me to be a contestant on the show and take him out." I waited for them to nod like my bobblehead dolls. "Except that you forget, I'd have to kill him in front of millions of viewers, worldwide. How, exactly, do I do that?"

Burma's crisp accent cut in. "That is why you are the only one for this job, Missi. As an inventor, you will most likely be able to stay on the program while others are voted out. And you can figure out a unique way to kill him that will look like an accident. That is, *if* he is who we think he is."

"And it's not millions of viewers, dear," Mom said. "It's more like thousands, actually."

"Wait a minute." Sometimes my brain processes information at lightning speed. This, however, was not one of those moments. "What do you mean *if*?"

Mom sighed as if I were a complete idiot. "We already told you—our client isn't entirely sure Beckett is a bad guy."

That's weird. I've never heard of a Bombay assignment that wasn't pretty clear-cut. "So do I kill him, or not?"

Mom smiled. "We'll let you know. Basically you'll be on the show to keep an eye on him until we get more information."

It was hard to digest this information. I guess what they were saying made sense, but it still pissed me off. I like a good reality television show like anyone else.

And like anyone else, I'd rather watch it at home, sitting on my couch, sipping red wine with the air conditioner on.

"You have some time to prepare before you're needed in Toronto. I'll e-mail you the dossier on Beckett and everything I have on the show." Mom winked at me. It was as if she were a normal mother talking to her daughter. Not an assassin ordering her daughter to stalk and *maybe* kill a man.

Back in my lab, I continued to blow up panels of drywall, but my heart just wasn't into it. I quit early and made my way to my apartment in the main building on the island.

My workshop is sacred to me, a place of peace and quiet . . . well, except for the explosions and stuff. I have a lot of strange paraphernalia in there, but mainly that is for inspiration. From the stuffed black jaguar to my collection of *A-Team* DVDs to my "Hang In There" poster featuring an adorable kitten hanging from a tree—it all makes perfect sense.

My home, on the other hand, is different. Being strange is one thing. Letting that impact my kids is another. Me and the boys have a great condo on the island. And this may sound weird, but I've worked really hard to make our living space look totally normal. It was tough at first, since it was completely against my nature to have fine art, leather furniture and Tiffany lamps, but I managed. I used a lot of color on the walls to compensate.

I just didn't want the boys to grow up too weird.

They lost their dad before they were old enough to remember him and they lived on a remote island where they were trained since age five to be assassins. A little normalcy was required.

Monty and Jack were sitting on the couch playing video games as I came in. Neither of them looked away from the screen, but both shouted, "Hi, Mom."

The fact that they looked like two kids from opposite sides of the gene pool always got people's attention. Monty resembled his father, Rudy, in looks and disposition. He was more cautious, more intellectual and at times could be more serious than his brother. Jackson's red hair was a recessive Bombay trait that skipped every generation. His shorter, athletic build came from my dad. His wicked sense of humor and penchant for getting in trouble came from me.

And I loved them like no other mother could. For seventeen years, they'd been my whole life. It would be really tough to give them up for college in the near future. Then I'd be alone. Huh. I'd never thought about that before. I hastily pushed that thought from my mind.

It occurred to me that I'd have to leave the boys here for a month while I was on the show. That was an unpleasant idea. The boys had just turned seventeen and were hell on wheels. If we'd had wheels in the jungle, that is. There was no way I could leave them.

I toyed with making Mom watch them, sending them to live with their father's parents in the States or for a brief stint in military school, or possibly just rendering them unconscious for a month. I could have done that last one, but there were some side effects involved and I didn't want them to have excessive facial hair or golf ball–sized warts.

I pulled a beer from the fridge and sat down next to them on the couch. Figuring out what to do with two adolescent, hormonal, teen assassins would be worse than doing the damn show. Either way, I was pretty sure that the one person who wouldn't survive in either case was me.

Chapter Three

Diplomacy is the art of saying "Nice doggie" until you can find a rock.

—Will Rogers

I was up early the next morning, doing my usual jog around the island. Santa Muerta's pretty small. It usually took about an hour and a half to run the sandy beach perimeter. Jogging always helps me think. I don't know if it's because more oxygen is going to the brain or whether I just jar it into action, but I don't question anything that works. Oh yeah, and I do it for the exercise too.

I'd never had good luck with exercise. Yoga twisted me into so many knots I spent a week at a chiropractor's in Florida funding the doctor's summer home in Aspen. That time I tried aerobics I ended up breaking my coccyx (the doctors still scratch their heads over that one). I swam for a while. We had a pool on the island in addition to the ocean. But that backfired when I was attacked by sharks. In the pool, no less. I always suspected Jack and Monty of that one but could never prove it. Other attempts proved disastrous, from general calisthenics (I got shin splints from push-ups—apparently I was doing them wrong), to Tai Chi (did you know that howler monkeys consider some of those movements *very* threatening?), but nothing seemed to work as well as jogging. It's boring as hell, but it does the job.

And speaking of jobs, this assignment had me worried. Because of the other work I do for the Council, I hadn't done a lot of fieldwork in the last five years. And my isolation on Santa Muerta had kind of turned me into a hermit. I could be social with the best of them, but really only for short periods of time. How the hell was I going to spend thirty days, 24/7, with a diverse group of Canadians?

So, I guess I was saying I was a rusty, antisocial assassin. Neither quality would lend itself well to this particular hit.

Another thing that bothered me was the fact that I didn't know what kind of environment I'd be in. The last couple of *Survivor* shows took place in the Arctic Circle and Gobi Desert. And since this was the first season of the Canadian program, I wasn't sure what they'd do. With my luck, they'd maroon us on the Bering Strait.

At least Burma was right. My being an inventor could make things easier. I had no doubt I could come up with ways to make my team's life a little better, and that would keep me on the show longer. Making stuff à la *MacGyver* (damn, I miss that show) came naturally to me and I loved doing it. The only problem was, I wouldn't have any tools with me, nor would I know where we were going until they threw us off the boat.

I was just about to the bungalows and still had no ideas, when I spotted two familiar figures sitting in the sand. Changing direction, I headed right for them.

"Mom"—I plopped into the sand beside them—"Aunt Carolina, what are you doing here?"

My mother and aunt smiled at me serenely. For a moment, I wondered if they were on something. Shit. I bet they found my little cannabis garden. *What?* I'm saving it up in case I get glaucoma someday.

Mom giggled and Carolina followed suit. There was a faint whiff of herb mingling with the salt sea air. Both women wore very modest swimsuits and, by the numbers on the bottle lying in the sand, a thick, impenetrable force field of sunscreen.

"Hello, sweetheart," Mom answered. "Lovely day, isn't it?"

"Uh, it's always a lovely day here. The weather is perfect year-round." All right, so maybe I didn't have to be so contrary.

"Are you looking forward to the job?" Carolina beamed.

I crossed my legs in front of me. "No, not really."

My darling mother ignored my comment. "Carolina was talking about her new granddaughter, Sofia. She just got her first tooth."

Oh hell. I knew what was going on. "Mom, you have grandkids. Monty and Jack. Remember them?"

"Oh, I know. I just thought it would be fun to have a baby in the family again." Her eyes narrowed meaningfully at me.

"I'm forty-five. I don't want another baby." I pointed at my aunt. "Borrow hers."

No one spoke for a minute and I haaaaaate uncomfortable silences, so I offered, "How's Louis?" I was referring to my aunt's other new grandchild, seven-year-old child genius, Louis Bombay.

Carolina beamed. "Oh! He's so adorable! My only grandson. I spoil him rotten. But I have to admit, I have no idea what he's saying most of the time."

I had to laugh at that. Louis was scary-smart. The long-lost son of my cousin Dakota, Louis was more like me than his father.

"I'd love to have him visit," I ventured. "He could work in the lab with me. Do you think I could borrow him sometime?"

"Of course! He talks about you a lot. You made a huge impression on him when he was here last."

I nodded, and changed the subject. All this talk about babies felt like fire ants breeding under my skin. "Mom, I think you need to pull a few more strings on that Canadian show. It would be easier if I knew where we were going to be. Then I could do some research and make some plans based on the lay of the land."

"Hmmmm, what?" Mom looked up, her mouth full of Twizzlers. Where the hell had they come from? "Oh yes. You'll be in Costa Rica, dear."

My heart leaped. "Really! That's terrific! I've been there about thirty or forty times!" It was true. Costa Rica was one of my favorite places. I'd been just about everywhere—the beaches, San Jose, the cloud rainforest, the volcanoes. I felt a wave of relief drown the aforementioned imaginary fire ants.

I frowned. "But if you know that and we find out what we need to know early, why can't I just go and wax Vic before the cameras arrive?"

She shook her head. "It just won't work, Missi. The producers will notice that Vic died and you disappeared. We don't want any untoward publicity."

I rolled my eyes. This from the same group that ordered my cousins Dak and Paris to come up with a marketing plan for the family business earlier this year, complete with a Web site and branding.

"Fine. At least I know where I'm going." I stood up and brushed the sand off my legs, getting ready to run back to my workshop.

"Missi," Mom said slowly, "why don't you pack your bikinis for the trip? You have a nice figure and might as well show it off. You never know who will be watching the show."

"Mom, this isn't a bizarre, jungle blind-date-athon. I'll be on assignment. I'm not there to pick up men."

She leveled her eyes at me. "Well, it wouldn't hurt to try. You've been without a man so long, you're starting to get, well, a little strange."

This was coming from a stoned, sixty-seven-year-old woman with a floppy hat, 150-plus-SPF sunscreen and a bag of Twizzlers.

"She's right, you know," added the woman who, up until this moment, had been my favorite aunt. "Look at Gin and Dak! They found wonderful spouses.

You don't want to spend the rest of your life alone, do you?"

I looked away, into the surf, repeating the silent mantra: *I won't kill them. I won't kill them. I won't kill them.* After a few deep, cleansing breaths, I turned back to their upturned and inquisitive faces.

"Well, I've got work to do, so I'd better get back. Nice to see you again, Carolina."

As I turned back and jogged in the direction of my lab, I realized that I'd finally figured out who would look after the twins while I was gone. And good luck to her. Mom wouldn't miss grandkids after keeping up with those two for a month.

That thought made me feel a lot better.

Chapter Four

MICHELE: *Hey Romy, remember Mrs. Divitz's class, there was like always a word problem. Like there's a guy in a rowboat going X miles, and the current is going, like, you know, some other miles, and how long does it take him to get to town? It's like, "Who cares? Who wants to go to town with a guy who drives a rowboat?"*

—*Romy and Michele's High School Reunion*

Sure. I wanted to find someone special again. But that was not first and foremost in my mind. I'd been married once. He was a great guy. Rudy could make my heart swirl, was fantastic in bed and he fathered two wonderful sons. Unfortunately, he'd had really bad timing while crossing the street in Dallas. It's said that when the bus full of evangelical teens hit him, you could hear him screaming a mile away.

I slammed a few drawers in my bedroom. Mom had to know she pissed me off with this crap. I decided a long time ago that I'd met my perfect match. And while it was unfortunate that fate intervened in the form of a busload of Christian adolescents singing "Kumbaya," my chance for love was over.

The accident left me a widowed mother of twin boys going through their terrible twos. I fled my life in Texas and moved back here. And that's how it's been ever since.

I was happy. Living on a tropical island was everyone's idea of a dream. It made it possible for me to pursue my first loves—science and invention. I had a huge trust fund (all Bombays did) and could travel whenever I wanted. Life was perfect. My stomach clenched. Where did that feeling come from? I loved my life on Santa Muerta.

Which might be why I wasn't looking forward to this upcoming trip. I scanned the collection of swimsuits now laid out on my bed. No, I wasn't going to wear any bikinis, no matter how bad Mom wanted me to. Not that I was worried about my body—I took care of myself and exercised. I even invented a skin cream that made me look much younger than I was. If I had to, I could turn the cosmetics industry on its ass. Even so, I chose a couple of one-piece suits and put the rest away.

It occurred to me that I didn't know what to pack. There were no instructions. Maybe we'd get to take a backpack? I'd heard somewhere that contestants were allowed to bring one personal item. What would I take? Deodorant? A toothbrush? Scissors? *Twister?* I love that game!

Hmmm. From what I'd seen before, the biggest trouble was making fire and cutting things. I'd need to come up with something that would hide flint and a cutting edge. That gave me the first glimmer of hope and I took off through the jungle to my workshop.

I went through boxes with my usual stab at organization—throwing crap everywhere. Truth be told, I wasn't very tidy. Oh, I knew where everything was—but I didn't know what I was looking for. *But I still haven't found what I'm looking for. Mental note—download more U2 onto iPod. I wonder if they'll let me take that with me?*

Hmmm. Surveying the clutter, I realized I'd need a plan. Well, I could always come up with some sort of flint scissors. No—I'd never be allowed on the airplane with those. Whatever I made had to get past security screeners. Of course, I could hide a blade in some sort of lead enclosure.

Oh brother. That's what I get for reading the kids' *Superman* comic books. In my own defense, I've always been a comic book geek. I'm still not sure how the boys got hold of an *Action Comics* no. 1 from June 1938. They were extremely rare and very, very expensive. Honestly, I didn't really want to know anyway.

Okay. What would Batman do? Bruce Wayne was an inventor. He had what I thought was the best superpower—a brain. Sure, Superman could fly, was bulletproof and strong. But he wasn't near as smart as Batman—who could do all those things, but with his BRAIN. Wait a minute. I don't mean that his brain was bulletproof and could fly. That would be ridiculous. I mean, where would it go?

GAAAAAAAAAAAAAAAAAAAAA! Focus, Missi! Focus!

Unfortunately, it was impossible. So I fired up the speedboat to head to the mainland for some supplies.

There was this great surplus store in Ecuador (hey! that rhymes!) where I filled up on flints and knives in various shapes and sizes. I was back home by evening and unloaded everything on the kitchen table while I whipped up some tapas for dinner.

"Cool stuff, Mom!" Jack and Monty burst into the kitchen like Siamese twins. Hmmm. I didn't know if I'd ever seen them apart. There was that stomach thing again.

"Is this for *Survivor*?" Monty frowned as he flipped one of the butterfly knives expertly back and forth. Most moms would be freaked out to see their teenage son do that, but I was proud. I taught them that trick when they were seven.

"It's *Survival*. A Canadian show. And yes. I'm trying to figure out how to smuggle them onto the program." I shoved a couple of plates toward them and we all sat at the breakfast bar to eat.

Jack picked up one of the flints shaped like a small rectangle. "Can you hide it in soap or something?"

I shook my head. Damn. These tapas were gooooood. I reached for the sour cream. "I don't think they let you take stuff like that. I think we get to bring a small tote bag of clothes, but I don't know if we're allowed anything else."

The boys looked at each other, then down at the stuff, then back at each other. I know this may sound weird, but I admired that connection. It was comforting knowing they'd have it for the rest of their lives.

Monty and Jack would never be alone. My stomach winced, and this time I reached for the antacid.

We continued to eat while picking at the pile of flints and blades. None of us spoke. But I knew that was because we were all trying to come up with a solution to my problem.

Wow. I'd never really thought of my sons as adults before. They'd had their training and first kills of course, but it didn't occur to me until this moment that they could help me with anything. Kinda brought a tear to my eye.

The phone interrupted this Hallmark moment and I picked it up.

"Gotta go, boys," I said, replacing the receiver. "The Council's got the scoop on the other contestants."

Jack leaped up. "Can we go?"

"Please?" Monty begged.

"I don't see why not." I shrugged. "After all, it doesn't really matter who anyone is but the Vic."

The three of us headed downstairs to the conference room to meet with the Council. Despite their age, my sons were very protective of me. Both taller than yours truly, they flanked me like bodyguards.

You know, it was sort of nice that the boys were interested in my assignment. I felt a bit of pride welling up. Someday maybe the three of us could work together. Neither boy had any interest in inventing, but their brains were as slippery as Lex Luthor's, and that made them smart enough to be helpful.

As we entered the room, I noticed that only Georgia and York were there, pointing to a cluttered table.

"He's a stud!" Jack pointed at the picture of one of the contestants.

"Yeah! Mom could actually get some!" Monty nudged his brother and they grinned at me. Okay. Maybe not so helpful.

"Get some?" I hollered. "Get out!" I pointed to the door and watched as they put on their saddest puppy-dog eyes and slunk out of the room.

I turned back to York and Georgia. Where was Mom? And the others?

Georgia smiled—she'd had two boys too. Unfortunately, I'd killed her evil son Richie a little less than a year before, but she didn't seem to hold it against me. She still had Coney—her son with a PhD from an Ivy League school, who up until recently was a carny. I heard he was on some sort of sabbatical now.

"Here's a list of the other participants." She brushed her dark brown hair from her eyes before continuing. "I managed to hack into the studio's server."

The table was littered with eight-by-ten-inch glossy photos and résumés. I picked up the one the boys had pointed out. Hmmmm. Lex Danby. Lex? Like the bad guy in *Superman*? I brought the photo closer. He was cute. I felt my face redden and quickly put it down. Looking up at Georgia confirmed my fear—she'd seen it. My aunt winked at me.

Isaac Beckett, the Vic, was there too. Apparently he claimed to be an expert poker player. I guess putting "terrorist" on his application might have made them think twice. He was almost as hot as Lex. But bad guys were verboten. Maybe it had been too long since I'd had a boyfriend. Of course that would mean Mom was right and there was NO WAY I'd admit that!

"Take these with you and study them," York interrupted with a yawn. Apparently I was boring him. "You should be getting your instructions in the mail today." He waved his hand, indicating with arrogant dismissal that I was done here. You know, being on *Survival* might actually be a nice break from dealing with the Bombays.

Chapter Five

OLIVE: *I'd like to dedicate this to my grandpa, who showed me these moves.*

PAGEANT MC: *Aww, that is so sweet.* (Audience applauds.)

PAGEANT MC: *Is he here? Where's your grandpa right now?*

OLIVE: *In the trunk of our car.*

—*Little Miss Sunshine*

I had to hand it to Georgia—she'd done a good job of getting those profiles. Sitting at the dining room table, I spread the sheets and photos out. There would be twelve of us in all. And except for one African American, it appeared that diversity was an afterthought. Oh well. I wasn't really there to save the world.

I was already bored. Isaac Beckett grinned at me from the tabletop so I thought it was time to play "Get to Know Your Vic!"

He was cute. Actually, he was gorgeous, with dark, wavy hair, an olive complexion and striking green eyes. The profile told me he was forty-one, single, a pro poker player from Toronto who liked Mexican food and had never been camping a day in his life. I squinted at the picture, as if that would allow me to see something I missed. It occurred to me that I didn't have a dossier on him yet. The Council was definitely slipping.

"Mail!" Monty and Jack shouted in unison as they dumped a pile on the table. I moved my stuff out of the way. I liked mail. Granted, we had to go to the mainland to get it, but the boys loved doing that.

"Hey!" Monty stared at a brown envelope on the table.

Jack grabbed it. "It's from the show!"

I snatched it from my son and opened it. All that was inside was a checklist of things I could bring. Damn. I could only bring a couple sets of clothes, eyeglasses and one personal item. The examples included a Bible (a Bible?), a toothbrush, or a photo of loved ones. I guess that if you didn't survive, you'd at least be able to see your loved ones for the last time, get last rites or leave the earth with clean teeth.

"You have to be there in two days!" Monty read (loudly, I might add) over my shoulder.

Again, I squinted, expecting a miracle of vision, I guess. "That can't be right! I should have more time than that!"

Jack shook his head with—did I detect glee? "You have to be in Canada the day after tomorrow." He pointed at the small print.

I threw my hands up in the air. "But I can't be ready in that short amount of time!"

The boys wisely said nothing. I picked up the phone and dialed.

"Mom! I just found out I have to leave tomorrow for *Survival!*"

"To survive what, dear?" My mother's voice was relaxed. Too relaxed.

"The show! I have to be in Canada for the show in two days!"

I could feel Mom smiling through the connection. "That's nice, sweetie. Drop me a postcard, okay?"

What?

"No, Mom, I can't. We won't have any contact with the outside world whatsoever." I took a deep breath. "I can't do this. There's no time to get organized. You'll have to call it off."

"Sorry, babe," Mom said in a sing-songy voice. "A job's a job. Oh! I knitted you a knapsack to take. Send the boys over for it, will you?" And then, she hung up on me. Yes, my own mother.

To say that panic had set in would be unfair. I was on the edge of full-blown hysteria. I started to pace back and forth while my children calmly watched me rant like a lunatic.

"I can't do this! There's no way I'll be ready in time! And why do I have to fly to Canada just to come back down here to Costa Rica? That would at least buy me a day or two! Who are these people? If I kill the producer would they drop the show?"

"It says here that you are a homemaker from Texas," Jack said quietly. In spite of his mischievous nature he knew when to avoid a joke at my expense.

"What?" I spun on my heel.

He sighed as if having to deal with me was some sort of chore. "You're a homemaker from Texas. Widowed. You went to college on a bowling scholarship and in your free time like to cook and decorate, and long to find another man to take care of."

"Bowling scholarship?" Monty asked, missing the point entirely.

"Give me that!" I ripped the page from my son. Yup. That's what it said, all right. Where in the hell had they got that? I can't cook, and decorating the condo damn near killed me. Mom! She must have written this. I'd kill her!

"You can't bowl!" Monty informed me.

I pointed at the door. "Go upstairs and tell Grandma I'm NOT going!"

A few minutes later, my son returned with the bag and a note from Mom that read, "Hope you like the bag, honey. Be sure to get waxed before you go. Can't get a man if you're hairy like a monkey." The tote bag she knitted for me said HOT TO TROT. GET ME WHILE I'M HOT.

If she weren't my mother, I'd have killed her.

Chapter Six

ELAINE DICKINSON: *There's no reason to become alarmed, and we hope you'll enjoy the rest of your flight. By the way, is there anyone on board who knows how to fly a plane?*

—*Airplane!*

Two days have never, in the history of womankind, gone so quickly. As my plane landed in Canada, I couldn't help thinking about how stupid this assignment was. Mom agreed (like she had any choice after I zapped her with a Taser) to take the boys. Monty and Jack exchanged a grin when they found out they were under Grandma's control. That made me worry.

Monty and Jack tried to contain their excitement that I was leaving. It's not that I'm the strictest mom, but those two can really cause trouble when they put their minds to it—which they do nearly 100 percent of their waking hours. And did I mention they are precocious?

"Mom," Monty asked, "how are you going to manage being around men?"

"What?"

Jack chimed in. "Maybe you should adopt a persona or something."

"What are you guys talking about?" Did they want

me to put on a brunet wig and pretend to be an ant farmer?

Monty looked at his brother, and they communicated telepathically. "It's just, maybe you shouldn't be so much like yourself."

"Yeah. You are a little flaky," Jackson added.

I tried to get mad, but they did have a point. "Why are you two telling me this now?"

"Well, you haven't dated in like—" Monty started.

"In forever." Jack finished. "And if you start spouting off about explosives or rambling on about snack foods you're gonna come off as weird."

I crossed my arms over my chest. Normally this would indicate I was pissed off. In this case, it was a stab at stalling before I could figure out what to say.

"Listen," I said slowly, "I'm on this show for one thing—to do a job. I have no intention of dating any of the other contestants." The photos of Lex and Isaac flashed through my mind and I winced. "Besides, I won't be on long enough to win. It's all about the job."

Monty stared at me. He was the introspective one, the dark-haired, serious son. If I was lying, he knew about it—sometimes before I even did.

"Mom," he said, "you're not getting any younger."

Jackson interrupted my impending rage. "And we'll be heading off to college soon. Do you want to spend the rest of your days with Grandma as your only companion?"

Touché. Damn.

"Just flirt a little," Monty begged. "What can it hurt?"

"Let me get this straight." It was about time I said something! "You guys would have no problem with me dating someone?"

Jack grinned dopily. My little redhead. He was the one who didn't take life seriously enough. "No. Why would we?"

"Just make sure to run him past us before you ask him to marry you," Monty finished.

Visions of my sons hooking up a future fiancé of mine to a lie detector, then waterboarding him afterward popped into my head. And why would I be the one to propose? I'm not old-fashioned by any means, but did they think I was desperate?

I hugged them and told them to quit hanging out with Grandma and her propaganda machine. That was the last time I saw them before I left for Canada.

I'd managed to make a cuff bracelet with a serrated edge that could be straightened and used as a saw. It was steel with large, grayish, flint stones dotting the surface. I have to admit, it was a damned good idea. Never once did security at the airport stop me. So, I had my cutting device and fire tool.

"Mrs. Bombay?" A thin, gangly kid in an ill-fitting chauffeur suit squeaked as I walked past. Turned out he was my driver. And in spite of five wrong turns, he got me to the studios in one piece.

Shouldering my backpack (I'd made a new one— like I was gonna use Mom's!), I joined the other eleven contestants on a soundstage. They all looked just like their photos. I'd memorized their stats before leaving.

"Can I have your attention, please?" a young woman with a clipboard shouted. She didn't need to. No one was talking to anyone else—which I thought was kind of strange.

"Uh, thanks." She forced a smile. "I'm Julie, your assistant director for *Survival*. I see you all brought a small bag with your belongings. If you would step over to that table"—she indicated a rickety card table in the corner—"our security will search your bags, removing anything that can't go. When you're all done, please have a seat over there." She pointed to a set of folding chairs against the opposite wall.

We formed a line at the table. I moved slowly so I could be at the end and observe my fellow contestants. I figured that the contents of their bags would tell me a lot about them.

Ten packages of condoms, five bottles of lube and two porn mags later, I realized that there were things about these people I didn't really want to know. I'll tell you this, these people were either very randy or extremely lonely. Ick.

I found it interesting that no one spoke during the whole thing. Had I missed something about a vow of silence in the memo? That would be a problem. Maybe the others were used to not speaking, but I tend to rattle on when nervous. At last they went through my bag, and finding nothing, moved me along.

"Wait," the security guard (whose name tag said

IVOR—Ivor?) stopped me and pointed at my bracelet. "What's that?"

"It's a religious artifact," I responded smoothly, a little proud of coming up with the idea. I mean, who in these über-PC times would question that?

"Really?" His eyebrows went up. "Native American?" By the smirk on his lips I decided he didn't believe me. I mean, it could definitely have passed for Native American. But with my blonde hair and blue eyes, that might have been in doubt.

My brain raced. I should've come up with a religion. Idiot! My mind grasped the first thing I thought of.

"It's one of the lesser-known faiths. FSM. I'm studying online to become a high priestess."

The guard looked as though he wanted to ask, but decided against it. He waved me on and I moved on wobbly legs toward my seat.

"FSM?" The question came from Lex Danby as I sat down. Damn. He was even hotter in person—tall and built with deep, chocolate brown eyes. His khaki cargo shorts and Ramones T-shirt gave him an air of casual sexiness. Something about his smile made an electric spark ignite inside me.

"Church of the Flying Spaghetti Monster," I whispered back. "I saw it on *The Daily Show*."

He extended his hand. "I'm Lex Danby."

I reached to grasp his hand in mine. I hoped he couldn't feel my heartbeat pounding through my veins. "Missi Bombay. Nice meeting you."

"You look a little too tan to be here."

"I'm not from here." I waved my arm as if that meant anything. "I live in the South." That seemed like a good enough explanation without having to give too many details. "So how did you manage to end up here?"

"Someone hit me over the head and I woke up here." He smiled. Lex looked right into my eyes in such a confident way it made me tingle. I liked him immediately.

I guess we had the same problem. "I wish that had happened to me. My excuse is an overly concerned mother with too many connections to Canadian broadcasting."

Lex laughed and I blushed. I loved the way his eyes crinkled in the corners when he smiled—like he smiled a lot.

I would've said more, but Julie was back with her clipboard.

"Now that your bags have been checked, we're going to go over a few ground rules before we get on the plane."

What? We'd just got here? And we were leaving again?

"We're heading for an unknown location." She stopped and shook her head. "I mean, I know where it is. You don't. Therefore, it's unknown to you. But not to me. I know where we're going."

I smiled. It was slightly reassuring to know I wasn't the only one who thought in tangled sentences. I liked this woman already.

"Anyway, we're about to get on the plane. The only rule for the flight is no talking. You aren't allowed to talk to the others until we land. Okay?" She asked even though we knew we couldn't question it.

No talking? How old do they think we are? Like they could really keep us silent.

"I'm passing out an agreement you need to sign before we leave. This contract says you agree to the terms of the program and will follow all rules and regulations."

Yup. That's what it said all right. I guessed they really could keep us silent. I signed the form and passed it to the end of the row. Julie told us it was time and we gathered our things and followed her to a bus. In silence. I'm not kidding.

The bus took us to a private hangar at the Toronto airport, where we got on a small plane. The other contestants closed their eyes and I decided to also. If you can't talk and the in-flight movie is some B-grade tearjerker about two lonely people in the Yukon, you tend to do that.

Chapter Seven

If a person offends you and you are in doubt as to whether it was intentional or not, do not resort to extreme measures. Simply watch your chance and hit him with a brick.

—Mark Twain

It was very dark outside when they rushed us off the plane and onto another bus. I would've thought we were still in Canada, had it not been for the heat and humidity. My stay up north lasted maybe thirty minutes and I was back where I came from. The whole thing made me a little grumpy.

Dawn was poking through the jungle and more and more of us were starting to wake up. The bus had no conveniences whatsoever, which added to my foul mood. The woman who sat next to me on the bus smelled like patchouli. She had long, straight hair, no makeup and a lot of jewelry. Not the good stuff, more like dragons-and-goddesses shit. From the photos I'd seen earlier, I figured that she was Liliana, an artist in her fifties. I still wasn't allowed to talk to her, which was good, since I needed all my lung capacity not to strangle on her perfume in the thick humidity.

"How long is this going to take?" I mused aloud.

Liliana looked startled. I'm sure she wondered if I was talking to her.

"No talking!" Julie hissed. She looked pretty miserable.

"I'm not talking to her," I replied. "I'm talking to myself. There was nothing in the contract about not talking to myself."

Julie's face twisted into a grimace. She looked at the pages on her clipboard, then at me. "Well, I'm making a new rule! No talking to anyone—and that includes yourself!"

"Technically," Lex said behind me, "you can't enforce that." Did I imagine it, or did he wink at me? Wow. A man hadn't winked at me in years. It was a definite turn-on.

"And you're not a contestant, dumbass. So we can talk to you." A thin, overly tanned woman with short hair spoke up. I recognized her from the files as Sami—a thirty-three-year-old electrician.

Soon the whole bus opened up with conversation. I guess my peers needed to get it out. No one said anything important, really. But it was clear there was a need to speak just for the sake of hearing our own voices. This went on for a few minutes until the bus jerked to a stop and we all fell forward.

Julie stood and brushed her hair off her face. "Great. We're here."

"Here" turned out to be the beach. As we got off the bus, everyone looked around, trying to figure out what was next. Apparently the novelty of speaking was replaced with the realization that we had, indeed, signed up for this stupid show.

We all watched as the bus backed away and drove off and a small Jeep pulled up. A man who was so attractive he looked a little surreal jumped out of the Jeep and walked over to us.

"I'm Alan, and I'm your host for *Survival*." Julie walked over to him, handing him a large bag.

"Welcome to Costa Rica!" Alan said with a smile. His cheerful welcome and gorgeous smile seemed to put us at ease. "This is where you'll stay, in two camps, for the next thirty days."

I raised my hand and Alan nodded. "Here? We're staying here?" I know it seemed like a stupid question.

"Well, yes, actually. The two tribes will be about half a mile apart, but you will be on this beach."

"But"—I bit my lip—"I can see a resort from here."

The whole group followed my gaze to see that not more than five hundred feet away was a luxury resort, complete with vacationers gawking at us.

"Um, well, yes," Julie stammered. "The Blanco Tigre is our sponsor. And that's where those of you who are voted off will stay until the filming concludes."

"So, they're just gonna be right there?" one man asked.

"How in the hell are we going to do this with a goddamned resort looking over our shoulder?" asked another. They were talking too quickly for me to identify.

"I signed on for a realistic survival experience! How can this be the real thing if we can see that?" a smallish man with a weasely face shouted.

Interestingly enough, none of the women complained. Maybe they were already plotting their demise on the show so they could spend the whole time at the resort.

Julie looked to Alan for help and he raised his hands and whistled.

"Look! You all signed the contract. This is our location. The Costa Rican government wasn't interested in giving us locations in the parks, so we went with this stretch of beach owned by the Tigre. Just pretend they aren't there!"

On his last word, two Jet Skis raced by blasting loud music. Yeah. Authenticity was going to be tough here.

"Now. We're going to divide you into teams, give you your buffs, and let you get started. The first challenge is tomorrow at sunup." He nodded at Julie who walked over to us.

"One, two, one, two . . . ," I kid you not. Julie numbered us off into two groups of ones and twos. No unique challenge, no test to put us into our tribes. None of the fun, weird stuff they use on *Survivor* to divvy us up. They counted us off like we were in grade school. I thought it was funny. Lex raised his right eyebrow at me. Apparently he did too. There was some serious chemistry there and I hoped it wasn't all part of my imagination.

"So," Lex leaned in and whispered, "can your mother with the Canadian broadcasting connections get us out of this? I think I've had enough already."

Not unless I take Isaac out now. And I couldn't do that until I was sure. "Nope. Looks like we're stuck here." And for once, I didn't really mind it.

Julie interrupted us with instructions to sort ourselves out based on our number. I wanted to complain about this *Sesame Street* method of organization. Do they have *Sesame Street* in Canada? Maybe they have something else. I dunno, like *Oregano Avenue*, and instead of Cookie Monster, they have Flan Monster. No, wait, that would be Mexico.

After we formed up (I was a "one"), I was very relieved to see that my team had both the Vic and Lex. I liked Lex. Maybe I could off Vic early and we could form some kind of reverse alliance to get ourselves kicked off and spend the rest of the month in the hot tub at the resort.

"Now that you have formed two tribes"—I looked up to see Alan had been joined by two Ticans (Costa Ricans call themselves that, although I have no idea why) dressed in primitive attire—"we will give you your team names that represent the culture of Costa Rica." He smiled at the two natives and reached into the bag, pulling out two bandanas, one white and one gray. Huh? Why no colors?

"Team One—you shall be the Ottawa tribe." Alan frowned, then looked down at the bandana again. "Ottawa? Inuit? What the fuck, Julie? Those are Canadian tribal names! Not Costa Rican!" Alan dangled the two bandanas, covered with images of salmon, grizzly bears and totem poles.

Julie looked like she wanted to pass out. Grabbing the bandanas, she looked at them as if they were poisonous snakes. "This can't be right! I told the interns we needed native stuff! Not this!"

Apparently, she'd failed to specify which native stuff she needed. My guess was the interns thought she'd meant Canadian. I found the whole thing amusing.

"Dammit! That ain't right!" the guy who'd complained about authenticity spoke up. "I want this to be 100 percent accurate! Not this bullshit!"

Oh yeah. That must be Silas. He was a hard-core Civil War reenactor. I'd heard of these guys. Everything had to be real, right down to the dysentery.

Alan held his hands up and the Ticans stopped dancing. "All right. It's a screw up. But since this is what we've got, we're going to go with it." He motioned toward the camera crew who'd gotten everything on tape. "This is the camera crew who will be following you around. There will be two cameras for every tribe and they will be on 24/7. Don't try to bribe them. They get paid a lot of money for what they do and will be fired if it's discovered that they became involved."

Julie whispered something in Alan's ear, then turned to us. "Okay. You have until morning to set up your site. Team Two—I mean the Inuit tribe—come with me."

The Ottawa tribe watched as the Inuit disappeared over the next sand dune. We turned and looked at the two-camera crew of three who said nothing, but began taping anyway. There were six of us, just standing there doing nothing. I thought it might be funny if we just did that all day. But no, one of my team members began to speak.

"Let's all introduce ourselves! I know a great icebreaker!" said a superperky young woman. "Everyone get in a circle and hold hands!" she tittered.

That must be Cricket—a summer camp director. Oh yeah, she wasn't driving me nuts already. If Monty and Jack were here, they'd have had her marinating in enough sugar to be carried off by the mosquitoes with her remains picked at by vultures. The *Parent Trap* twins had nothing on my boys. I missed them.

"You're out of your goddamned mind, bitch." Sami shook her head.

Silas piped up. "They didn't do no icebreakers in the Civil War. And unless it's something people would do when stranded in the wild, I won't do it either."

Cricket bit her lip and frowned. Apparently, she was unable to deal with adults.

Lex stepped forward. "I'm Lex." He pointed at me. *Ooh! He's pointing at me!*

"Oh! My name is Missi." I did a little wave and felt like an idiot.

"I'm Isaac." That was all my Vic said. Damn, he was cute. And he had one of those deep, gravelly voices.

Too bad he might be evil and then would have to be destroyed.

"Hell. My name's Sami. And don't any of you assholes even think of calling me Samantha."

I realized that from here on out, virtually everything Sami said would be bleeped.

"Name's Silas," the skinny reenactor said grumpily.

We stood there in silence, sizing each other up. This sure was a surly group—except for the überperky Cricket. I was pretty sure we weren't going to get along very well. With the exception of me, Lex and Isaac, that is. A ménage à trois popped into my head and I struggled to stifle it.

"I'm just trying to help," pouted Cricket. What kind of name is Cricket, anyway? Seems her parents doomed her to become a camp counselor from the start by naming her that.

"Look," Isaac said, "I think we just got off on the wrong foot. Let's start over." It was kind of cute how he did that, making Cricket feel better. *Stop it! He's the bad guy and you will probably have to kill him!*

"As I mentioned earlier, I'm Isaac. I play poker."

Sure, if by that you mean you deal a generous deck to terrorists. Hey! That's pretty good! Too bad I can't really say that.

Isaac pointed at me and grinned. I was in danger of liking the bastard.

"Oh. Um, I'm Missi and I'm"—what was I? Oh yeah—"I'm a widowed mother of two and I live in

Texas." The Gloria Steinem within just wouldn't allow me to claim homemaking as an occupation.

"I'm Lex, and I'm a bartender originally from Iowa, now living in Windsor." Lex also winked at me. I took that to mean two things: (1) we had already formed an alliance; and (2) he saw me as the goddess I truly was deep down, toga and all.

"Well, hell," Sami swore, "I'm Sami and I'm an electrician from Newfoundland."

I wondered how an electrician was going to do in a place with no electricity. Or maybe this was what she considered a vacation.

Silas glowered. That's exactly what I expected him to do. "I told ya my name. I'm a private in the Union Army—a professional Civil War reenactor. And I came on this show because I wanted to try living an austere life. I 'spect everyone will follow the rules."

Obviously Silas was going to be the biggest pain in the ass.

"I'm Cricket, and I'm a camp counselor from upstate New York! I'm SO excited to be here! I know lots of fun games and songs to keep us busy!" She actually bubbled on the spot. In my imagination, Monty tied her to a tree while Jack let loose the fire ants. The thought made me smile.

It appeared that Silas had come in a distant second to Cricket as "Most Likely to Irritate Me." The woman actually ended all her sentences with exclamation marks.

"How about you boys?" Cricket chirped to the camera crew.

The three young men looked at each other nervously. Apparently, they couldn't decide what to do.

"Maybe they can't talk to us," I said. I knew they couldn't interfere in anything that happened—which was not at all reassuring.

"I'm Jimmy," the tall, skinny kid answered. "That's Bert and Ernie."

"Like the Muppets?" Cricket asked. She seemed so excited to have found something kid relatable, I was worried she would burst into flame.

Bert and Ernie looked at each other. "Who?"

At that moment I realized I was officially "old." When twentysomethings don't know about *Sesame Street*—my crack cocaine as a kid—it's time to make funeral arrangements.

"We can't really talk to you," Jimmy said as he shouldered his camera, "so go and do something we can film."

Huh. I guess we were boring them. It occurred to me that if we ever wanted to interrupt the filming, we could just talk to the cameraman. *I'll stash that nugget in my brain files under* X. *It doesn't mean anything. I just like the letter* X. *X marks the spot.* X *stands for danger! Two straight lines crossing over in the middle . . . Oh damn. I'm channeling* Sesame Street *again. Thank God no one said "Mahna Mahna" or I'd really be in trouble. Great. Now that song is stuck in my head. . . .*

It was then when I realized that Isaac had been talking.

"So we'll just get started on our shelter, then. Anyone have an idea just how we can cut down those bamboo trees without an axe?"

Chapter Eight

If we run out of food and anyone has to be eaten, you will be first.

—Ernest Shackleton

I slowly raised my hand, and it made me feel like I was back in school, half-afraid of what my teacher would say should I get the answer wrong.

"Um, I know how. It's pretty easy. You see, bamboo trees have air pockets in their joints and in the wood itself. You just set a fire at the base of the tree, piercing the chambers first—or, as I'm sure you know, it would just explode." The only problem was, how could I start a fire using my bracelet with the camera crew there? I'd have to find some way to distract them.

"We'll need some stuff," I started slowly, because I was pulling this out of my ass as I went. I pointed at Cricket and Silas. "You two go get big leaves and fronds for the roof." I turned to Isaac, Lex and Sami. "And you three get me some tinder, kindling, any kind of dead stuff." I pointed in two different directions so the cameramen would have to split up and follow them.

Once everyone left, I let out the breath I didn't know I'd been holding. It only took a few moments to size up the right tree and get what I needed together.

A few strikes against the flint in my bracelet and I had a small spark. After blowing on it for a few moments, I had a fire. And no one saw me cheat. Excellent.

"How did you do that?" Lex's voice breathed in my ear, causing lots of quivering in lots of places.

I decided to trust him, mainly because I wanted to sleep with him. I'm sure that's not a good enough reason, but oh well.

"And you had no problem smuggling that in?" He looked impressed. At least, I wanted him to be impressed as he checked out my bracelet. "I thought it was an artifact from the Church of the Flying Spaghetti Monster." His smile gave me goose bumps in spite of the heat.

I giggled like an idiot and made some stupid "aw, shucks" motion with my hand. Ugh. Okay Missi! You don't know anything about this guy and you're already proving your mother right. Snap out of it!

"And," Cricket's voice squeaked a few yards away, "I can build a fire like nobody's business." She emerged from the jungle with a really pissed-off Silas in tow.

Cricket and Silas stopped short, gaping at my fire.

"How on earth did you do that?" she cried.

The cameramen, Jimmy and Bert, looked at me with their mouths hanging open. Obviously, I'd tripped the monkey. On *Survivor*, the players had to do challenges to earn flint for fire. They wanted to know how I managed it and likely knew they'd be in trouble since they hadn't been there to get it on tape.

"Damn," was all Jimmy said.

I shrugged. "I just rubbed two sticks together and poof." Lex stifled a grin as he turned to feed the fire.

"Can you do it again—so I can at least capture it on film?" Bert pleaded. *Aha, I knew it.* But now I was in trouble. I'd need their compliance throughout the taping, but in all honesty, I cannot rub two sticks together to make a fire. I swear, the whole idea of it is a hoax dreamed up by some sadistic Boy Scout.

I shook my head. "No. I can't guarantee it. I just got lucky, that's all. Besides, we need to keep this fire going so we can topple the tree."

The cameramen didn't even try to hide their disappointment as the other two joined them. Isaac and Sami made it back with an armload of dead plant matter in time for my physics explanation. I was pretty impressed with myself—but I could tell the others were suspicious. That is, until the tree fell on Silas.

In hindsight, I guess we should've been watching for that, but Silas wasn't hurt, and actually, the minor injury seemed to make him happy. Okay, so he looked more constipated than blissed out, but I'll take what I can get.

It took the rest of the day to fell enough trees and gather enough leaves to make a pretty decent lean-to. Sami and Cricket managed to weave some thick mats for the floor, and once we were all done, I had to admit we had a really nice place. Dinner consisted of coconuts. Tomorrow would be our first challenge and we needed to get some sleep.

"Well I, for one, am glad Missi's on our team." Isaac

startled me by talking. We don't really talk to our Vics . . . ever, really.

Lex nodded. "I think, overall, we have a pretty good group."

"We're supposed to call it a tribe!" Silas barked.

"Does anyone want to do any team-building exercises or sing?" Cricket offered, in a way that implied she meant to be helpful.

"Fuck off, bitch," Sami said, and the rest of us hid our grins.

"I'm still amazed at what you did today, Missi," Isaac continued.

"Well, I just hope it was the right thing to do," Silas grumbled. "Everything needs to be authentic or I'll get acid reflux."

For some odd reason, I got the feeling Silas enjoyed heartburn, but I left that unsaid and turned to Isaac.

"No big. I was lucky enough to know what to do. I'm sure everyone will have a moment like that." Okay, so I was lying. I didn't really think some of us were capable of doing much, to tell the truth. Cricket could be counted on to drive us to murder with her inane camp psychobabble, and Silas would only be of use if we had to take on Robert E. Lee.

Nobody really had a response, so I stood up and headed down the beach.

"What the hell are you doing?" Sami asked. I was getting used to her language—at least enough to realize she meant nothing by it.

"Mashing up coconut to get the oil. It protects against

the salt in the water and as a bonus it works as a mild sunscreen." Once I had the paste, I smeared it on my arms and legs before plunging into the ocean's surf. I was sweaty, hot and tired and knew I couldn't sleep without at least a little dip.

My tribe had a harder time adapting. Maybe it's because I'm from a tropical area and more acclimated to the weather. But this bunch was having a hard time with it.

Silas's skin turned a bright pink after only half an hour in the sun. Weirdly enough, he seemed to like it. Apparently misery and suffering were part of the authentic experience.

Cricket wasn't having too much trouble with sunburn. My guess was that years working outside helped her. But the mosquitoes thought she was a virtual blood buffet and proceeded to feed on her like mad. By sundown, she was covered in red welts. For just a minute I wondered if the boys really were here.

Sami had so much melanin stored up in her skin it didn't seem to affect her. And the bugs apparently thought she was toxic and avoided her. Isaac and Lex had a little sunburn and a few bites, but neither one complained.

Sleeping that first night was pretty awkward. There were three men and three women in a pretty small shelter. Somehow we managed to segregate, with the girls on one mat and the boys on the other. But it was still weird. After tomorrow, I thought we'd be so exhausted it wouldn't even matter.

Actually, this was a strange *Survivor*-esque show. There were only a few people in their twenties—the rest were older. I squeezed my eyes tightly as if that would help me remember my files so I'd know who we were up against in the Inuit tribe.

I'd already kind of met Liliana, the artist. Let's see, there was Kit—a model who was the first to go home on two different seasons of *The Bachelor*. My guess was she was a little reality show nuts.

Kit and Liliana were the only girls on the team. They bunked with Bob, the career politician; Brick Phoenix—I'm giving you his full name because (1) it was completely ridiculous, and (2) his real name was Norman Finkelstein—an actor, of course; Moe, an unemployed and overweight thirty-year-old who still lived at home (well, at least not that month); and Dr. Andy, a therapist.

Yeesh. The Inuit tribe was younger than we were, so I figured that might be a problem the next day.

"I'll git you, Johnny Reb!" Silas cried out in his sleep.

This was going to be a loooooong four weeks.

Chapter Nine

I tried to sleep. Really, I did. But it was impossible. It appeared that some of the members of our team talked, shouted and sang in their sleep—except for me, Lex and Isaac. I'd have to figure out a way to deal with that. Otherwise, I'd drop dead from lack of sleep.

It was so early the sun wasn't up yet. I had no idea what time it was, so I climbed to my feet and slipped out of our lean-to.

The fresh, salty air felt so good I didn't want to do anything. Jimmy, Bert and Ernie were nowhere to be found. They probably got to stay at the resort. Oh well.

A five-foot-long piece of bamboo lay near my feet. I snatched it up and decided to do a little fishing. After looking both ways, I took off my bracelet and snapped it into a straight saw. As quietly as I could, I split the end of the stick into four sharp tines, reinforcing them by binding them at the base with some leftover hibiscus bark. It looked pretty dangerous, I thought proudly, as I unhinged my bracelet and put it back on my wrist.

It took me a while to get the hang of spearfishing.

There were a couple of tidal pools with trapped fish, so I wasn't completely hopeless. I had to smile remembering the first time the twins had gone fishing. They'd used so much C-4 that the one lake on Santa Muerta was unusable for ten years. Sigh. Memories.

By the time the sun rose, I had a fire going and six cleaned fish lined up beside me on a large palm leaf. I was able to throw the spear to dislodge three coconuts, so we had coconut milk for breakfast. I even managed to split the shells into bowls for roasting the fish.

"What the hell?" Sami joined me by the fire. "Did you do all this?" She was fidgeting with her fingers, and I realized she was a smoker. Wow. She was quitting cold turkey here. I had a sneaking suspicion that her language was going to get saltier as time wore on.

"Yup. Want some? I marinated it with coconut. There's some milk too." Actually, I was pretty proud of myself. I was the Martha Stewart of *Survival*.

The others slowly joined us and pretty soon we were all eating breakfast. Silas was particularly interested in the spear I'd made. I couldn't tell if he was suspicious or impressed. Somehow, I knew this was going to be an ongoing problem.

"You're funny, resourceful and you can cook? You're too good to be true," Lex teased. I fought the urge to flirt back. After all, I was here to do a job and there was no way I could admit Mom was maybe a little bit right about me.

"You should see me change the oil on a car sometime." Okay, I guess I just couldn't help it.

He smiled. "I'd like to see that." He ran his hands through his hair. "I can't figure out if you're our savior or planted here to catch us off guard."

"Are you serious? Who in their right mind would be here when they could be over there?" I pointed at the Blanco Tigre.

Lex's eyes glimmered. "That's a good point. But then, why didn't we just book vacations instead of signing up for this sad excuse for a show?"

"I don't know. Apparently we were coerced and then brainwashed to think it was our idea all along."

"You're probably right," he said, as he helped Sami and Cricket to another serving of fish.

I watched how Lex took care of the others without them realizing that was what he was doing. He cared about the team. He didn't have to. That's not the way the game is usually played, but he did. There was no condescension in his actions. No one suspected Lex was coddling us because he wasn't. It's hard to describe, but he made us feel safe without making us think we needed him to do it.

It reminded me of my late husband. Lex had a quiet dignity that I adored. And then there was the fact that he'd picked me to befriend—obviously the man had good taste.

"Where's Cricket?" I asked. How did I not see her slip away during breakfast?

"Fuck if I know," Sami answered. "The bitch is always missing."

"I noticed that too," Isaac said. "Silas went off to look for clams."

I sighed. "I suppose we should get something collected for dinner later."

Lex and Sami started working on the fire as Isaac and I went for coconuts. It felt strange to be alone with a possible Vic. No, not strange, awkward. The idea that I was friendly with someone I might have to kill very soon seemed like a breach of common courtesy. I hoped there wouldn't be any conversation.

I was wrong.

"I can't tell you how great it is that the four of us have an alliance." Isaac smiled in utter sincerity. Damn.

"Yeah. I think so too." I hoped he would get the hint.

He didn't. "What's up with the other team? Did you get a load of them?"

"Um, not really." *Take the hint. Take the hint!*

"First there's the Dr. Phil clone. And then the woman who smells like a crystal shop. That Moe guy seems okay, but I don't know about the others." He grinned, punching me lightly in the arm. "Hell, I think we might be the only normal people on the show!"

I tried very hard to hate him. I imagined him poisoning kittens, eating dolphins, causing global warming . . . anything to avoid liking him. Isaac was in my alliance for one reason only—so I could keep him around until I had to kill him.

"So what's your story?" he asked as he picked up another coconut.

"I don't have one." I shrugged and giggled, which made me look like an idiot.

Isaac laughed endearingly, damn him. "Everyone has a story, Missi."

"Not me. I don't believe in them." What a weird thing to say. But maybe that was good and he'd just write me off as weird. I could live with that.

"Okay. I get it. You play things close to the vest. No problem." He gave me a little sad smile and walked away.

I got what I wanted. But I felt horrible. This was obviously a great assignment. Thanks, Mom. I wandered back to camp to find our camera crew had finally arrived.

"Oh man! Are you kidding me?" Jimmy looked pretty stunned as he joined us with Bert and Ernie in tow. "How did you get food? Coconut-marinated fish?" He squinted at me. "Did you get this from the resort?"

"No." I shook my head. "I couldn't sleep so I made this"—I pointed to the spear—"and caught these."

The crew was disappointed. They began filming anyway, but I heard Ernie muttering that they would be here first thing tomorrow morning to catch me in the act of . . . of what? I wasn't doing anything wrong. I mean, the bracelet was sort of like cheating, but I didn't see anything wrong with that. Especially when I didn't want to be here in the first place.

When breakfast was over, my tribe thanked me. Isaac smothered the fire and I showed them all how to smush up the coconut and smear it on their skin as a sunscreen.

"Hey!" Julie appeared beside us, clipboard in hand. "Are you ready for your challenge?" She grinned. "I'll bet you had a rough night with no shelter. . . ." Her voice faded off as she saw the very nice shelter we'd made with mats on the floor. "Well, you're probably pretty hungry and thirsty. . . ." Then she noticed the fish skeletons, coconut husks and remains of a fire.

It was obvious we'd taken the wind out of her sails. She expected to find us on the brink of death, and instead we had shelter, fire and food. And she looked pissed.

"What? How? How did this happen?" she shrieked at us. No one spoke. I mean, wasn't this the point? We were supposed to find ways to survive . . . right?

Julie turned to the camera guys. "Tell me you got this on tape!" Maybe she figured she could salvage it if we'd done something dramatic, like made a pact with Satan for the food and shelter—something explainable like that.

Jimmy blanched and shook his head. Bert and Ernie winced, fearing what would come next. I felt a little sorry for them. It was my fault. Somehow, I'd have to find a way to give them a big scoop. Otherwise, they were likely to work against me. And I certainly didn't want them dogging me—especially when I took out Vic.

"So, what the hell's next? Do we get a goddamned challenge or what?" Sami barked.

Julie winced. "Please don't swear so much Sami. Or you'll be edited out."

Sami winked at me and I smothered a giggle. I really liked her. Before I had kids, I had saltier language than a pirate with Tourette's syndrome. Once the boys turned five, however, they decided that I had to clean up my act. The institution of a "swear jar" was pretty ingenious. Within three months, they had enough to buy a car. Of course, five-year-olds can't drive, so that doesn't make sense, but you know what I mean. Don't you?

"We do have a challenge for you this morning, and it is for reward. I can't tell you any more than that, so if you'll all just follow me—SILENTLY—you'll find out soon."

We all shrugged, which was weird, then began talking loudly as we followed her into the jungle. You can't treat a bunch of adults like kids, and we resented her—so we acted like kids. Might as well have a little fun with it.

The chatter seemed to annoy Julie, which in turn amused us. Nobody really had anything to say, so we pointed out every damn tree and bug as though we'd never seen anything like it in our lives.

After about ten minutes, we entered a clearing that looked suspiciously like a resort volleyball court. At opposite ends of the court were two dark tanks filled with water. Connecting the tanks was some sort of balance beam–obstacle course. Dead center was a square platform. So this was the challenge?

There was no time to question Julie, because our smarmy host, Alan, showed up with brilliantly white teeth and a—no doubt—resort-enhanced tan.

"Today's challenge is for reward." Our host looked meaningfully at both teams. We pretty much rolled our eyes.

"One of you stands on the platform and you form a bridge to the tank." He pointed along the balance beam. "You hold on to each other however you can, without anyone falling off."

Huh. That seemed easy enough. Until I spotted the fulcrums. Apparently, the balance beams weren't secure—they were, well, balanced on fulcrums all the way across. It looked like they could move in any direction, too. How very Hogwarts. Damn.

Alan motioned for Bert and Ernie to demonstrate. The men sighed and put down their cameras, then climbed the platform. And while they were as coordinated as blind epileptics with inner-ear problems, I didn't see how we were going to do any better. The beams swayed back and forth, coming apart where they were connected. We'd have to use our bodies to hold them together. Fantastic.

"Once you get everyone across to make the bridge, the one on the end has to use their free hand to find the pearls in the water and pass them along the bridge to the guy on the platform, who will place the pearl in a bucket. When you have ten pearls, everyone has to work their way back to the platform for the win. At any time, should any of your teammates fall, the whole team has to go back to the platform and start over."

Wow. I was impressed. What a sadistic challenge. So, all we had to do was hold onto each other. I didn't have great balance, so I immediately volunteered to be the pearl diver for the team. Everyone nodded. Whew. At least I wouldn't have to keep two people balanced. I just had to stick my hand in that cloudy water and sift for pearls. How hard could that be?

Once the teams figured out who would do what, Alan started talking. "Okay. Remember the rules. Want to know what you're playing for?"

Of course, we all nodded. What did he expect us to do?

Alan walked over to a table covered with a tarp, and with an obnoxious flair for the dramatic, lifted it. "You are playing for mani/pedis and a haircut at the resort's salon!"

"Are you shitting us?" Sami said what we were all thinking. "What the hell do we need our nails done and our hair styled for?"

She had a point. It was a useless reward. And it wasn't like we'd been here a month. It was only thirty-six hours ago that I'd had a good shower. Man, this show sucked.

Alan looked like his leg was being humped by a porcupine. "It's a good reward—and you'll work hard for it," he said through clenched teeth.

With little interest, we all climbed onto the platform, waiting for the order to begin. Whatever.

"When we get halfway through the challenge, there will be a twist. So think of getting across as quickly as possible." Alan grinned, then shouted, "Go!"

Our team huddled for a moment and Isaac came up with the idea that we go one at a time, climbing across the bodies connected before us. It sounded reasonable. Hell, shooting Alan and Julie sounded reasonable at this point. Cricket took her position as the first person in line, standing half on the platform and half on the first beam. Silas took her hand and stood on the next beam. Isaac gingerly crept in front of the two and managed to add himself to Silas, firmly gripping his hand. The three of them were holding hands, and looked pretty steady. Sami went next. And even though she swore colorfully the whole way, she was very nimble. Must be from scrambling up telephone poles, bridges and stuff for her work.

With a big grin, she grabbed Isaac's hand and shouted, "Come on!" to Lex.

I was a little concerned at this point. Lex was a fairly large guy and the beams were really swaying. Sheer luck was holding them and our team together. I looked over and saw that the other team was doing better.

I flinched as Lex very slowly and very carefully moved his way down the course, clinging to each teammate. I started to get a little excited, thinking of his body against mine. I would have that chance very soon. Maybe Mom was right. Of course, I would *never* tell her that!

There really was a certain chemistry between us—for which I was grateful. I mean, Isaac was cute too, and if I'd been as attracted to him as I was to Lex, I would have had bigger problems on my hands. Why wasn't I interested in Isaac? It was probably that big bull's-eye I saw superimposed over his heart. Knowing you have to kill someone and the fact that he's probably evil are definitely a libido buzzkill.

But why was I attracted to Lex? Had it really been that long since I'd been interested in a man? Maybe it was just because we were close in age and had the same sense of humor? I was a little hesitant to read too much into it. Besides, on *Survivor*, people lied all the time to each other just to make alliances. How did I know he was sincere? I barely knew him!

Panic struck, and not in the good way, when I realized I'd be next. I chose the end spot because it was securely on a platform and I wouldn't be likely to let go of my teammates that way. I'd forgotten that I had to get there in the first place. Shit.

"Come on, Missi! It's not hard, you can do it," Lex called out with a wink. I got a little choked up thinking about how the possibly future Mr. Missi Bombay was being so supportive!

With a deep breath, I stepped from Cricket and the stability of the first platform to Silas. As I kind of shimmied past him I could see that his mind was elsewhere. I wondered if he was busy concentrating on the joys of gangrene, or plotting to start another Civil War. Good luck getting everyone to wear wool and fight with bayonets.

I almost fell as I clung to Isaac, but he saved me by looping his leg around my thigh, squishing my body to his. For a second I looked him in the eye. I almost let go out of shock, when I realized I'd never been so close to a Vic before.

Sami broke me out of my thoughts with a sharp, "Get a move on, dumbass!"

I climbed across her body onto Lex's. For a moment, I let my hands linger on his body. Damn, he felt good. Finally, I made it across, standing firmly on the other platform. I was covered in sweat and shaking, but I'd made it. Yay me!

"Now that *everyone* has made it . . . ," Alan said a little too sharply. How long had it taken me? Of course, I'd have stayed longer with Lex if I could have.

I shook it off and Alan continued, "Here's the twist. Inside these tanks are several fish. Most of them are harmless."

Most?

Chapter Ten

ANNOUNCER (directing men in a police lineup):
Turn to the left. (Suspects turn to the left.)
Turn to the right. (Suspects turn to the right.)
Bird dance.

—*The Vacant Lot*

"Also inside the tank are two piranhas. That will make it harder to find the pearls." The smug bastard smiled.

"Are you out of your fucking mind, you goddamned psycho?" Sami had managed to articulate the words I was thinking—but she'd done it so much more diplomatically. I looked at the tank and realized I couldn't see anything in the water.

"Of course I'm serious!" Alan's face turned red. "It's supposed to be a challenge!"

Isaac spoke up. "I think we should refuse to go any further. I don't want Missi getting hurt for some idiotic spa treatment."

Lex added, "She is *not* doing it. We'll just bow out."

"You bet your ass, we will!" Sami exclaimed. "We won't lose any members until we do the immunity challenge. This is just too fucking retarded."

I got a little choked up. They were fighting for me! We really were a team! Or they didn't want the woman who'd caught and made breakfast to lose a hand. And how could I get a decent manicure anyway if a damned piranha chewed my fingers off? It just didn't make sense. Although the idea of making my own prosthetic arm was intriguing. *Hmmm. Maybe I could trick it out with an index finger that shoots lasers. That would be really cool.*

Julie started screaming. "Look! We have to keep the show competitive! Just do it!"

Wow. She snaps easily. Good to know.

Cricket was turning green thinking about it, and Silas looked a little too happy. No one from the other team spoke. Maybe they hoped we'd drop hands and they'd win the spa treatment by forfeit.

Alan narrowed his eyes. "You will do it, or you will send two team members home—tonight!" By the way the veins in his forehead bulged, I guessed he was serious.

"Look, guys," I said, "it's okay. Piranhas rarely attack humans. I'll be fine. Let's just get it done." I looked across to my counterpart and saw that Moe, the unemployed thirtysomething who lived at home, just shrugged. Apparently, when your mom washes your underwear and getting up to go to work just means shooting for higher scores on your PlayStation, something like this doesn't bother you.

The team looked at me with either admiration or

concern. It didn't matter which. I'd been around piranhas before. I figured if I moved slowly and didn't threaten them, I'd be okay. Chances were the other fish had more to fear than I did.

"I don't know," Isaac said slowly. I realized I was in danger of liking him. And that would be bad. *Focus, Missi. Piranha first, deal with Vic later.*

I shook my head. It would be far worse to have to vote two people off and risk losing challenges. I needed to stay in the game until I could figure out whether or not I was to take Isaac out.

"Let's just get this over with. I can do it," I said resolutely.

"You heard the lady," Alan said with a grin that made me want to beat the crap out of him. "The first team to have all of their pearls wins. Go!"

I slowly dipped my hand in the dark water. Moving fast would have seemed threatening to the piranhas. Although as nasty as this water was, chances were they couldn't see anything either. Maybe I'd get lucky and they'd be extremely nearsighted. Can fish be nearsighted? I mean, who's going to give them an eye test? It's not like they'd recognize a giant *E*, or for that matter, be able to communicate it if they did. . . .

My hand brushed lightly against the scales of a fish, bringing me back to the here and now. I felt two pearls on the bottom. Very slowly, I pulled them up and tried to figure out how to give them to Lex. We weren't supposed to let go of our hands and that meant they had to travel down the line some other way.

I looked him up and down—maybe a little too intently. The other team hadn't figured it out either. So, I let my hormones decide and popped the two pearls into my mouth and kissed Lex, rolling them off my tongue onto his.

Electric current ripped through me and I realized it really, really had been a while since I'd kissed a man. At first Lex looked surprised, until he felt the two pearls. He looked at Sami and the rest, who were completely shocked. Briefly, he opened his mouth and showed the pearls to Sami. She grinned and leaned toward him, taking the pearls from his mouth to hers.

I must admit that I was a little jealous. Then I realized I should be trolling for more pearls. So I slowly dipped my hand in again and pulled up two more. Happily, I popped them in my mouth and kissed Lex again. This was way too much fun. Maybe all our challenges could involve the connection of two body parts.

A shout of disgust came from Silas, who didn't look too pleased to have to kiss Isaac for the pearls, but he sucked it up like a good boy in blue.

Moe put a pearl in his mouth and leaned over to pass it to his teammate, Brick Phoenix. Brick refused, citing it would hurt his future acting career to be seen Frenching a man. I was a bit surprised to see Moe shrug and spit the pearl into the hand he was holding with the actor wannabe. Brick leaned down to put the pearl into his mouth and I decided we were doing okay.

I carefully slipped my hand into the water, this time finding three pearls. Was it wrong of me to put only two in my mouth to pass to Lex? I mean, you gotta take what you can get when you can get it, right? While Lex was giving the pearls to Sami, I put the third one in my mouth.

Did I imagine it? Or did Lex's tongue lightly stroke mine? Woo hoo! Could we ditch the cameras later for a total make-out session? Suddenly, my idea of throwing the game to spend the rest of the time at the Blanco Tigre seemed like the best idea in the world!

Unfortunately, the other team was down to two pearls left. We had three. I knew this because Alan gleefully announced it. Julie looked pissed that no one had lost a finger yet. She seemed especially upset that I wasn't bitten. Oh well.

I reached into the water again, scraping the bottom to try to find all three remaining pearls. Something sharp slashed at my fingers and it took all I had to keep my hand in there. I found two pearls and pulled out.

"She's bleeding!" Cricket squealed, pointing at me with her free hand. I'm sure she was thinking, If only I had my camp first-aid kit—I'd save the day!

Huh? Oh yeah. I was bleeding. And the dirty water wouldn't help. My fingers were all intact, but there was an ugly slash across the knuckles.

"Don't do it, Missi," Lex said seriously.

The others nodded. I was touched by their concern. However, I desperately wanted to kiss Lex again and I wanted us to win this challenge. So I slid my hand into the water once again. For a second, I allowed myself to check out Moe's progress. He hesitated briefly. He must have realized there really were piranhas in there. His team seemed a tad less supportive. I gathered this mainly because they were yelling at him to hurry up.

My fingers closed around the last pearl and I brought my hand out a little too quickly, which accounted for the piranha attached to the fleshy part of my palm. Stupid fish. I put the pearl in my mouth and closed my eyes for the kiss—piranha firmly attached to my hand.

Lex froze a little at the sight of the fish, but then took the pearl from my mouth and ran his tongue lightly over my lips. I sighed and watched as it was delivered to Cricket and she happily dropped the last pearl into the bucket.

"Ottawa has all of their pearls and just needs to get everyone back on the main platform!" Alan threw his arms in the air. Julie smirked. Obviously, she'd gotten her wish.

I had to go first and I still had that fish riding sidecar. Oh well, it would have to go with me. I climbed in front of Lex, my eyes on his as I slid across the front of him. I let go and held onto Sami, eventually making it back across. As my teammates crept back, one by one, I tried to dislodge the fish.

Unfortunately, he wasn't budging. The bastard. He just gasped his last breath, refusing to let go. The little shit died right there, embedded in my hand. I tried to separate his jaws, but if I pulled too much, my skin would tear and I'd likely need medical attention and might get booted from the show.

Tempting as that thought was, I decided to let him stay. It didn't really hurt, since their teeth are razor sharp, and he didn't pull or tear the flesh. I concentrated instead on helping the rest of my Ottawa tribe get back.

"Ottawa wins!" Alan announced.

The Inuit tribe looked pissed, but somewhat in awe of the fact that I continued on with that damned fish attached to me.

"Go ahead and follow Julie—she'll take you to your reward. Inuit—go back to your campsite. Tomorrow we'll have our first immunity challenge."

"Let me see that." Isaac took my hand and the fish in his. "He's in there really good. I'm afraid to dislodge him without tearing your skin."

The rest of the group gathered around me, all offering suggestions that were completely useless. I mean, how many Canadians knew how to get rid of a piranha? It was invariably decided that we could figure something out at the spa and we reluctantly followed Julie—mostly because she was screaming for us to do so. I wondered if I'd get in trouble for taking her out too?

Chapter Eleven

SIR ALEXANDER DANE: *By Grapthar's hammer, by the sons of Worvan, you shall be avenged.*

—*Galaxy Quest*

Guess what? Nobody at the spa knew what to do either. And Julie was completely useless. Either that, or she refused to help. Needless to say, Bert and Ernie filmed everything.

I can't tell you how weird it was to get a manicure with a dead fish attached to my hand. Imelda, my manicurist, politely worked around it as if it weren't there. I decided to name the fish Bob.

The best part of the reward was taking a shower and putting on the fluffy, white robe. Getting my hand through the sleeve with Bob was difficult, but I forgot all about him once I saw Lex in his robe.

During my pedicure, Bob started drying up a bit. I was sitting next to Isaac, and he was still trying to come up with a solution. I was trying to get annoyed with him, but he was so sweet.

"I just can't understand why no one has offered you medical attention!" he said loudly, hoping the staff might react. They didn't.

"Well, I'm hoping that when he dries up, we can just snap him off. He's a little heavy," I replied. The glassy, lifeless eyes were staring at me. Sigh. Poor Bob. He died for that last pearl.

My hairdresser turned out to be an American expat named Gloria with a giant, blonde bouffant hairdo and a beauty mark that seemed to move a few millimeters every five minutes or so.

The minute she saw the fish, she seized a pair of shears and carefully snipped Bob off at the lips. Poor Bob. As she styled my hair (which she said really needed some work), she soaked my hand in some type of clear solution. While my hair was setting under the dryer, Gloria carefully pried the teeth out of my hand, covered the wound liberally with Neosporin and bandaged it, slipping me three ibuprofen under the table. I felt so much relief (and a little sadness) at having Bob removed, I didn't really notice the pain.

"Um," I said slowly, "can I have those?"

Gloria laughed. "Sure, honey. I'll be right back."

Ten minutes later, Gloria returned with the teeth strung on a bit of leather. She presented them to me like it was the Nobel Prize. Then she took the curlers out of my hair.

We looked ridiculous, walking the beach back to our campsite with these high, curly coifs and bright polish on our fingers and toes. No one spoke at first, and not because Julie warned us, but mostly because it was a stupid reward.

"I'm really pissed off they didn't help you," Sami said on the way back.

"I have to admit, that was really rude," Cricket chirped.

"You got a lot of moxie," Silas begrudged. Apparently he approved of the way I suffered.

"I'm going to punch Alan in the face when we see him tomorrow," Lex murmured.

"I'll hold him down for you," Isaac said.

It was as if I already had a boyfriend and a big brother on the team. I didn't say much—just fingered Bob's teeth, now tethered around my neck. Two things were on my mind. First of all was my explosive attraction to Lex. I was seriously turned on from hugging his body and kissing him earlier. Granted, everyone else got kissed too, but what happened between us was special. Right?

And secondly, I was very worried I was becoming friends with the Vic. I was on this stupid show for one reason and one reason only. He was a bad guy. I had a job to do. But Isaac was sweet. He was looking after me. And that made me very nervous.

When a Bombay gets an assignment, we act upon it from a distance. We rarely know much more about the Vic than his dossier.

In this case, I was spending 24/7 with Vic. Hell, I was catching and cooking fish for him! That had to be a first. And it was going to be a lot harder.

The rest of the group seemed to interpret my silence as dealing with the pain or not feeling well. The spa staff had fed us fruits and finger sandwiches for dinner, so there wasn't much to do when we got back to camp.

I sat down on the mat in the shelter and suddenly felt dizzy. My hand started to throb beneath the bandage. The ibuprofen must have been wearing off. I lay down and started to force myself to sleep. Somewhere in the night, someone put some fronds over me and whispered, "Good night, Missi." Either someone smoothed my hair, or I was hallucinating. It didn't really matter either way.

The next morning found me wandering off into the jungle to see if I could find any fruit other than coconut. My hand was a little sore and I needed some alone time away from my team.

Remember when I said I didn't know how I'd react to being around a group of strangers constantly? Well, it's pretty damned exhausting. Especially when I'm the one who always seems to make things happen.

The other thing was that I was missing my boys. At first I thought some time off from being a mom would be great. But honestly, I hadn't really been away from them all that much. And soon, they'd be heading off to college. There was a blind sense of panic washing over me as I realized that this would be what the future holds. Once they went off to school, it would take a miracle (or at least the promise of greasy food and for me to be their personal maid) to lure them back. And I'd have the condo all to myself.

I shrugged off my homesickness. My alone time

wouldn't last much longer and I did need to get some food. Spotting a mango tree, I pushed all thoughts of Monty and Jack from my brain.

I was just reaching up to grasp a large fruit when it just plopped into my hand. Did I just imagine it, or did I hear someone say, "Mom"? *I must have an infection.* I examined my bandaged hand, but it didn't seem to be swollen or seeping. I reached up and grabbed another mango and thought I heard it again.

This time, I looked around. I'd have bet it was those cameramen, messing with me. But I didn't see anyone. Just a couple of howler monkeys, and I could do without them.

Have I mentioned that I'm not fond of monkeys? I mean, they're okay, but there's something about them that bothers me. Some people are afraid of the dark, others are afraid of clowns. My irrational fear is more like a nails-on-chalkboard kind of thing. I can't stand pictures of monkeys dressed as people. Especially chimps. I don't know why, but it makes me want to gag. I once threw up in a spectacular, Technicolor fashion when my college roommate papered my walls with a "Chimps of the Office" calendar for my birthday. Let's just say she was not as amused as she thought she'd be.

"Mom!" a voice called rather urgently, causing me to drop my mangoes.

"Hello?" I said, staring around me. That's it. I've lost it. Completely lost my mind. And on a cheap, Canadian knockoff of *Survivor*, no less. I knew this day was coming. I just hoped it would be sooner than later. Not that I'd be the first Bombay to flip out. My great-great-great grandma told everyone that sunflowers yelled at her all the time and developed a scorched earth policy on all flowers. Hell of an assassin, though. She once took out a Russian hitman with one finger. No lie.

"Jeez, Mom! Up here!" The voice was louder now. I guess everyone has a breaking point. Apparently mine involved a piranha named Bob.

Something began to unfold from a branch above me. It only took seconds for me to recognize Monty, hanging upside down from the mango tree. *Oh. So I'm not crazy. Huh.*

"What are you doing here?" I whispered loudly at my son.

Monty broke into a wide grin. He looked like a bat, hanging upside down like that. Jackson unfolded himself next to his brother with the same smile.

"We wanted to help!" Monty said.

"You're supposed to be back on Santa Muerta with your grandmother! Does she even know you're here?" I did feel a flicker of satisfaction thinking of Mom realizing the boys were gone. And I will admit, it did my heart good to see them.

"We told her we were going camping up near the ropes course. She never goes there," Jackson said. That was true. Mom wasn't big on nature. Well, except for her recent interest in my glaucoma stash.

I looked around. "You are going to get me in trouble. I've got a job to do and we aren't supposed to have any contact with outsiders!" Yeesh! I sounded like that bitch Julie.

"At least come down here and give me a hug!" I added.

The boys shook their heads. "This is safer," Jackson said.

"Cool!" Monty pointed at the teeth around my neck. "Where'd you get those!"

I sighed and filled them in. My sons announced that they thought I was the coolest mom ever, which made me happy.

"We're going to help you," Monty announced.

"Here." Jackson tossed something down to me.

I looked around before opening the small brown bag. It was filled with chocolate protein bars—twelve in all. Good boys.

"We're staying at the resort," Monty added.

"We've got Grandma's credit card." Jackson grinned.

I couldn't hide a smile. My boys.

"Well, get back before anyone catches you. I can't have them filming me talking to trees."

The boys laughed and pulled themselves into the upper recesses of the tree.

I shook my finger at them. "Just because I can't see you doesn't mean I don't know you're there!"

"Uh, who are you talking to?" Cricket's voice brought me up short. I slowly turned to find her and the cameramen staring at me.

I carefully shoved the bag into my shirt. "Oh, just a couple of monkeys. They threw mangoes at me." I grinned, holding up the fruit and hoping they would buy it.

"You are so weird," Cricket said. Bert and Ernie said nothing, of course. "You have to come back to camp. We got our sea mail."

"Sea mail?" I asked, realizing it was the rip-off's version of "tree mail." Cricket looked at me in disgust and walked away. What had I done to piss her off?

Bert and Ernie stayed with me. So I looked up into the tree and said, "Bye-bye monkeys! I'm watching you!" Of course they filmed the whole thing. But I had to say something to Monty and Jack. They were my sons, after all. I stopped for a minute, then looked up again.

"Love you!" I said to the tree, then headed back to camp, ignoring the strange looks from the cameramen.

Chapter Twelve

MICHELE: *For me, it's like I've just given birth to my own baby girl, except she's like a big, giant girl who smokes and says "shit" a lot. You know?*
　　—Romy and Michele's High School Reunion

Everyone was huddled around something when I got back. Lex saw me and broke off from the group.

"Are you okay?" he asked as he checked out my hand. "Cricket said you were talking to monkeys."

I smiled. "Just trying to freak her out. It was nothing." I was relieved to see him smile back. In six months, when this aired, he'd see that I was, in fact, talking to a tree. But I'd have time to explain before then.

Sea mail consisted of a piece of parchment in a bottle. How original. There was a map that would lead us to a clearing in the jungle where we would have an immunity challenge. The losing team would vote a member off tonight. We had a couple of hours before making the trek.

I managed to slip protein bars to everyone but Silas without the cameras seeing. It was obvious he would disapprove, but we needed a little boost before the challenge. I told my teammates I'd gotten them from the spa yesterday.

One by one, the cameramen took us off to talk to

the camera about the game, our chances, strategies, etc. When they returned with Sami, shaking their heads, I figured she'd cursed a blue streak, leaving them with nothing but bleeped-out language.

When it was my turn, they took me off to the ocean and asked me to sit waist deep in the water and talk about the show so far. I hate staged photos. You know how the newspapers do it, right? The guy who woke up to find a bullet hole in his car is usually standing there, staring through the stupid hole, looking all serious. That is so stupid.

But I sat there, in the water, in my swimsuit, not knowing what to say.

"Just tell us what your strategy is for winning the game," Ernie begged.

I shrugged. I mean, I could hardly say that my game was over once I killed Isaac and that my goal was to be naked in a hammock with Lex, drinking margaritas, now, could I?

My hand went up to the piranha teeth and so I said the only thing I could think of.

"I named the fish Bob. He was okay. I figure I just moved too fast on that last pearl grab and it startled him. I mean, he's just hanging out in the completely murky depths of a plastic pond and wondering what the hell is going on, right? I still feel sorry for him. Gloria up at the spa made this necklace for me. I guess I'll always have a piece of him."

It was kind of like having an out-of-body experience. Why couldn't I just shut up? No. I had to keep going on about some dead piranha like an idiot to a cameraman who'd recently seen me tell monkeys that I love them.

As we walked back to the group, I realized that *I* was the fish out of water here, not Bob. If only the Council had selected my cousin Dak, or Gin. They'd have been ten times better than me.

"Let's go!" Cricket called. She looked like she was badly in need of a clipboard.

"About goddamned time!" Sami grumbled.

Isaac took the map and the lead, with Lex and me trailing behind him. I was torn between studying my Vic and flirting with my new boyfriend-who-didn't-know-he-was-my-boyfriend.

"So, what do you think, Missi?" I realized Lex was saying something to me very quietly.

"Huh?"

"About the alliance? You, me, Sami and Isaac?" He looked a little frustrated.

"Oh. Yeah. Sure."

Isaac looked back at me and winked and I smiled involuntarily. This was getting worse. And I had no idea how to fix it.

According to his dossier, Isaac was a bad man. A cold-blooded killer. But my gut was telling me that he was one of the good guys. What the hell was going on here?

"I'll fill Sami in after the challenge," Lex said.

The challenge. Right. I could figure out a solution after the challenge. After all, I was on a mission, and that mission involved staying on the show until I could off Vic. Isaac. Vissac. Hmmmm.

My brain was exhausted by the time we came to the clearing where the immunity challenge was to take place. The protein bars were starting to kick in, and I could see the other team was struggling. It was highly likely they hadn't had any food or water (or protein bars dropped from seventeen-year-old primates), so this looked to be fairly easy.

"Welcome back," our snarky host, Alan, said. I wondered if I could kill him instead. The whole show was a joke.

"Listen!" Julie shrilled. Oh yeah. She was already dead to me.

Alan continued, "This challenge is for immunity. The tribe that wins goes back to camp. The losing tribe will vote someone off tonight."

He pointed to the course and I started laughing. Did Mom set this up? It was an exact replica of the ropes course on Santa Muerta! How weird. Although I wouldn't put anything past the Council—they wanted to ensure I'd get the job (the one I no longer wanted to do) done.

"You'll work as a team to get through each of the segments of the course. At the end, you'll zip-line to the finish. The other team members can help, but the last one through the course has to fasten themself on to the zip line and join their team for the win."

Julie was glaring at me and I realized I was still

laughing. I stopped and acted like I was paying attention as Alan went over each leg of the course.

"What?" Isaac whispered.

I leaned close so Julie wouldn't get too pissed. "I've worked on a course exactly like this one. I know what we have to do."

Isaac grinned and nodded at Lex, who'd heard everything I'd said. Standing between them, I felt a little like a Missi sandwich. Kind of like a grilled cheese— all goey and warm. Or maybe like a Fluffernutter with peanut butter and Marsmallow Fluff. Or possibly like . . .

"You have five minutes to discuss strategy with your teammates. When I blow this whistle, you can begin." Alan smirked. I bet he really thought he had us this time.

"Missi's got a plan," Lex was explaining to the group.

I nodded. "I've worked on this exact same course many times before." Images of helping my cousin Richie through the spider-web segment made me shudder involuntarily. "It's pretty easy—there's just a slight trick to each part. When we get the zip line, I'll set it up and send everyone. Then I'll go."

Cricket looked doubtful. What did I need to do to convince this bimbo, for crying out loud?

"Trust me. I've done all of this before." I'd barely finished when the whistle sounded, making me wonder if it really had been five minutes.

As a team, we raced to the first challenge. Two sets of long two-by-fours with ropes attached lay at our feet. Working quickly, I lined the boards up parallel (parallelly?) and had each person stand in a line, one foot on each plank. I took the end and told everyone to bring the ropes up over their shoulders. I'd explained that we needed to walk as one group, kind of like a dyslexic centipede (actually, more like a dodecapede) across the course.

I called out the directions as we went, telling the team which side to lift as we moved together. A quick glance over my shoulder told me the Inuit tribe was now copying our movements. That figured. They'd probably do that the whole way through.

It only took a few minutes to get to the next challenge, with the other team close behind. Sami clapped me on the back, but there was no time for congratulations.

The spider-web course would be a little harder. Basically, it consisted of ropes woven vertically between two posts, kind of like, well, a big spider web. But without the giant spider—although that would be really cool, wouldn't it? The web had large and small holes peppered throughout, and knots that could piss off the saltiest sailor.

The goal was to get everyone through it without touching the ropes. This might sound easy, but the web started four feet off the ground. And, you could use each hole (there were six) only once.

"I've done this one before—at camp," Cricket said

slowly. I could tell that she wasn't completely convinced that it would be easier with adults than with nimble, elastic kids.

"Good. You first," I answered. It would help to have someone who'd done this on the other side.

With a quick nod, Cricket leapt headfirst through one of the smaller loops, ending in a beautiful dive roll on the other side. My jaw dropped.

"Well, Holy Shit," Sami said. Somehow, I knew she was capitalizing her words as she swore.

I pointed to Lex. "You next. We'll need some brawn on the other side to help some of us across."

Lex sized up the web. He was the biggest of all of us. Not because he was fat or anything —he was compact, but muscular. The center hole was the obvious choice for him, but I wanted to save it for the end since it was the easiest.

Isaac pulled Silas over to the web and the two put their knees together, thighs bent, for Lex to use to climb. With a nod, he stood on their legs (looking a little like a transvestite cheerleader) and hurled himself through the second-largest loop to the other side. Lex landed with a thud, but stood up to reveal he was okay. And he hadn't touched the ropes.

I thought about my options. Sami and Silas were pretty wiry. It wouldn't be hard to get them through. Isaac again seemed to read my mind. He told Silas to make himself as stiff as a board. Ooh! Remember that from slumber parties—stiff as a board, light as a feather?

I dragged my brain back to the task at hand. Isaac, Sami and I then lifted him and fed him through one of the loops to Lex and Cricket on the other side. We did the same thing with Sami. It was much easier. She must've weighed just under one hundred pounds.

Now we just had Isaac and me left. Isaac was in really good shape, and I was struggling to figure out who should go next. I heard Julie yelling at the Inuit tribe. Apparently they'd touched one of the ropes and had to do it all over. I didn't even look, not wanting to break concentration. We had more time now, but what would be the best way to do it?

"I could boost you through the middle," Isaac suggested.

I shook my head. "No. You need to go next. The last person should be the smaller of the two."

There were only two holes left we hadn't used. The large one in the middle would easily accommodate Isaac's frame, but that would leave me with the smaller one, which was also about five feet off the ground. Getting Isaac through that one would be more of a challenge, but if we did it, I could take a running high jump to get through the larger, center hole.

I walked up to the web and got down on my hands and knees.

"Climb on my back," I said. "The others will help you through."

"No. There has to be another way."

"There isn't any other way. I need to jump through the center hole. I need the extra clearance. Go ahead and climb on my back. The other side will get you through and down."

Lex looked doubtful this time, but Cricket took up the charge.

"Get on Missi's back. Step through with your right leg. Back through it scrunching up your body as you go. We'll hold you and pull your left leg through last."

She was right. That was it exactly. I braced myself and nodded to Isaac.

He stood gingerly on my back and I tried to imagine that my spine was made of cement. It hurt. Isaac was heavy and I don't think I've ever had a man stand on my back before. My fists and feet dug into the dirt and I tried to keep silent. If I flinched or groaned, I was pretty sure Isaac would stop.

I felt him lift his right leg and he wobbled as he tried to thread it through the hole.

"We've got you," Silas encouraged. Was he actually being supportive? Maybe my suffering impressed him.

Isaac's weight shifted as he tried to keep himself steady. My back felt like it was in a vise. My shoulders and legs were starting to tremble, but I said nothing. It seemed like hours before he lifted off me completely, and I waited in that position to make sure he didn't need to step back on me.

"It's okay, Missi. We did it," Lex's deep voice murmured. I slowly started to straighten out. My muscles were screaming. I knew I had to do a couple of stretches before making my way through the web.

As I stood, I fought to keep a grimace off my face. Isaac looked so worried and I didn't want to upset him. It occurred to me that this was unusual behavior for an assassin toward her Vic.

There was no time to dwell on it. There was no guarantee I could jump high enough to get through that hole. What would MacGyver do? I thought about that a lot. He was kind of my hero. Of course, he'd create a ramp using hairspray, a toothpick and home-made cement. Hmmm. I had an idea.

There were five large rocks in a decorative pile a few yards off to my left. I dragged two over to the front of the web. Then I grabbed the two planks from the previous challenge and propped them up on the rocks. Two more rocks secured the planks at my end. See where I'm going with this?

I walked back about five feet, then ran up the make-shift platform and launched myself through the center hole. It felt like I was soaring through mud and I be-came aware of every inch of my skin as I passed through the large loop. My arms were extended in front of me, and for a moment I thought I must look a little like Superman. Well, Superman with boobs, that is.

My hands hit the dirt, followed ungracefully by my head, as I watched my toes clear the hole.

"You did it!" Lex cried as he and Isaac hauled me to my feet. I thought somewhere in the distance I heard someone say, "Way to go, Mom!" but I couldn't be sure. I may have been hallucinating.

"No time for champagne," I said as I raced to the zip line.

Cricket and I climbed into our harnesses, instructing the others to do the same.

"No helmets?" Cricket gasped. She was right. Safety obviously wasn't a concern on this show. Bastards. At least she seemed to have some experience with the zip line.

I hooked the pulley up to the line and safety line. Cricket set up the lanyard and carabiners, securing them to Silas's belay. Before he had any idea what was happening (and I guessed before he had the opportunity to protest), we hurled him off the platform. I must say I'd never heard a man scream like that.

"Good job," I said to Cricket and she nodded.

Sami went next, and at the end of the line I saw her and Silas struggling to get out of their harnesses. The other team was having a hard time figuring out how everything worked. And for a moment I panicked. People have *died* on these things. You had to get the combination exactly right. What was this stupid production company thinking?

Lex went through, and then I sent Cricket. Over on the other platform, it looked like they had the first person, Kit, ready to go. Unfortunately, they'd done it all wrong and in a matter of minutes the girl was about to fall twenty feet to her death.

Isaac was standing in front of me on the platform, grinning. It occurred to me that I could take care of him right there and then. All I'd have to do was mess with the carabiners and he'd plummet to his death.

"Are you okay?" Isaac asked.

I realized I was stalling. The job could be over and I could go home. The idea pounded in my brain as I held his fate, quite literally, in my hands. Isaac smiled at me and my stomach turned inside out. I couldn't do it. Quickly I secured him, then sent him safely to the other side of the line.

Something snapped as I saw that the other team was about to inadvertently kill one of their own. I leaped over the edge of our platform and ran toward Inuit, waving my arms and yelling, "Wait!" I climbed the steps two at a time and in a few moments had completely reorganized their zip-line system. I sent Kit and she rode the line to the end in silence. After sending two more of their team members safely, I realized what I was doing.

"Do it just as I did!" I shouted as I raced back to my platform. I avoided eye contact with my tribe—who remained strangely silent. I clicked the second carabiner into place and stepped off the platform.

Shit. I'd forgotten to release the safety line! I was just dangling in midair a foot away from the platform. A quick glance at the other team told me the last person was getting ready to go. If they won, I'd have blown it big time.

Reaching up for the line, I scrambled to get my feet back on the platform. I managed to lessen the tension just enough to unhook the carabiner and slid to the ground on the other side.

"Ottawa wins!" Alan shouted and I collapsed to the ground. It was over. After a few moments, I opened my eyes and saw a variety of emotions on the faces of my teammates. I couldn't tell if they thought I'd behaved nobly or idiotically, and I didn't care. We'd won and everyone survived. Literally.

Chapter Thirteen

If I ran for a position of leadership in this town, my platform would be "A howler monkey in every home," because nothing says community like a whole mess of howler monkeys.

—Todd Welvaert, journalist

Back at camp, I found myself at the mango tree talking to myself. "Dammit. I choked. I froze. What the hell?" I repeated this over and over, like some twisted meditation.

"Mom." Jackson's voice came from above.

After looking around to see if any of the camera crew was there, I looked up.

"Hey, kids." I didn't feel much like chastising them. I was too happy to see someone I knew . . . someone who I knew loved and supported me.

"We saw what happened," Monty said quietly. "It's okay."

"Yeah," Jack piped up. "It can't be easy to take Vic out when he's a friend."

I shook my head. "I'm pretty sure I can't do it at all, guys."

"It's okay." Jack unfolded himself so his red hair hung upside down. "We're going to help you."

Monty appeared beside his brother. "Don't do anything until we can think of something." I'd be lying if I said I wasn't a little *verklempt* at their attempts to comfort me.

There was an idea. "Hey, will you guys do me a favor and look into Vic for me?" I asked. "He just doesn't seem to be the type we usually axe. Maybe my judgment is clouding up from being so close to him, but I need more motivation. Can you get me the scoop?"

Monty grinned. "Roger that."

"Yeah! We'll get right on it," Jack echoed.

I wanted to hug them both, but couldn't risk it. I just turned away and headed back to camp. This would work, I told myself. The boys would figure something out. And their research would make my job clearer. A small, but significant sense of relief crept over me. At least I could put plans on hold until I heard back.

I was just about to camp when I spotted Lex leaning against a tree. The way the sun came down, illuminating his face, turned my skin to gooseflesh.

"I was waiting for you," he said. "I think what you did today—rescuing the other team like that—was amazing."

Before I knew what was happening, Lex pulled me into his arms and kissed me. It was one of those brain-melting kisses that I haven't had in years, I might add. My arms slid around his neck and I kissed him back with everything I had.

I was just starting to come to my senses and drag him off into the bushes for a quickie when something went clunk and I felt Lex flinch.

"Whoa!" He pulled back and began massaging his head. On the ground I spotted a hard, unripe mango. Looking up into the trees, I thought I saw a flash of red.

"Damn monkeys!" Lex cursed with a smile.

Yeah. Damn monkeys, I thought. Damn monkeys with red hair.

"Are you okay?" I asked, reaching up to touch the lump that was forming on his head.

"I'm fine." Lex smiled and it looked like we were going to make out again. Yay!

"Missi! Lex! Jesus Christ, where the fuck are you bastards?" Sami's voice was nearby.

We broke apart quickly as she joined us. Looking from one to the other, Sami got this "wink, wink, nudge, nudge" look.

"We're celebrating back at camp." She jabbed a thumb over her shoulder. "But I think I interrupted some private celebration here."

"Sami!" I started. "You didn't swear once in either sentence!"

She grinned. "Guess I'm losing my goddamned touch." Sami turned and raced off, leaving Lex and me to walk back to camp.

"Tell me about yourself," I teased. In all honesty, I didn't know that much about him.

Lex looked at me sideways and smiled. "What do you want to know?"

"Whatever." Gak! I was too new to this dating stuff. I didn't want to sound like an idiot—I just couldn't help myself.

"Okay. I'm a bartender and former stuntman. I don't really live in Canada. My brother thought it would be funny to sign me up for the show. I had no idea until I got the letter in the mail. By then I thought, why not? And here I am."

"That's funny. My, um . . ." I paused, wondering how much to tell him about my family. I didn't want to tell him the Bombays sent me here to kill Isaac. I was pretty sure that was a first-date no-no. ". . . mom and sons did the same thing to me." I filled him in on Monty and Jack's saying that they thought their mom should live a little. Not totally a lie. In fact, it was embarrassingly close to the truth.

Lex laughed. "Do you think that's how the others got here?"

"I suspect Cricket's fellow camp counselors were debating between this and killing her. I think Silas enjoys pain and suffering a little too much."

"What else should I know about you?" Lex squeezed my hand.

"Oh. Well, I'm a widow and live in Texas." There was no way I was going to tell him what I really did for a living, but I figured there was no harm in a little truth. "I'm an inventor. I like to make things."

"Like what?" he asked. Of course he asked. What the hell was I doing? It's not like I could claim credit for Post-its. Although I've always been jealous that I didn't come up with them. That and those plastic sleeves menus come in so they don't get messy.

"Oh, this and that." I tried to change the direction

a little. I couldn't talk about my disintegrating bullets or exploding Wacky WallWalkers, now, could I? At least, not yet.

I pulled my bracelet off and straightened it. "I invented this for the show." I pointed out the saw, the flint stones, and other handy applications.

"I'm impressed. So that's how you've managed out here. And that explains the resourcefulness in the challenges."

Lex's reply made me sigh with relief. Maybe he wouldn't press. And now that we were back at camp, there'd be more people to distract him.

"Great job!" Isaac called as we rejoined everyone.

"I think it's really cool that you saved Inuit like that," Cricket chirped. "But we have to be careful. We don't want them to win."

Silas nodded. "That was honorable. Damned challenge wasn't very authentic."

Julie interrupted our little party, casting a dour malaise on everything.

"Ottawa's presence is requested at Tribal Council," she said as if announcing the Queen of England.

"Why?" Lex stepped forward. "We won. Why should we have to go?"

Julie put her hand up in his face. "You get to watch the other team vote off a member. And you really have to be silent this time!"

We looked at each other. That seemed rather cruel. Leave it to Julie to come up with something like that. What a sadist. She'd fit right in with the Bombays. I was starting to wonder about her lineage, when Isaac broke in.

"When do we go?"

"Now," Julie answered. She turned and marched imperiously into the jungle. No one followed her, mainly because we hated her.

She returned, red-faced. "I said, NOW!"

It only took a few minutes to get to the pool at the Blanco Tigre. A little section was roped off for us and a luau for the guests was in full swing. Now that was cruel. We stared, drooling at the clean, well-dressed tourists gobbling down roasted pork, fruit kabobs and more. I was salivating over the iced-down beer, but that's just me.

"Are you fucking kidding?" Sami said to Julie. "We have to do this here? And we have to watch all those goddamned bastards eating like that?"

"Sami!" Julie turned red again and I wondered if her head would pop off. "Please stop swearing! If you don't, I'll have to dub your voice on the tape!"

Sami winked at me. "Whatever, bitch."

"She's got a point," Silas started. "This ain't authentic at all. How can we go through with this if ya ain't followin' the rules?"

The rest of us nodded and it was clear that Julie wanted to be somewhere else. But we weren't letting her off the hook. This was mean and stupid.

At that second, who should round the corner with a plate of food but Alan. He was flirting with some blonde, a cold beer in one hand and a mouth full of barbecue.

"You know," Alan said to the blonde, "I work in television. I'm a big star up north."

I figured that he was implying the U.S., because who the hell cares about a big star in Canada? The girl giggled and—oops, will you look at that? Her dress strap *accidentally* slipped from her shoulder.

Julie cleared her throat obnoxiously and Alan froze when he saw us, looking like a kid who got caught with his whole arm in the cookie jar.

"Julie, could I see you for a moment please?" His voice was strained and I couldn't help but giggle. As a group, we followed her.

"Guys—" Alan started, smearing barbecued pork–stained fingers on a napkin. He had a big glob of it on his face. We didn't tell him. "Just Julie, okay?"

Sami shook her head. "I don't fucking think so, you bastard. It's torture enough being here. Might at least have a little goddamned fun."

Ernie shouldered his camera and whispered, "Don't worry. I'll catch it. I'll share it with you if you give me a little footage of you performing one of your miracles later." I winked my response and he followed the two off into the jungle.

The second they were out of sight, the Ottawa tribe scrambled for the buffet table. Without a word we stuffed as much food as we could into our bags. To my surprise, Silas scooped up enough beer for us to get pretty drunk later. I guessed he was getting sick of the show too. Either that or they'd had a kegger at the surrender at Appomattox.

We were all seated and looking innocent when Alan returned, barbecue glob still on his face. Julie looked seriously pissed. Ernie was grinning. I guess we could add entertainment to the booze and food later.

"Will the Inuit Tribe please enter the Tribal Council area?" Alan boomed, raising his arms like he was some kind of god.

One by one, the other team filed in, looking with surprise at us, and with horror at the luau going on around them. Several of the resort guests dragged chairs over, with full plates on their laps.

"Inuit," Alan intoned, staring not at the team, but at the bimbo in the audience. The lump of sauce on his face quivered respectfully. "You lost the immunity challenge. Therefore, you have to vote off one of your members." He pointed dramatically at them and his voice got even louder. "One of you will be going home tonight."

"Kit," Alan said, "you've spent these first few days without food or drinkable water. How are you feeling?"

Kit sniffled. "Well, Alan, it's pretty hard, you know?" She looked at our host—who, in turn, looked pissed off that she'd used his first name—then burst into tears. "I can't get voted off! Not tonight! I've been the first one voted off two other reality shows! Please, please, please, don't vote for me!" the leggy brunette pleaded with her teammates.

The resort guests stared at her, eyes wide open, and filling their mouths with food. I hoped they'd get trichinosis.

"Um, okay." Alan squirmed (which made me happy). "Brick. How about you?"

Brick turned in his seat toward the camera and stared at it thoughtfully for a moment. Or at least, acting like he was staring thoughtfully at it. I noticed Moe rolling his eyes and smiled.

"Being stranded, here in paradise, with only the simplest of needs met, I find that I—Brick Phoenix—am like a child lost among the tempest storm of life . . . itself." He frowned at the camera, then turned back to Alan, who looked a little shaken.

"Liliana?" Our host squeaked.

This Inuit member rose to her feet, startling everyone else. "My body is my art. Food and water are the media I use to sustain my art. Without these tools, my body will no longer be art." She sat down dramatically.

I was starting to think everyone on Inuit had some form of heatstroke. Alan didn't seem to know how to respond to any of this.

Moe raised his hand and spoke before being asked. "I think it sucks." He reminded me of the character Ed, in *Shaun of the Dead*. "Especially with the resort so close by. But I'll do whatever I have to do to win the twenty-five thousand dollars."

What? We were playing for only twenty-five thousand dollars? The other show at least gave you one million dollars if you won. These poor bastards were playing for practically nothing! My empathy level spiked for Inuit and I cursed the producers.

"I think what you have here is our struggle with our inner selves," Dr. Andy piped up, using his hands as he spoke. Obviously he thought it gave him more of a stage presence. He was an African American Dr. Phil wannabe. "In living so primitively, we are literally starving the part of our ego that demands entitlement. It's very therapeutic when you look at it that way."

I could have used some therapy. I wished I could have talked to Dr. Andy just then about my problem. Of course, I couldn't—but there was something comforting in knowing he was right there.

Bob seemed to realize he was the only one who hadn't spoken, so he threw in his two cents. No politician could stay quiet for long, but I wasn't surprised he'd waited to get in the last word. "I suggest that no matter what, we do this democratically, for the right reasons. I see no reason why we have to get political about this. That's just partisan politics."

Okaaaaaaaaaaaaaaaay. Now that I saw that the Inuit tribe had all been recruited from the "short bus," I didn't feel so bad about what I was dealing with.

"Just go vote!" Alan shouted. He was very flustered. I wished I had some popcorn. The kind with movie theater butter. I love that. No salt though, because if you salt the top half you end up drinking most of your pop, which means you'll have to go to the bathroom every five minutes, and for what you pay for tickets these days, you might as well just go home. . . .

"Now I'll tally up the votes," Alan stated loudly,

regaining some of his composure. Gee. That went fast. How long was I thinking about popcorn?

Kit burst into a fresh round of tears as if anticipating the inevitable as Alan opened the large clay pot and pulled out the first vote.

He lifted the first slip of parchment out and read, "Kit. The first vote is for Kit."

Kit immediately added loud sobs.

"The second vote is for Liliana." Alan said. "One vote for Kit, one for Liliana."

He reached in and pulled out the third slip. "Bob. One vote for Kit, one for Liliana and one for Bob."

Kit howled. My guess was that it just hurt having been the first vote and hearing it over and over again.

"The fourth vote is for"—Alan frowned as he read the paper—"Dr. Andy. One vote for Kit. One vote for Liliana. One vote for Bob. One vote for Dr. Andy."

Julie was turning a little green at the gills. I guessed she didn't like the suspense. But I figured it wasn't hurting the show to drag it out to the last vote.

"Brick received the fifth vote." Alan looked pretty worried as he again parroted the vote so far. Really, there only needed to be one more vote for any of those names and they'd be out of the game.

"And the last vote is for . . ." Beads of sweat broke out on Alan's forehead. "Moe? Are you joking?"

We just stared in shock. No one had been voted off. Everyone had received one vote. What were the odds of that happening?

"Do you even know how to play this game?" Alan

shrieked at Inuit. "You're supposed to form alliances! This kind of crap isn't supposed to happen!"

I started laughing. Lex squeezed my knee (which is very close to *you-know-what*). Isaac winked and Sami whispered a *goddamn*.

"All right!" Julie took charge with the ease of a storm trooper. "We'll just have to vote again!" She pointed at Moe and he slowly rose to go to the ballot box.

"You're out of paper," he said simply.

We all looked over and, true enough, there was no more paper. Obviously, there was no backup plan.

"Will this work?" A cabana boy threw a resort stationery pad at Alan. I noticed with a start that the resort audience had doubled in size. Kind of like that scene in *The Birds* where Tippi Hedren is sitting on a bench outside the school? And with each puff of her cigarette, more birds landed until she turned around and found the monkey bars coated with crows? Kind of like that.

Julie handed the hotel stationery to Moe and he wrote down his vote. One by one, everyone went up to cast their vote.

"Now, I'll read the votes." Alan pulled the whole handful out of the jar and flipped through them, reading as he went. "Kit," he recited, causing Kit to start wailing again, "Moe, Liliana, Bob, Brick, Dr. Andy, goddamn it! You did it again!" He slammed the lid of the jar to the ground, causing it to splinter into a million pieces.

So, we watched as Inuit voted two more times, and

each time, each person (starting with Kit every time for some strange reason) received one vote and no one was voted off.

At first I thought it was some very clever strategy on Inuit's part to avoid losing a teammate. And then I thought they were each writing their own name down in hopes of being voted off and hitting the buffet. But as we went on, the looks of complete surprise and frustration on their faces (especially Kit's) led me to believe they really warranted that short bus.

"That's it!" Alan's face was turning red. "I'm thinking of a number between one and twenty."

Julie turned toward him, stunned. "Surely you're not going to just have them guess a number!"

I don't know, it sounded pretty smart to me. I was getting sick of sitting in the hot sun with a bag of food hidden under my chair probably breeding all kinds of nasty bacteria.

"Yes, I am!" Alan stamped his foot. He pointed at Kit first (I guess it just seemed automatic at this point) and shouted for her to choose a number.

"Um"—Kit choked back a sob—"nineteen?"

One by one, the six of them told Alan a number.

"Ha!" Alan's frown turned into a creepy-looking grin. "It was seven! Bob is the first person vot . . . I mean removed from *Survival*. Now bring me your damn torch and we're done."

Bob stood and nodded to the team, then walked his torch over to Alan.

"Yadda, yadda, yadda," Alan babbled as he doused the man's torch. "Bob, the tribe has spoken."

Julie escorted Bob off the set and into the main resort building, where I guessed she was checking him into a room. Lucky bastard. We were still sitting there when he came outside with a grin and loaded up his plate at the buffet.

"The rest of you go back to your camps. Tomorrow we will have another challenge." Alan had regained some of his professionalism, but I thought I saw a spark of madness around the eyes. The blonde had disappeared and the barbecue glob had fallen and smeared down the length of his white, linen shirt.

Chapter Fourteen

NARRATOR: *Even a poisonous snake isn't bad. You just have to keep away from the sharp end.*
—The Gods Must Be Crazy

"That was a hell of a thing," Sami muttered through a mouthful of fruit.

Everyone nodded as we sat on the beach eating our contraband food. Silas had managed to hide a bottle of beer for each of us and we were all feeling pretty mellow. For a second I thought about my glaucoma stash on Santa Muerta.

"At least we have this," Isaac raised his banana-leaf plate.

Lex nodded. "I still can't believe Julie didn't notice us walking out of the pool area leaking barbecue sauce."

I elbowed him gently in the ribs. "She's too concerned about the nonvote and Alan's extracurricular activities." For a moment, I wondered if Julie was in love with Alan. Then I threw up in my mouth and the feeling was over.

"Do you think we should do that when we go to Tribal Council?" Cricket chirped.

Everyone laughed and we continued eating. I was feeling all warm and gooey—like marshmallow crème. At one point, Sami and I volunteered to get more kindling.

"Why are you here?" Sami asked me once we were too far away to be overheard.

I shrugged. "It seemed like something to do." *My family set me up to knock off Isaac* just didn't have the right ring to it.

"How about you?"

Sami coughed and I heard her thoughts rattle around in her chest. She may not have been smoking anymore, but the damage was done.

"I know you think I lead this fucking glamorous life as a traveling electrician. . . ." She politely paused as I giggled. "But behind the tiaras and French champagne was a woman who screamed for a fucked-up adventure."

I nodded. "Yeah. It was just like that for me too. I couldn't believe my luck to get a crusty Civil War junkie and psychotic camp counselor in the same deal."

Sami looked off into the ocean. "Well, I guess we're on the same goddamned page. Hell, we're practically twins."

"Oh yes," I added. "Definitely separated at birth."

Neither of us spoke for a moment.

"Fact is," Sami said quietly, "I'm getting too old for this shit. I could use the money before some health problems force me to retire before my time."

I was stunned. It never occurred to me that Sami would open up about anything. Her trust in me almost made me tell her I was an assassin. Almost. Okay, I never really came close, but the conversation touched me.

"Do you want to talk about it?" I asked, not really knowing what to say.

She shook her head. "Jesus Christ, I've said too much already, bitch!" A sad smile tugged at the heavily lined corners of her mouth.

"Did you say something?" I feigned. "I'm sorry. I wasn't listening."

Sami laughed and clapped me on the back. "Shit. Let's get outta here. I'm sure Lex is waiting for you."

I looked at her quizzically. "What do you mean?"

"Aw, fuck. Everyone knows he's hot for you. Don't give me any bullshit, because you know it too."

We headed back to camp and I realized Lex and I hadn't been as cautious as we thought. Oh well. It didn't really matter in the end.

After the food was gone, everyone started to get ready for bed. Tomorrow would be another challenge and we didn't want to go down like the other team did. The cameramen never did show up. Maybe they had more to film at the other camp, or perhaps they blended in at the luau for some ill-gotten time off.

Lex and I took a moonlit stroll along the beach. As he held my hand, I thought this couldn't be more perfect. Well, except for being on the show and having to kill Isaac . . .

He sat down in the sand, pulling me down beside him. "I talked to Isaac and Sami about forming an alliance with us. They both thought it was a good idea."

A Bombay forming an alliance with her Vic. Now, that had to be a first.

I nodded. "That's good. What do you think about the other team? Anyone there look like a prospect?"

Lex stared out at the ocean for a moment before responding. "No. They all looked like they were nuts."

"I'll agree to that."

The two of us sat there for a moment, listening to the surf pound the shore. I really liked Lex. I mean really, really liked him. My mind turned to that scene in *From Here to Eternity* where the couple make out, rolling around in the surf. That would be *awesome*. Of course, then we'd be covered in seaweed, choking on salt water and digging sand out of various crevices for days. I guess it didn't sound so romantic when you put it that way.

"Any guesses on tomorrow's challenge?" I steered the subject clear.

"I don't know. Could be anything really. These guys don't seem to have a clue. For all we know, we could be playing shuffleboard at the resort."

I scratched the side of my nose. "That would suck. I'm no good at shuffleboard."

"What are you good at?"

I thought about that for a moment. I mean, there's only so much I could tell him. "I'm great at killing people using nothing more than a rectal thermometer and sunflower seeds"—that would probably be more than Lex wanted to know.

"I'm good at thinking outside the box," I answered truthfully. Technically I wasn't lying.

"Yes, I've seen some of your work." He laughed. "Is that what you are passionate about?"

"What do you mean?" What did he mean?

"Well, is that what you've always wanted to do—invent stuff? Fit a square peg into a round hole?"

"Actually, I can do that. And yes, I guess it is my passion." It surprised me that I'd never really thought about it before. Being creative and inventing things were just in my blood. I couldn't imagine doing anything else.

Lex said, "You look confused."

"No. Not really," I lied. "I guess I just never had a dream about doing one big thing. I just love inventing."

He looked at me for a moment. "There isn't something you'd like to do with your talents? Invent the perfect mousetrap?"

I laughed uneasily. "I guess not." It always bothered me a little that my inventions would go unrecognized by the world due to the highly secretive nature of the Bombay family business, but I wasn't about to say that. "What about you? Any lofty goals for your life?"

Lex shook his head. "I don't have it all together like you. Maybe I never will. My biggest goal would probably be just to find happiness. That's all that really seems to matter."

Damn, he had me there. Wasn't that what everyone wanted in life? Sure, some people wanted fame and fortune. But this gorgeous hunk of man just wanted to be happy. How cool was that?

"There is one thing we both seem to be good at." He grinned and leaned toward me.

My lips met his, and oooh la la! As Lex's arms slid

around me I chastised myself for going all these years without a man.

My hands were just sliding up his nice, muscular arms when we heard shouting down the beach.

I wanted to ignore it until I recognized the word *help* being screamed over and over. Lex and I jumped up and ran down the beach toward camp.

Imagine our surprise when we found our shelter in flames. Sami tossed water onto the fire as Silas and Isaac tried to beat it out with giant leaves. I snatched up a couple of empty coconut halves and raced toward the sea while Lex joined the other men. For a moment I realized that Cricket was nowhere to be seen.

We worked silently for what seemed like hours. Sami and I ran back and forth with water and the men stamped out the remaining embers. Our shelter was reduced to ashes.

"What happened?" I asked when I suddenly realized I didn't know.

"No fucking clue," Sami began. "I went into the jungle to take a piss and I came back to see Silas and Isaac trying to put the fire out."

Lex and I turned to the other men.

Silas shrugged. "I don't know either. We didn't have a campfire tonight cuz of all the food we got. I was collecting fruit and saw the smoke. Isaac showed up a few seconds after me."

Isaac nodded but didn't add anything.

"Where's Cricket?" I asked.

Everyone shrugged. Lex examined the charred remains of our site. It was too dark to determine what caused the fire and I was more concerned with our missing team member.

"We can figure this out later. Right now, we should find Cricket," I pressed, startled that I found myself so concerned about her.

We started combing the beach, shouting for our missing teammate. Nothing. It was far too dark to enter the jungle alone with no light. I was getting a little worried.

Lex pulled out the emergency walkie-talkie Julie had given us on our first day at camp. He was just turning it on, when who should walk out of the foliage but our little wayward camp counselor.

"Where the hell have you been, bitch?" Sami shouted. I thought I detected more concern than contempt in her raspy voice.

"What?" Cricket said a little defensively. "I was out getting mangoes for breakfast."

That would've been a reasonable explanation, were it not for the fact that she had no mangoes whatsoever.

"How do we know she didn't start the fire?" Silas squinted at her suspiciously.

"What fire?" Cricket squeaked.

"How did you find your way through the jungle without any light?" Isaac asked. I thought it was a pretty good question.

"What's your problem?" she asked. "I told you where

I was, what I was doing. I didn't start any fire." Her eyes trailed the length of camp and stopped on the charred shelter.

"What happened?" Cricket made a slight movement with her right hand—it looked like she pocketed something she didn't want us to see. Then she ran over to what remained of our sleeping area.

"All right," Lex started, "let's just calm down. We don't know that she's not telling the truth and we don't know how the fire got started."

Isaac nodded. "And we won't know until morning light. Let's just give everyone the benefit of the doubt and try to get some sleep for the challenge tomorrow."

The others nodded grudgingly and we silently dug our own spots in the sand. Silas was snoring within seconds, but I had a feeling that everyone else was awake, listening for . . . what, exactly?

"I don't want you to get cold," Lex's voice purred in my ear as he settled in next to me. His arm slid over me and I could feel my temperature rise a few notches. As I heard his breathing slow down to sleep tempo, my mind wandered.

What had happened here? Had someone deliberately started the fire? If it had been an accident, I was pretty sure one of my teammates would have owned up to it. And where had Cricket been? How had she maneuvered through the pitch-black jungle? And what was she concealing in her pocket that she didn't want us to see?

My brain repeated these questions over and over until I realized that someone was moving around the camp. Very gently, I lifted my head and looked around. A dark shadow was moving against the canopy of trees. I couldn't make out who it was, and I was pretty sure whoever didn't want anyone to know what it was doing. Slowly I turned my head to see where the rest of my teammates were sleeping. I just barely made out the dark clumps of bodies, but had no idea who was up and around. One, two, three . . . yup. The shadow was one of us.

Lex rolled onto his back and I lay down with my head on his shoulder. It was probably just someone going to use the bathroom. Or maybe one of my team was trying to solve the mystery. After a couple of shuffling noises, the sounds ended. Whoever it was had gone to sleep.

The urge to jump to my feet was doused by the realization I might be overreacting. Everyone had to get up sometime in the night for the bathroom. What was I going to do, tie them up one by one and force them to confess under the threat of torture? All I had on me was the bracelet and fire. No, that was too Spanish Inquisition. All I really needed was some water, a coconut shell and some copper wire. . . .

This train of thought was going nowhere. The fact was that we didn't know what had happened. In order to stay in the game to do my job, I had to keep my teammates happy. And I was pretty sure they wouldn't be happy with me if I was grilling them about their latrine usage. I needed more evidence, so I turned off my inner Nancy Drew and tried to get some rest.

Chapter Fifteen

JOEL: *If you don't understand it, shoot it.*
                    —Mystery Science Theater 3000

My eyes popped open at daylight. I have this weird inner alarm clock that goes off when I need something. In my imagination, it's a Raggedy Ann clock that says, "Wake up, wake up you sleepy head—it's time to start our day." I don't know why it's Raggedy Ann. I never liked her. Something about those red and white–striped socks seems creepy.

I sat up and looked around. Everyone was still asleep. I stood up slowly and moved quietly to the burned-out shelter to see what I could find.

At first glance, everything seemed to be normal. I mean, a fire like that wasn't exactly normal, but nothing looked out of place. I couldn't smell any accelerant, like gasoline. There was no trace of foul play. Maybe it really was an accident.

Glancing over at my slumbering team, I thought I saw something shiny out of the corner of my eye. I got down on my hands and knees and peered under the floor of the shelter. Half-buried in the sand was a smooth, black oval. It took me two sticks to reach it and I managed to drag it out from under the ruins and slip it into my pocket as Silas woke up.

"Morning," he grumbled.

I nodded. "Sleep well?"

"Yeah, right." Silas stood and tottered off toward the jungle.

As soon as he was out of sight, I pulled the object out of my pocket. It was a cigarette lighter. Where had that come from? It certainly implied that the fire had been deliberately set. But why? Who? It really bothered me that I didn't know. Especially since I was the past president of the Nancy Drew Fan Club. Of course, that was back in 1975, but it still counts and I still had the ID card in my wallet.

Sami rose next, winked at me, then headed off into the jungle. It was that time of day when everyone had to turn the jungle into a latrine. I followed her with my eyes. Sami was a likely candidate. I was convinced she was a smoker. Maybe she smuggled some cigarettes and the lighter onto the show? I could just picture her sitting on the corner of the shelter, lighting a smoke and dropping it as someone came into view.

But why wouldn't she admit it? We'd all had contraband the night before, so it wasn't like we were going to geek out and turn people in.

Duh! Of course she wouldn't want anyone to know! She might think it could get her voted off somehow.

Isaac and Lex woke up simultaneously. In a few minutes they had snatched up the spear to fetch fish for breakfast. Sami and I went in search of coconuts and fruit. Silas hadn't come back and Cricket was still asleep. As I climbed the tree to collect mangoes, I toyed with the idea of handing Sami the lighter. For some reason, I just couldn't do it.

Cricket finally woke up and Silas returned to find fish sizzling over a fire. Our perky little camper didn't say a word about where she'd been the night before. In fact, she didn't say anything at all. Maybe we'd come down too hard on her.

"Well," said Isaac as he stood and stretched, "I guess we'd better get started on another shelter."

Sami nodded. "I am itching from all that damned sand."

Lex and I wandered off to find what we needed for a new shelter.

"What a team," I moaned. "How did I end up here?"

"They aren't so bad. I think it would be worse to be on Inuit."

"Are you serious? Between Cricket the camp counselor and Silas the Civil War reenactor, we're doomed."

"Oh, I wouldn't say that. At least we have someone to lead a suicide charge should we find ourselves in combat."

"I hadn't thought of that," I admitted.

"And if one of the challenges involves knots, Cricket can probably lead us through it with a song."

"Well, I *was* feeling better."

"Didn't you ever go to summer camp as a kid?"

I wondered how much to tell him. The Bombays do their own kind of camping. Capture the Flag usually ends rather badly, and our songs tend to have bloodthirsty military cadences.

"Nope. And from being around Cricket I can tell I really missed out."

"Well, I went to camp. And it wasn't that bad."

You know, it was kind of cute how he stuck up for everybody. But I didn't have time for this.

"There's some brush over there." I pointed and he grabbed it. "How about reenacting bloody carnage? Ever do that?"

"I was a stuntman in Hollywood for years. It was my job to make the guys who got hit by cannon fire fly through the air and not get hurt."

"Silas wouldn't like that. He seems like the type who'd love to get sun poisoning by playing dead on a battlefield all day."

"I worked with some reenactors on a period piece once. They drove me nuts with their demands for authenticity. I eventually had to replace them with actors. They called them 'farbs'—people who don't follow the tradition to a T."

"What didn't they approve of?"

"We had pads for the actors to land on so they wouldn't get hurt. And they were pissed off because the boots all fit. No one got any blisters—and that is some kind of badge of honor with them."

"Did you work on any movies where you kill off camp counselors?" I asked hopefully.

"No. I didn't do the *Friday the 13th* stuff. I worked on some television programs, but mostly action flicks."

"Anything I'd have seen?"

I listened as Lex listed a string of movies from the early 1990s.

"Are you serious? *Bad Blood* is one of my favorite films! Your explosions were top notch! How did you manage to make that water tower blow?" He was hitting on my territory now.

"Mostly C-4. You like explosions?"

Do I! How could I phrase it without sounding like the Unabomber? "I guess I can really appreciate a good bombing scene. Most of them are so unrealistic."

Lex nodded. "Now everything is done on computer. Very little is real these days."

I sighed in agreement. We were almost back to camp.

Lex put his hand on my shoulder. "Let's give Cricket and Silas a chance. If they blow it, I'll be the first to admit I was wrong."

My knees went a little weak. He was far more mature than I was. And he was right. Getting along with everyone was crucial to doing my job. Gorgeous, compassionate, responsible *and* he liked to blow things up. I was definitely in trouble.

We had just gotten back when Julie came out of the jungle, clipboard in hand. She surveyed the burned remains and looked at us.

"Have a little trouble last night?" She didn't wait for us to reply. "I hope Bert and Ernie got it on tape." Huh. She didn't ask if anyone got hurt. Bitch.

Her eyes rested on me and it occurred to me that Julie wasn't my number one fan. I shuffled my feet trying to buy time. I didn't want to rat out our camera crew. If I told her they were AWOL last night, she'd probably shove them up our asses for the rest of the time.

"Yup, they got it," I decided aloud.

I noticed the rest of the team staring at me. "We screwed up and accidentally caught our shelter on fire. Silly us!"

No one else spoke. Apparently, they thought I should run with this alone.

"Well," Julie scowled, "I'm glad to hear they're finally doing their jobs." She squinted down the length of the beach. "Where are they now?"

"Oh," Sami said, "they needed to get some more batteries or some shit like that."

"Yeah." Cricket added.

"Fine." Julie looked at her clipboard. "We have the first challenge this morning, followed by the immunity challenge and Tribal Council." She was reading as if she were our cruise director. *Julie the Cruise Director. Ooh! Lex could be Gopher.*

"When this morning?" Cricket asked, her head cocked to one side. Suspicion reared up when I saw her and I suppressed it. There was no evidence she had done anything wrong. Maybe sneaky, but not wrong.

"Now," Julie said a little too angrily. "We're heading there now."

"Wait a minute," Silas interrupted. "We have two challenges in the same day?" Apparently, he was the only one smart enough to catch that.

Julie nodded. "Yes, that's right."

We all began to protest at once and Julie threw her hands up in the air.

"Look! There will be no argument on this! Let's go!"

Everyone followed her down the beach. It was hard to see where all this was going. Two challenges and a Tribal Council in the same day? What the hell was going on? Were we shortening our stay? I wasn't ready to take care of Isaac yet. In fact, I didn't want to take care of him at all.

A looming sense of panic bloomed in my stomach. I was running out of time and options. I prayed Monty and Jack would have something for me soon.

"Any ideas about the fire?" Isaac whispered to Lex and me as we lagged behind the rest of the group.

I pulled the lighter from my pocket. "I found this."

Lex took it from me and, after examining it, handed it to Isaac.

"Do you think maybe it came from the camera crew?" Isaac asked. Huh. I hadn't thought of that.

"Where was it?" Lex asked.

I told them where I'd found it but kept my suspicion of Sami to myself. She was part of our alliance and I didn't want them to vote her off should we lose our immunity challenge.

"It was probably just an accident," Lex mused.

Isaac nodded. "We're just getting paranoid. We really need to focus. Two challenges in one day is a lot."

His words died off when we realized we were suddenly in the middle of the Inuit camp. They were located only about five minutes down the beach! Was this whole show being planned by monkeys? That made me think about monkeys in suits and I shuddered.

Now, when I say "camp," I'm using the word very loosely. This team never built a shelter and barely had a working fire pit. Where did they sleep? It looked like they just crashed in the sand—just as we had last night. Yeesh.

Julie collected the Inuit members and we took off, heading further down the beach. The other tribe said nothing. Actually, they looked incapable of thought. I wasn't certain they'd eaten anything since we got there. They appeared to be too weak to take on one challenge, let alone two in the same day.

The other members of my team looked just as shocked as I did. Sure, you wanted to beat out everyone else for the money—but you didn't want them to die of starvation and exhaustion in the process. Lilianna looked thin and tired. I was worried about her the most. What was happening to these people? They really weren't going to survive at this rate.

Chapter Sixteen

HELEN: *Gort! Klaatu barada nikto!*
           —The Day the Earth Stood Still

Julie stopped suddenly, causing us all to crash into her like the Keystone Cops. She, of course, didn't fall over. Evil never does.

"Hello." Alan stood on the beach, waving his arms to reveal nothing around him.

Where was the challenge course? This couldn't be it . . . could it?

"Welcome to your reward challenge," Alan intoned.

We looked around us. There was nothing but sand and surf. How in the hell could this be it?

"As you now know, we have two challenges today. This one is for reward. Want to know what you're playing for?"

No one nodded. No one did anything. Alan ignored us dramatically.

"Bavarian beer!"

Julie grunted as she dragged a keg out of the jungle.

Absolutely everyone cheered. Being drunk was a much better option than being sober in this situation. And the beer we'd had the other night was warm and flat by the time we got back to camp.

"Real German brew," Alan continued. "This stuff has the highest alcohol content possible. And the keg is completely chilled, so it should stay ice-cold all day."

I started drooling at the mention of ice-cold. I hadn't had anything ice-cold (except the cold shoulder from Julie) since we left Canada.

Jimmy, Bert and Ernie stumbled out of the jungle. But where was the other camera crew? In fact, our three boys looked pretty bad. Big party last night, perhaps? That would explain their absence last night and this morning.

"Here's what's going to happen." Alan pointed at each team. "You are going to play charades. Each team member will act out the item listed on their card. The first team to guess all six answers wins the beer."

Charades? On a reality show? Seriously? In my mind's eye I now saw the aforementioned monkeys screaming with glee.

Julie separated the two teams and we were asked to select our first player. No one volunteered. I guess we all thought we sucked at this stupid game. Inuit chose Lilianna. This was going to get really interesting.

"I'll do it!" Cricket chirped a little too eagerly. We nodded our assent and she jumped up and stood in front of us. Julie started the stopwatch.

"Go!" Alan shouted.

Cricket nearly mauled Julie for the card and squinted at the writing. Suddenly, she leaped forward, eyes open wide, wiggling her arms and prancing about in circles in front of us.

I had no idea where to begin. Was there even a theme to this?

"A jellyfish with seizures?" I guessed.

"Jesus, bitch!" Sami shouted. "Are you wiggling your arms or flapping the goddamned things?"

Cricket frowned and I even thought I saw her middle finger go up briefly. She went back to her galloping spasms.

"Johnny Reb with a bullet in the heart?" Silas asked. Wow. How did he come up with that? Maybe everything looked like a Civil War reference to him.

"A butterfly!" Isaac called out—bringing my thoughts back to the present.

"A parrot?" Lex asked.

I really wanted that beer. But for the life of me, I couldn't figure out what the hell she was. I looked over at Inuit and saw Lillianna making some similar movements. Hers made sense.

"She looks like a hummingbird," I said quietly.

"That's it! Ottawa wins the first guess." Julie forced a grin.

That's weird. I was just looking at the other team and . . . oh my God! They gave us all the same cards! How completely stupid were they? The monkeys in suits did backflips in my head.

I jumped up and took my card. My mind was still reeling from the fact that both teams had the exact same clues. A few yards away, Kit was getting her card. Damn. I didn't have much time.

The card said I was a volcano. Okay—so there was a theme. I couldn't tell my teammates or let them know that if they couldn't figure it out by looking at our team, they should look at the other team.

So, I erupted. Well, as a volcano, that is. Never the one who excelled at party games, I gave it my best shot. After making what I thought looked like a pointy mountain over my head, I crouched down and then kind of shot upwards, flinging my arms open at the top. I even threw in this kind of jazzy move where my arms slithered down like hot lava. I was pretty proud of myself.

Of course, I faced five completely blank faces. So I did it again. Nothing. Not even a guess from Ottawa. Obviously they didn't appreciate my genius.

I glanced over at Kit. Apparently her team hadn't yet figured out that we had the same clues, and she didn't know a different way to portray a volcano any more than I did.

Completely exasperated, I simply made the *V* sign with the first two fingers of my hand.

"Volcano!" Lex shouted.

I smiled at him. What a great guy! As I took my seat and Silas stood up, I whispered what I knew to everyone else. From the shock on their faces, I guessed they couldn't believe it either. We were just starting to discuss it when Alan shouted out that Inuit got the suggestion. There were now two points for Ottawa and one for the other team. Silas glowered as he sat down, probably because we hadn't paid any attention to him.

Sami stood up and took the card from Julie. She looked pissed when she read it. So, she turned to look at Brick/Norman to see how he was faring.

Sami got our attention and pointed at the other team. Brick was sliding forward, then back in a weird flowing motion.

Isaac yelled, "The tides! The sea tides."

Sami grinned and rejoined us, slapping him on the back.

"Wait! That's not fair!" Julie shouted, her face turning red. "They guessed what the other team was doing. Sami didn't play, she just pointed to Brick!"

Alan looked from us to Inuit and back again. "Well, they did get it right."

Brick and his teammates looked stunned. I guess they just now realized what we'd known all along.

"I say we give the point to Inuit!" Julie snapped, winning her no favor with us.

"Hey! It's not our fault you're too fucking stupid to give each team separate suggestions!" Sami got right up in her face. "We won. We played by your rules and I motioned. Isaac guessed it. Our point."

Julie took a step back. Maybe she realized that Sami would beat the shit out of her. I had no doubt about it, myself.

"Ottawa wins the point. Let's continue," Alan answered.

Isaac rose to take his card for the next round. Julie gave Moe his card but held on to ours.

"Knock it off, Julie," Alan said when he saw what was happening. But Julie started running in circles, keeping the card out of Isaac's hands. Inuit was working hard on guessing Moe's word. He looked like a beached whale, lying on his side in the sand.

By now, Alan had joined in and both he and Isaac were chasing Julie around the beach for the card. The guesses were coming fast and furious from Inuit. We didn't have much time.

I stood up as Julie ran toward me and clotheslined her in the throat with my extended arm. She dropped to the ground and I stood on her neck until she released the card to Isaac.

Moe was now on his arms, dragging his body across the beach. Isaac hung his arms in front of him and loosely made a clapping motion.

"A sea lion!" Cricket said.

I pulled Julie up to her feet and dusted the sand off her. She clung to her clipboard as if it would save her life.

"Four out of six answers right!" Alan smiled at Julie. "Ottawa wins!"

Julie snapped her clipboard in half and marched off into the jungle.

"Ottawa, you win the reward. But there is a twist.

You have only two hours to drain this keg before the immunity challenge. If it isn't completely empty before the challenge—you lose automatically. The losing team votes a member off, tonight."

Oooh. That was bad.

"Whatever, dumbass." Sami was already dragging the keg back toward our camp. Isaac and Lex jumped in and soon the three of them were practically running across the beach.

Lex tapped the keg with a speed I felt might have broken the laws of physics, and within minutes we were gulping down the frothy brew. No one spoke. I was actually afraid that someone from the resort would show up and take it away from us. I wouldn't have been surprised if Alan had swiped it from some vacationing Berliners.

"Mmmmm . . ." I groaned in delight after polishing off another coconut husk of beer. It felt so good going down. We just lay there in the sand, nursing that keg.

Sami filled her fifth mug of beer without any obvious effects of drunkenness. Maybe we could pull this off after all.

Cricket vomited for the third time. Okay. Maybe not. But Lex was doing okay. Isaac seemed a little bombed. Silas passed out after his third.

My buzz was kicking in. This beer was seriously potent. I nursed another mug as I watched Sami go for her eighth. She had an amazing tolerance.

I looked down at the stopwatch Julie had left behind. Only an hour to go and we still had half a keg.

"Maybe we should give up," Cricket hiccuped.

"How mush had you have?" I mumbled. Okay, so I was more than a little buzzed.

"Oh," she thought for a few moments, then turned back to me. "Did you shay something?"

"I think we should take a break," Lex said. "Some of you need to throw up to get this out of your system."

Oh yeah! He was a barfender. I pictured him in a G-string.

"Especially you." Two Lexes quivered in front of me as they took the huskkkk out of my fands. Blahh-hhchhhh.

"I'm good." Sami poured herself another one.

Lex led me off down the beach a little ways. I jammed my finger into my throat and puked into the surf. We stumbled back to the rest of them.

Sami, Isaac and Lex continued working on the keg while Cricket, the unconscious Silas and I watched. I plopped backward into the sand and stared up at the clouds, which resembled monkeys in suits for some reason.

"Missi?" I heard a voice murmur in my ear.

My eyes opened to see Lex, a little less blurry and only one of him, standing next to me.

"It's time to go," he continued.

I stumbled to my feet and saw that Sami and Isaac were carrying Silas. Cricket just looked green.

"Ish the keg gone?" I asked his lovely blue eyes.

"Yup."

Jimmy the cameraman grinned and seemed to have

sprouted two heads. Bert and Ernie looked more like the Muppets than themselves. How much had I drunk?

We followed the crew into the jungle. Thank God it was a short trip or we wouldn't have made it. Every single one of us was bombed. Even Sami couldn't walk straight.

"This is a twisted show," I complained as Lex walked into a tree.

We came into a clearing with an extremely complicated obstacle course. Oh shit.

The Inuit tribe took one look at us and smiled. Things were looking up for them. I, for one, desperately had to pee.

"Ottawa!" Alan shouted, making us all flinch with pain. "You have to sit one person out. Who will it be?"

Silas answered by passing out, face down in the sand.

"I guess it will be Silas," I said.

Alan explained the course in some dialect of the Tagalog language, while we struggled to stay upright. I have no idea what he said. I've never been to France. Wait. They speak French there. Tagalog is something else. It begins with an fffff. Philippiano?

They led us to a raised platform where we would begin the course. The stairs were particularly challenging. Alan shouted and we began.

Sami took one step on the balance beam and fell off into the sand below. She didn't move. Neither did we. If she was dead, we didn't want to take any chances.

So, we watched as the Inuit tribe won their first challenge. It was nice to see them jumping up and down together with glee. I was happy for them. And I wanted a nap, a toothbrush and complete darkness.

Somehow we made it back to camp. It hadn't really hit us that we had to vote someone off in a few hours, just that the banging of the surf on the sand was making so much noise. I lay down, pressing my forehead against the cool metal keg. It felt wonderful. The rest of me felt like shit.

At that moment, an annoying little voice in my soggy brain told me there was something wrong. That was weird. I'm usually pretty good about sizing up a situation. Figurative alarm bells were going off and I had no idea why.

Sitting up, I looked at my teammates—all passed out in the sand around me. No one else seemed concerned. I tried to ignore the nagging intuition, but there was no use. Bombays rely heavily on instinct. When you feel that something is wrong, chances are it is.

But what in the hell was it? I leaned against the steel keg, my head throbbing. Maybe my senses were over-reacting. I mean, it's not like that hasn't happened before. Like the time in the pool on Santa Muerta with the sharks. Oh. Wait. There really had been sharks in the pool.

"Get up!" I shouted as I jumped to my feet. No one responded.

"Get up! Now!" I yelled louder, and then grabbed my head as it ached.

Lex leaned up on an elbow. "Missi, can't you just let everyone die in peace?"

The alarm in my brain was getting louder. Something very bad was going to happen. I kicked, pushed and dragged my teammates toward the jungle. I didn't know why exactly—a fact that they didn't seem to appreciate. I had just pushed Isaac into the trees when the keg I'd been leaning against exploded and shot up into the sky.

We all watched as what was left of the smoking metal crashed to the sand. After a few minutes, we emerged from the trees to inspect the bomb that had been in our midst (and inconveniently pressed to my forehead earlier).

"Holy fucking shit!" To my surprise, that came from Silas, not Sami.

I took two of the discarded coconut shells and gingerly turned over the twisted metal. A small, smoldering lump was attached to one side. C-4. Somebody had tried to kill us using the old "bomb in the keg" trick. This was far more serious than sabotage.

Isaac raced to the resort and found the crew. Bert and Ernie were more than happy to have something to film . . . an enthusiasm I found slightly creepy. Alan contacted the police, and we all sobered up quickly during the interrogation. By the time they left with the twisted wreckage of the keg late that afternoon, our hangovers had turned into exhaustion. Lex talked me into trying to get some sleep.

"I'll take the watch," he said.

I looked at him sharply. "Do you think we're in danger?"

He shook his head. "Most likely someone just wanted to scare us." I couldn't tell if he was lying to make me feel better. Eventually I succumbed to sleep, my head in his lap, grateful for his presence.

Chapter Seventeen

KING LEONIDAS: *Spartans! Ready your breakfast and eat hearty . . . for tonight, we dine in hell!*

—*300*

I came to as dusk settled on the beach. My head was pounding, my mouth felt like I'd eaten a monkey—fur and all—and I noticed that half my team was asleep out in the sand. I never did well with hangovers, being a lightweight and all. Amid all the commotion of the afternoon, the effects hadn't seemed so bad, but now they were back full force.

"Missi!" Isaac whispered and I crawled over to where he and Lex were sitting with a bunch of bananas and a couple of coconut halves filled with water. I drank and ate like I'd never had food and water before.

"We're trying to decide whether to vote off Cricket or Silas tonight," Isaac murmured. We quickly looked over our shoulders to see Sami, Cricket and Silas still out.

Oh. Right. In spite of the explosion, we still had a game to play. And we still had Tribal Council coming up that night.

"I was thinking we should vote off Cricket." Lex put his hand on the back of my neck and began to massage. I started to melt.

"But what about Silas?" Isaac pressed. "He's just as bad as she is. They are both moody, surly and awkward during the challenges."

Yeesh. I had no ideas for them. "We could pull what Inuit tried yesterday?" I suggested.

Lex shook his head. "No. They'll be ready for that."

"But I don't want to vote anyone off!" I was getting a little whiny.

"Neither do we, but something has to be done."

Isaac was right. We'd all signed contracts, agreeing to play the game as it was. There was no getting out of it.

"Fine. I vote for Cricket then. Silas at least pulls his weight around camp and we can use him in the physical challenges."

Lex nodded solemnly. "I'll wake Sami and tell her."

I felt like shit. I didn't want Cricket to go home. She had been pretty helpful during the ropes course challenge. But she was also conveniently missing when the shelter caught fire. If she was the saboteur, it would be good to get rid of her. And if she wasn't, at least she'd be safe at the resort. Either way, voting someone off was a bad situation. The beer was wearing off and my tongue was starting to shed, but I still felt awful.

Silas came to and skittered over to me, taking a banana.

"So." He peeled the fruit slowly and popped it into his mouth. "Who's it gonna be?"

I didn't have the heart to mess around. "You are staying. Cricket is going."

Silas looked at me quietly for a moment. He'd never

really spoken to me before. I felt like I was seeing him for the first time.

"Okay," he said. "How much time have we got?"

"Not long," Isaac replied. "They should be here any minute to take us to Tribal."

I wandered off into the trees to clear my head. Birds shrieked, snakes slithered and monkeys chattered, all amplified by my alcohol-addled brain. Within a few minutes I found Monty and Jack's tree—at least the tree I usually saw them in.

"Boys!" I managed a stage whisper, then looked around uneasily.

"Hi, Mom." Jackson unfolded himself upside down like a giant, red-headed bat. Monty was hanging next to him.

"You wouldn't happen to have toothbrushes, would you?" I asked hopefully.

Monty laughed and handed me a bag. Inside were six toothbrushes and toothpaste, six sticks of deodorant and a bottle of aspirin. Damn, I love those boys.

"We don't really have any info for you," Jackson said.

"It's hard to find out about Isaac. It's like he doesn't exist. I've found a few references to an Isaac Beckett who worked in Vegas a few years back, but the info is old and a lot of it is sketchy at best. There's nothing about the kind of work he did, which is weird. It's like he tried to have all records of him erased," Monty finished.

"Well, that would fit his MO." I tapped my chin. It

was very likely a bad guy would be hard to trace. My fingers itched for my special computer equipment, but unless I knew how to power a laptop using a banana, it would be useless. Now lemons, I could work with. I used them to power radios all the time.

"Hold off till we find something on Vic," Jack said.

"And there's something else," Monty added. "I think one of your teammates is sabotaging the show. I saw—" He cut off his words, shrinking up into the tree.

"Missi!" Sami was right behind me. I turned slowly with a grin.

"Hey, Sami." I tried to be nonchalant. Maybe she hadn't seen the boys.

"What the hell are you doing here? The dumbasses are gonna come and get us soon. You hear about Cricket?"

I interrupted her. "Sami, what do you think about Isaac?"

She looked up with a grin. "Hell, you want to fuck him too? Damn, bitch, you are greedy."

I shook my head quickly. "No! No, I mean in the game. I don't think of Isaac like that." No. More like dead victim, really. Dead victim I was in danger of liking.

"He's okay. I don't think the son of a bitch is all as good a poker player as he thinks."

"What makes you think that?" I didn't recall any poker games around the campfire.

"He's just not good at bluffing. You can read him like an open book. Like the times you've given him the cold shoulder—he tried to play it off like he didn't care, but you could see he didn't like it. Like I said, bastard's got no poker face."

I smiled. "Oh, and you do?" I felt a little bad that she'd noticed my avoiding Issac. But Sami was a different animal altogether, and I had yet to figure her out.

Sami stopped what she was doing and gave me a hard look. "Well, I haven't made it this long as the only female electrician in my union without bluffing."

It had never occurred to me that Sami might have had trouble in her profession. I mean, I worked in a usually male-dominated field with no worries. Of course, I worked alone and only the Bombays knew what I did. And if they gave me any trouble they knew I was a bitch at paybacks.

"How bad is it?" I was curious and I liked Sami.

"I could tell you stories that would make you shit your spleen."

I didn't press, mainly because I didn't want to shit my spleen.

Sami continued anyway. "You know, folks think times have changed, but nothing could be further from the truth. Men are real bastards. They want to be able to say they have a woman working for them, but they treat you like a whore or an idiot."

"I didn't know it was that bad." And you wouldn't think so, would you? "Do you have any recourse through the union?"

Sami laughed angrily. "The union ignores me. When I complain about sexual harassment, they call me a bitch. When I tell the guys I work with I don't want to sleep with them, they call me a whore. It's a no-win situation."

"How do you deal with it?"

Sami grinned. "I call their wives or threaten to tell their daughters how they act. It isn't a huge threat, but it works."

I shook my head. "That's horrible." Suddenly I wanted to kill male electricians. I was lucky in that I didn't really work in a sexist environment. Things tend to even up real fast when there's the chance you can electrocute them with the lawn sprinkler. Actually, the Bombays have been pretty progressive over the centuries. I always suspected that went back to the beginning when the family realized the women were just as deadly as the men (if not more so).

"Yeah, well, dem's da berries." Sami stood. "Enough of this whiny shit. Let's get back."

As I followed her, I had a newfound respect for the woman. My guess was that very little in her life came easily. While I was impressed that she'd chosen such a male-dominated field, I was even more impressed that she hadn't cracked. Or maybe she had. Maybe that's how she ended up here.

The crew was AWOL again, so I doled out the toothpaste, toothbrushes, deodorant and aspirin to the group. Again, no one questioned me. That was weird. By the time Julie arrived we all smelled better. She looked at us suspiciously, but said nothing.

Each of us grabbed our torches and followed her in

the direction of the Blanco Tigre. Even though we had minty-fresh breath, we were pretty miserable (and by miserable, I mean hungover). Voting a member off was not something any of us wanted.

And then there was that other matter. The boys had said they'd seen something or someone that looked like the show was being sabotaged. From the mysterious fire, lighter and disappearance of Cricket to the exploding keg fireball, I had too much to think about.

I really didn't care about the show. Alan and Julie were useless as far as I was concerned. But I was worried about one of the contestants getting hurt.

That concern, added to the fact the boys hadn't been able to dig up anything on Isaac, made me very nervous. I wasn't going to kill him without some real evidence of his wrongdoing.

This whole mess was just going wrong. Well, except for the Lex part. He was smokin' hot. And he liked me. But I could work on that after the show was over.

As if he read my mind (which made me a little nervous, considering the fantasies I'd had about him recently), Lex put his arm around my shoulders.

"Are you okay?" he asked quietly.

"Oh, sure. I love screwing over a teammate. I'd do it every day if I could."

Lex shook his head. "No, I mean after last night. We haven't had much of a chance to talk about it."

I nodded. "I'm fine. It just . . ." Just what? Freaked me out? Worried me? What should I say? "I guess I was a little shaken up. I'm okay now."

"I think it's pretty amazing that you saved us like that. How did you know the keg was a bomb?" he asked.

"I didn't. I just had a bad feeling that something was wrong. It was pure gut instinct." That was true. That and my superintuitive superpowers.

"Well"—he gave my shoulders a squeeze—"I don't know what I'd do if something happened to you, Missi."

I was just about to launch into an "Awwwwwww!" moment when that prick Alan spoke.

"Welcome to Tribal Council, Ottawa." Alan had a torch lit directly under his chin to give him a scary face. How long had my mind been wandering? I didn't even realize I was there. I had to try to stop doing that.

"As you know, one of your members goes home tonight. Missi!"

What? Did I do something wrong?

"Missi, what do you think of my little twist on the reward challenge this afternoon?" He smiled. Apparently he felt this was solely his show.

"Well, Alan, I thought it was dangerous of you to insist on alcohol poisoning. Using extremely strong beer and giving six people two hours to drain a whole keg is grounds for a serious lawsuit. My attorney will be in touch."

Okay, so maybe that was a bit rough, but it was true. And I have to admit there was more than a little satisfaction in watching his face turn purple as I said it.

"Yeah, dumbass!" Sami shouted. "What kind of

morons are writing this fucking show anyway? I'm gonna kick your ass when this is over."

Lex chuckled softly behind me. Isaac winked at Sami and me. Silas was quiet as usual, and Cricket, probably realizing her number was up, said nothing.

"Well . . . um." Alan tottered. "Let's get on with the vote. And don't try to pull what Inuit did last time."

Julie pointed at me and I walked over to the pad of paper. They were using the hotel stationery again. But the pen said HAPPY JOE'S PIZZA. Real authentic. I wrote Cricket's name down, wincing as I did.

One by one my teammates cast their votes. No one looked happy. It was sad, really.

"I'll go tally the votes." Alan retrieved the lidless, clay pot and turned his back on us to hide the fact he was looking at the votes prematurely. Obviously, he didn't trust us. And we felt the same way about him.

"The first vote is for Cricket," he said, as if he hadn't already read them.

I looked at the camp counselor for a reaction, but her face was impassive. She was holding up pretty well each time Alan read her name.

"And the last and final vote is for . . . Cricket?" He looked at all the tallies then looked at her. "You voted yourself off?"

Damn. Wish I'd thought of that. Here I'd been feeling sorry for Cricket and she wanted to go! In spite of my hangover, I felt a little better.

"You can't vote yourself off! You're supposed to want to stay!" Alan threw his hands up. Clearly the game wasn't being played the way he wanted. "What is wrong with you people?"

Cricket grabbed her torch and walked up to Alan, who stood there ranting and raving while she waited. After a few moments, she grabbed his snuffer and snuffed out her own torch.

"Me," she said, "the tribe has spoken." And then she walked off to the resort, leaving a stunned Julie to follow in her wake.

"Right. We're done. Off you go." Alan waved us away and we walked unescorted back to camp.

Chapter Eighteen

Clothes make the man. Naked people have little or no influence in society.

—Mark Twain

"Man, this game is fucked-up!" Sami said with a smile once we got back. Bert and Ernie hung with us, but they didn't have their cameras on.

"Hey! Where were you guys last night? Not that we mind or anything. And where's Jimmy?" Isaac asked.

Bert and Ernie shrugged. It was clear they weren't going to answer. I had no idea why they were even here.

Lex and Silas built a nice fire and we opened up a few coconuts. Not a big feast, but the taste of Bavarian brew still lingered in my brain.

"How come you motherfuckers aren't filming us?" Sami asked Ernie point-blank.

"Nothing's really happening," said Bert.

"Okay," I began. "Do you have any idea why we had to run through two challenges in one day?"

"We're going over budget," Ernie said. "Looks like we'll be shaving a few days off the schedule."

Isaac asked the question on our minds. "How in the hell did you go over budget? You aren't overspending on the challenges. Charades costs nothing. And the rewards are lame."

"Yeah!" Sami kicked in, "where's the money going?"

"Well," Ernie said, squinting as if he didn't completely trust us, "Alan's using the presidential suite at the Tigre and running up huge bills with all the liquor and prostitutes."

We just kind of looked at each other. Poor Inuit was starving to death and Alan was paying women to have sex?

"And then there's his Hummer"—I assumed they meant his vehicle—"his driver, his daily hot stones massage . . ."

"I don't think I can take much more of this. Please stop," I begged. Picturing Alan naked with prostitutes was bad enough.

I told the group I needed to find coconuts and headed down the beach. Lex caught up with me.

"So, do you still think we made the right decision on our alliance?"

"Yeah. Sami is kind of a go-to guy, and Isaac seems okay." *Oh yeah, and I need him in my alliance so I can maybe kill him later.* I thought I'd leave that part out.

Lex looked at me for a moment. "Something's bothering you."

"No, it's not." *Yes, it is.* "Aside from being on the world's silliest reality show, hosted by a narcissist on a beach near a resort, I'm fine."

"You just seem a little distracted."

"You don't know me very well. According to my family, I always seem a little distracted." And I usually am when I'm about to kill someone. That's just par for the course.

"All right." Lex seemed to drop the issue. In all honesty, I was flattered that he was concerned about me. On the other hand, if he could read me like a book, that would be a problem.

"Changing the subject," I said, fumbling for a segue, "what does a stunt man like to do for fun?"

He smiled. "You mean like on a date?"

I could feel all heat flushing to my skin as I floundered, "N-No! I mean, for fun. Leisure stuff." I ended with a nervous giggle and hiccup. Real smooth.

"You'd be disappointed. I'm a pretty laid-back guy. I like hiking, going to movies, eating out."

All date things! "By yourself?" Gak! Why did I ask that?

"That's how it turns out most of the time. How about you?"

"Well, pretty much the same, really. I'm kind of boring that way." What was I doing? "I mean, not that I'm saying you're boring! I'm sure you aren't! I mean . . ."

Lex brushed my hair out of my face. "It's okay, Missi. I think I understand what you're saying. And I don't think you are boring either."

"Okay, do you have any hobbies?" Why did I have to open up that can of worms? I sure as hell didn't want to answer that question!

"I used to do a lot of sailing when I lived in California. I'd like to get back into that someday, but I'm kind of landlocked right now."

Distract him! "Um, what did you like about sailing?"

"I love being outside. The sounds of the ocean are very relaxing and I like the rocking of the waves. There's something very humbling about the whole experience."

I could relate to that. I loved time to myself. Living on an island, there was always someplace I could go to work through my thoughts when I was working on a project. And being the mother of twins made alone time sacrosanct.

"And you? What are your hobbies?"

Oh, you know, killing people in mysterious ways. Confounding CSI. The usual. "I like to knit. And I travel whenever I can. I jog for exercise. Nothing as profound as you."

Lex smiled. "I think anything we do for ourselves is profound. It's easy to forget how valuable life is sometimes."

Damn. He was getting to me. Smart and philosophical too? I couldn't stand it!

The howler monkeys began hooting it up as dusk settled around us. The fading sunset was spectacular. On Santa Muerta, I usually enjoyed these scenes alone. It was weird to share it with someone. Especially a man like Lex.

"I suppose you even find the howler monkeys soothing?"

He shook his head. "No. And I can't understand why they aren't extinct here."

I laughed. "I'm with you on that one." The yowling

grew louder. "What I wouldn't give for a blowgun right now."

"I could make you one," Lex offered softly. My immediate reaction was, Oh yeah? So could I, buddy! But it had been so long since someone offered to make something for me. Well, no one had ever done that. I was the one everyone came to for ingenuity. It was kind of nice to have someone else do it, so I just nodded.

Lex walked into the jungle a ways and returned with a foot-long piece of bamboo. I watched in amazement for ten minutes as he turned it into the perfect peashooter. Now, I would've done it a little differently, but I kept my mouth shut and helped him search the sand for pebbles.

A howler monkey dangled overhead at just the right moment. Lex put a pebble in his mouth and fired through the tube. The monkey howled in protest as he fled the scene. I knew the animal wasn't hurt, just angry.

I kissed Lex on the cheek, and he pulled back in surprise.

"What do I get that for?"

"Because that is the nicest thing anyone has ever done for me." It may have sounded dramatic, but it was true. This man was the first person who ever made something for me. And I thought it was terribly romantic.

We decided to head back and show everyone our new howler-monkey deterrent. Isaac, Silas and Sami were sitting around the fire.

Sami sighed as we joined them in midconversation.

"Those poor bastards over at Inuit. I don't think they've eaten anything but fruit for the past few days."

I sat up. "I've got an idea." I pointed at the crew. "We'll let you in on it, providing you don't show the footage to anyone until the show is wrapped."

Bert shrugged and Ernie nodded. Clearly loyalty to the show was a small matter to them.

I filled everyone in and they immediately agreed. Well, Silas mostly agreed. He'd apparently had enough of the bullshit.

Bert followed us with the camera as we made our way to the Blanco Tigre. I made my way to the front desk, trying to look like I didn't just walk off a reality show.

It only took a few moments to book the El Conquistador guesthouse (I have the number memorized on my black American Express Card). Once I had officially checked in, I gave Lex and Isaac the thumbs-up and they left for the beach. Sami, Silas and Bert followed discreetly behind as the concierge showed me to the cabin. After explaining all the amenities, she left and my three coconspirators joined me.

"Jesus Christ!" Sami sank into one of the leather-bound easy chairs. "This is more like it!"

Bert grinned. Ernie was most likely at Inuit, filming the arrival of Lex and Isaac as they escorted the tribe here. This was going to be great when they revealed this footage during the editing process. I would have given anything to see Julie's and Alan's faces in the editing room.

I ordered ten surf and turfs, white wine and extra towels, fluffy robes, toothbrushes, toothpaste and deodorant. Then I took a quick shower before my guests arrived.

Being independently wealthy has its advantages. With a huge trust fund, I could make this show a little more livable. The guest house was a smaller version of the hotel, with five bedrooms and five bathrooms. It was completely isolated, and I had it reserved for the whole stay.

Ernie promised he'd get the other camera crew on board (it helped that I'd created a drinking tab on my dime for them for the duration of the filming) and swore that Alan and Julie never left the Tigre at night. The bastards apparently didn't see any reason to leave when they had peons to take care of everything for them. They also expected us to live by the honor system. I was just coming out of the shower in my fluffy robe when a confused Inuit tribe walked in.

A couple of seconds after that, room service showed up with the robes, towels and toiletries and I sent everyone to shower up before the food arrived.

Lex came up behind me while I poked around the kitchen. He wrapped his arms around me and I could smell Irish Spring soap. That was interesting. I leaned back against him, closing my eyes.

"I think it's great you're doing this. But how can you pay for it?" he asked.

"Well, I charged it all to Alan's room. I guaranteed

a thousand-dollar tip to the front desk if they kept it off the daily bill until we left." Now, this wasn't true, not yet at least. But I didn't want any questions.

One by one, the rest of the contestants stumbled in, squeaky clean, wearing warm, fluffy robes. There was a knock at the door and Lex answered it, ushering in three waiters with carts full of lobster and steak.

I warned Inuit to eat lightly so they wouldn't get sick. No one spoke for a while. I think they were afraid they'd wake up from a dream to a mouthful of sand.

Sami finished first, pushing away from the table. "Now that was fucking fantastic."

The others nodded and for the first time, some of them smiled.

"Here's the deal," I began. "Everyone will have their own key to this house. Eat, drink, sleep, whatever. Just don't get caught. The cameramen will film us here, but no one will see that footage until this is over and we are safely home."

I explained that there were five bedrooms with bathrooms, so we needed to pair up. Lex and Isaac took one room, Sami and I another. Liliana and Kit, Brick and Dr. Andy, and Silas and Moe took the other rooms.

We sat and talked for a little while. EVERYONE thought this was a good idea. Around ten P.M. I called the front desk for a six A.M. wake-up call and ordered breakfast, and suggested we all get some sleep.

"Thank you—" Liliana started, but I shushed her.

"We all decided to do this. Get some sleep. We'll probably have a challenge in the morning."

One by one everyone drifted off to a bedroom but me. I wasn't even tired. And I had some thinking to do.

I poured a vodka tonic and slipped out onto the patio. While I felt good about helping the others and sticking it to Alan and Julie, I still had a lot to worry about.

Somehow I still had this contract on Isaac. And there was the boys' comment about a saboteur. What if someone got hurt? I really didn't like the chances the show was taking with our lives. And the thought of sabotage was ugly.

"Can't sleep?" Lex's voice came from behind me and I jumped.

"Not yet. Just trying to puzzle things out, I guess."

He wrapped his arms around me and I leaned against him. Damn, he felt good. I just wanted to melt into his skin until morning.

Lex's hands stroked up and down my back, igniting a fire I haven't felt in years. Ooh, I wanted this man.

"Lex, I . . ." I started to speak but he smothered my lips with his. This man could kiss. And I didn't get kissed very often. Actually, not since Rudy.

My brain started swirling as his hands slipped under my bathrobe and I remembered that I had no clothes on. I pulled away for a second.

"I'm sorry," he said. "Too fast? It's just been a long time and I don't know how . . ."

This time I crushed his lips to mine and slid my hands under his robe. I guess that answered his question and mine. I pulled him to a chaise lounge and within seconds we remembered how this sex thing was supposed to work. It was a quickie, to be sure. But oh man, what a quickie. With a houseful of guests and a jungle full of monkeys and jaguars, I felt like I was kind of in a hurry.

It seemed so simple until he entered me. Then it started to get very complicated. Well, not physically complicated. But my brain seemed to wake up from a coma. I kissed him as he rocked into me and it didn't take long for me to explode (figuratively, for once, since most of my explosions are actually quite literal).

We lay there in each other's arms for a long time, staring at the stars (with a cautious eye for jaguars). For some reason, words seemed useless.

"Wow."

I turned to face him. "Wow?"

"What? Is something wrong with *wow*?"

"I'd just rather hear something more dramatic, I guess," I said, and he chuckled.

"Missi, I want you to know that it has been a long, long, long time for me. I hope I didn't force it on you."

I sat up and turned toward him, closing my robe. "You didn't. What do you mean it's been a long time?"

"What? You think I do this all the time? I haven't made love to a woman in seven years."

"Really? Are you sure?" Of course I felt like an idiot as soon as I said it. Duh! I think he'd know if he'd done it since.

"Yes, I'm sure. My wife died seven years ago. It's not something you'd forget."

"Wow."

"Wow? Is that all you have to say?" He chucked me under the chin teasingly.

"I'm a widow too. My husband died about fifteen years ago. I guess it's been a long time for me as well."

It occurred to me that this was a strange conversation and probably one we should've had before the hot sex. Why hadn't it come up earlier?

"Surely you haven't been celibate all this time!" Lex feigned mock horror.

I hit him with a pillow. "No. But my love life is staggeringly dull. Fortunately, my twin, teenage sons keep me busy." Oops. I didn't mean to mention that.

Lex leaned back, staring into the inky sky. "Fiona and I never had children. We just kept putting it off for later."

I leaned against him. For once, my overwhelming motherhood seemed like a blessing.

"I bet you would've been a great dad."

I could feel him smile. "Thanks. I needed that."

"What, the nookie or the compliment?" I asked.

He smiled again and kissed my forehead. "Both. Definitely both."

Out of the corner of my eye I spotted one of the bedroom lights going on. Lex and I scrambled to our feet, kissed briefly then went off to our separate rooms.

Sami snored as I drifted off, thinking about sex, Lex and the fact that they rhymed.

Chapter Nineteen

The greatest happiness is to scatter your enemy, to drive him before you, to see his cities reduced to ashes, to see those who love him shrouded in tears, and to gather into your bosom his wives and daughters.

—Genghis Khan

The drill worked like a charm. Everyone got up at six, put their old clothes on, wolfed down breakfast and scrambled toward the beach to their campsites before Julie or the camera crew would arrive. Lex and I grinned goofily at each other the whole time. I felt like there was a balloon in my chest, swelling with helium. It was a very good feeling.

"When do you think they'll merge us?" Silas asked me as we followed Julie to another challenge.

I was a bit shocked. Silas had never asked me anything.

"I thought you were mad at me."

His right eyebrow went up. "Why would you think that?"

"Because of the"—I looked around to make sure Julie couldn't hear—"guesthouse. Not very authentic."

Silas nodded. "Yeah. I was mad at first. But this durned show is lame. I don't really care about that anymore."

Wow. That was bizarre. Silas actually appeared to be three-dimensional. Maybe it was a good omen.

Howler monkeys screeched as we entered a clearing full of equipment. It was kind of like they were our heralds—you know, like when the king enters the ballroom?

"Today's challenge is for reward. Tonight, both teams will go to Tribal Council and you will both vote off one member." Alan intoned.

Oh shit. We were losing two this time? The budget must be dwindling faster than I thought. I looked over at Isaac. He winked and I returned it. With all that was happening, we were becoming close. Hell, he was in my alliance with Lex and Sami. And worse yet, I liked him. My gut was telling me he was a great guy. But my head countered with the fact that despite what Sami thought, Isaac knew how to play a person like a poker hand. Either way, I was definitely running out of time on this job.

"We will put you in teams of two. Each team has to figure out a puzzle. The first team to solve the puzzle gets reward." Alan grinned. "Want to know what you're playing for?"

Nobody nodded or said anything. It was obvious to everyone that the rewards were lame when we had a sweet guesthouse waiting for us back at the Blanco Tigre.

Our host frowned. "The winning team will go marlin fishing this afternoon."

Open-ocean fishing? That was a reward? Who were

these people? I didn't think even Silas would enjoy sweating in a rickety boat in choppy water to catch a huge fish.

"And Missi, you'll be with Kit. That's it, take your places!" Julie whined. I realized I hadn't been paying attention again.

Each team stood in front of a table. They had blended the tribes, and I noticed that Lex was paired with Moe, Liliana with Sami, Isaac with Brick, and Silas was with Dr. Andy. Lex sketched me a wave and I goofily waved back—looking like a complete idiot.

"You may begin," Alan, the real complete idiot, said.

Kit's lower lip trembled. And we weren't even at Tribal Council yet. Two long poles, pointed on one end each, were lying on the ground. A thick, blue piece of rope was draped over the table, labeled "1." Next to it was a green and yellow piece of rope labeled "2," and next to that was a red rope labeled "3." I half-expected to see a bottle that said DRINK ME, and would've given a kidney to see a cake labeled EAT ME, but that just wasn't the case.

Sorry! Where was I? Oh yes. Kit filled me in (because I hadn't been paying attention—remember?) that somehow, we were supposed to figure out how to use the poles and rope to solve the puzzle.

I was completely lost. Looking around, the other teams had no idea what to do either.

"No one knows what to do. . . ." Alan spoke his commentary for the cameras.

Lex tried coiling the ropes around one of the poles

to see if a pattern emerged. Nothing. Liliana tried to tie knots in the various ropes and Silas was, I guess, measuring it using the length of his arms.

"Ten minutes in, and no one has got it right," Alan continued.

I seriously thought about impaling him on the end of one of our poles. That would have been fun. Did you know the Bombays were indirect relatives of Vlad the Impaler? According to family lore, he was a real prick—but very good at killing people.

"Dammit, Lil!" Sami cursed her partner. "Now we have to untie all those fucking knots!"

Big tears began to roll down Kit's perfect cheekbones. A crying model. Lucky me.

"Don't cry," I started, patting her clumsily on the back. "No one else knows what to do either."

Of course, I was right. Frustration was running very high on this challenge. For once, the show was doing something tough.

"Twenty minutes and no clue among the players." Alan was really getting on my nerves. In fact, everything was getting on my nerves. I was so stressed, I—

That's when it hit me.

"Kit, grab your pole and hold it at an angle."

The other teams weren't paying attention, but I had an idea. Carefully, I made a slipknot out of the blue rope and slid it over the end of the pole. Then I put ten loops on the pole, took the other pole and pushed the pointy end through the first stitch, front to back, wrapped the rope around it and pulled it backwards through the loop, pushing the one on Kit's pole off. I now had a loop on my pole.

"You're knitting?" Kit asked, sucking in a deep breath.

"I think so." I didn't say anything as I finished off the first row. Damn, this was hard. The poles were huge and hard to control. It took my whole body to make each stitch. I was really, really hoping I wouldn't have to purl the next row.

"Missi, figuring it out . . ." Alan seemed happy that someone was. I wondered how the other teams were going to manage if they didn't know how to knit. It hardly seemed fair, and I wasn't that excited about marlin fishing, but I wanted to see if it worked.

The other teams paid attention, but unless you knew how to knit, you were screwed. It appeared that I was the only one. So, they all sat down and watched me struggle with my giant needles. Great. Apparently they didn't want to go marlin fishing either. And since both tribes were voting someone off, I guess they all figured they really had nothing to lose.

After two more rows, we'd used up the blue yarn and started in with the green and yellow. Immediately I could see a pattern starting to emerge. I thought about giving up, but now everyone was staring at me, so I couldn't.

It took me all the way to the color variations in the red rope before I realized I was knitting letters. Kit did nothing but stand there, but that was okay. I was completely exhausted as I knitted the last row.

"Missi and Kit win the challenge!" Alan shouted.

Yay us. I looked at the swatch of knitting. It was pretty good work, if I do say so myself.

"Op?" I asked. "What does that mean?"

"Open! It's supposed to say 'open!'" Alan was turning an interesting shade of red.

Julie started rooting around the other teams' rope. "It should say that. I wonder if we got the rope mixed up?"

"Well, it doesn't matter because now they know the clue."

I turned to Alan. "The clue to what?" This game was really pissing me off. I looked at our camera crew. They all three shrugged simultaneously. That looked pretty cool.

"The clue to the hidden immunity idol!" Alan sputtered as if I were four years old.

"Why didn't you just tell us that?" I asked.

"I did!"

Kit and I looked at each other, then at Julie.

"Um, sorry, Alan," she said very quietly, "but you must've forgotten."

The host threw up his arms, negating whatever sense we had of his being in charge, and stormed off.

"Okay," Julie stammered, "I . . . I . . . guess I'll finish up then. Missi and Kit, for a twist, you get to pick another team to accompany you on the fishing trip." Her voice grew louder as she realized the boys were taping her. "The rest of you can go back to camp."

"We want Lex and Moe!" Kit shouted to my complete and utter surprise. Could she read minds? I was going to pick them anyway, but she didn't even ask me. I didn't know whether to be angry or grateful.

Lex and Moe joined us as the rest of the two tribes tried to hide their glee about going back to camp. If I'd had to hazard a guess, I'd have reckoned that the camp wasn't where they'd end up.

"Just couldn't stand the thought of doing this without me?" Lex asked with a smile that now had the power to turn my knees into jelly.

To my complete shock, Kit slipped her arm through his, batting her eyelashes. "No! We couldn't."

Oh shit.

Chapter Twenty

Nobody will ever win the battle of the sexes. There's too much fraternizing with the enemy.

—Henry Kissinger

"Oh my God!" Kit giggled, snuggling up to MY boyfriend. "You are sooooo funny!"

I sat there, simmering in the heat, hoping my next cast would accidentally toss her into what I hoped were shark-infested waters.

Lex looked pained as he pulled away for the one millionth time. There was absolutely no privacy on this boat. And for some reason we'd silently made a pact not to mention our budding romance. Now I regretted opening up the beach house to Inuit. Somehow, we'd have to get Kit voted off tonight.

"Hey! I caught something!" Moe shouted.

It was kind of a miracle, because we'd spent three hours already, getting a nasty sunburn and nothing so much as a nibble. My hopes soared, imagining he'd caught a shark I could feed Kit to . . . slowly.

"You know," Kit said, "these shows really like it if two of the contestants hook up. It makes for a really good drama."

That's when I finally noticed how beautiful Kit

was. Long, brown hair, blue eyes, long legs. Why hadn't I noticed that before?

"Really?" Lex asked, his eyes boring into mine.

"Oh man! It's huge!" Moe screamed.

"Oh yes." Kit slid her arm through his for the seventeenth time since the challenge. I know, because I'd been counting. When she got to twenty, I was throwing her overboard—accidentally rendering her unconscious before she hit the water.

"Hey guys! Help me out here!" Moe begged. Rollo, our boat's captain, stepped forward.

"In fact, it makes for really good ratings." Kit tried to look thoughtful. "Did you know I'm a model?"

I ground my teeth and pictured killing her.

"I heard that." Lex looked clearly uncomfortable but had no way out of the situation. I was trying to figure out if Kit's interest was real or whether she was trying to form an alliance. I had no proof but was pretty sure the alliance she was trying to start with Lex had nothing to do with the game.

Don't get me wrong. I'd liked her initially. Even felt sorry for her. But right now, that bitch was coming on to the first man I'd had sex with in . . . well, in more than a decade.

"Here it comes!" Moe yelled as he and Rollo landed a huge fish. It flopped violently all over the deck. There wasn't a lot of room for us to begin with.

Kit let out the fakest scream I ever heard and leaped

into Lex's arms. Poor bastard. He'd had no choice other than to catch her.

"Wow!" Moe stared at the fish and I started to feel a little sorry for him. We should have been happy for him. This may have been the most successful thing he'd ever done.

Lex kept trying to put Kit down but she scrambled to hang on, feigning fear.

"Good fish." Rollo slapped Moe on the back.

"Thank God you were here to save me!" Kit cooed to Lex.

I turned my attentions to Moe. It was either that or punch her in the throat—and she wasn't my Vic. The Bombays kind of frown on making hits without Council approval.

"That's really cool, Moe." I smiled at him.

He looked so happy. "Thanks, Missi! I'm so glad you invited me!"

"Well, I didn't, but I would've, had Kit not said it first."

Moe grinned. Hmmm. Maybe I could influence him to get his tribe to vote off Kit tonight. I turned to Rollo.

"Do you have a camera so he could have a picture with the fish?"

Rollo nodded and pulled a digital camera out of his cargo pocket. I helped Moe hoist the now-dead fish up in the air. It was almost as long as me.

"I'll e-mail it to the show," Rollo said, after snapping the shot.

Lex managed to escape the Kit-octopus to help the captain put the fish belowdecks. Kit followed them, going on and on about Lex's muscles. Yeesh.

The truth was he had very nice definition. Lex was a fine example of a man. This was good for me (who doesn't want a smoking-hot lover?), but bad for me in that the idiot Kit had also noticed him.

"Do you guys know who you're voting off tonight?" Okay, so I'm not subtle. I only had a few minutes to influence Moe.

He frowned, shaking his head. "I have no idea. Do you?"

I feigned innocence. "Me? No! I don't even know who I'd vote off in Ottawa."

Moe looked toward the hatch. "Frankly, I'd like to get rid of Kit. She cries all the time. I just want to smack her."

I laughed. "Yeah, I guess that would get annoying."

He nodded. "She and Liliana really hate each other. Kit's easy on the eyes, but does nothing around camp. Brick and Andy are okay."

I only had a few minutes to work my magic. "I'm pretty sure after this vote we'll be merged. If Kit's bothering you, you should convince the others to get rid of her tonight."

"Well," Moe said slowly, "I could do that. But only if you'll let me into your alliance."

"Alliance? What alliance?" Did I mention I'm not a good liar?

"With Lex and Sami. I think Isaac's in, too." Okay, so Moe wasn't as dumb as he looked.

A high-pitched giggle came from the hatch. I offered Moe my hand.

"You've got a deal."

Chapter Twenty-one

Pray that there's intelligent life somewhere up above
because there's bugger all down here on earth.
　　　　　　　—Eric Idle, *Monty Python Sings*

Lex and I dropped Moe and Kit off at their camp.
(Kit blew him a kiss. Bitch.) We were just out of their
line of vision when he pulled me off the beach and
into the jungle.

"I am so sorry about that," he began.

"You didn't look like you were having fun," I offered.

"No. Not with her."

"Do you have fun with me?" I pouted a little.

"Most definitely." Lex pulled me against him and
kissed me. I wrapped my arms around him and
kissed back.

"Whoa!" He jerked backwards, rubbing his head.

I squinted into the trees and spotted a flash of red. At
our feet was a small mango.

"You know what?" I said, "I think I have to go to
the bathroom. You go on ahead to camp and I'll catch
up. Okay?" I really didn't want him to go, but apparently two twin monkeys did.

"Are you sure?" He rubbed his head. "It seems kind
of dangerous out here."

I grinned. "Oh, it's just a capuchin monkey. Nothing I can't handle. Besides, you need to see what the buzz at camp is for who we're voting off tonight." I waved him away. "Go on! I'll be there in a few."

Lex looked doubtfully up at the trees, then at me. After a few seconds, he left.

"Boys!" I whispered loudly, "I know you're there!"

Jack jumped down, followed by Monty. They both stayed out of reach.

"Hey, Mom!" they said simultaneously.

"Stop hitting Lex! If it was a coconut it could have killed him!" It's true. Did you know that a little, two-pound coconut falling from a high tree can have a landing weight of one ton?

"Okay. Finc," Jack said, pouting.

I changed the subject. "Did you find anything out about Vic?" It was hard to be mad at them for too long.

Monty shook his head. "I'm going to try some aliases. There's a strong chance his name was once Bruce Wayne—which is totally Batman cool. I've also found some mentions of him in Interpol files, but a lot of the wording is blacked out."

"And we still don't know anything about the sabotage," Jack piped up. "But it's a real threat. Alan and Julie have been talking to the police."

"What? Why? What's happened?" I felt like I was completely out of the picture.

The twins grinned and I thought for just a moment how I'd like to know where they got their information. This was fleeting, and rational thought took over— aka, I didn't want to know.

"Someone took out an ad in the local paper claiming they burned down your shelter," Jack answered.

"And there have been a couple of death threats," added Monty.

"Rumor has it that the show might be completely shut down. I guess the head honchos at the network are considering it," Jack said.

That could be good news. I could get off this low-budget mess. Lex and I could get to know each other, shack up for a while . . .

"Is the Council asking questions?"

The boys looked at each other, communicating silently with that twin telepathy of theirs.

"No." I think they both answered.

"Mom . . . ," Jack began.

"We're worried about you," Monty finished.

Jack nodded. "We don't want you to get hurt."

I waved them off. "Don't worry. I'll be fine. I don't really care about the saboteur. But I do need to figure out what to do about Isaa . . . I mean Vic." The Council has zero tolerance for failure, meaning I could get taken out if I failed to do the job.

"We're on it!" Jack shouted as they ran off to who-knows-where.

Back at camp, Sami was waiting for me. No one else was there.

"What's up?" I asked.

"Isaac and Lex took Silas on a banana hunt so I could fill you in. Fuck Silas. He's out."

"All right." It's what I'd suspected anyway. But why did I feel so sad?

"Man," she continued, "I heard about that bitch Kit climbing all over Lex on the boat. What the hell?"

I shook my head. "Well, I made a deal with Moe. He'll try to get her voted off and we'll add him to our alliance."

"Fuckin' A!" Sami laughed, and started smothering the fire.

I helped her. I was feeling a little stupid for being so petty about Kit. Anger flashed and I remembered how blatant she'd been. Okay. I didn't feel too bad.

The men returned, and we sat around talking about the challenge.

"I'm really impressed with what you've done here, Missi," Isaac grinned. Damn. He was trying so hard to become my friend and I was trying to hate him.

"Thanks, Isaac. Just doing my part."

"Yeah, well, I just wanted you to know you are appreciated." Isaac gave me a thumbs up and walked away.

"You know," Lex said, "for someone who wanted him as an ally, you sure act like you'd rather not be on Isaac's team."

"Really? I didn't realize I was giving that impression."

"Did he do something to make you angry?" Lex asked as he rubbed my thigh. I tried to remain focused.

"No. He's been fine."

"So why the cold shoulder?"

"Honestly, I didn't think I was acting that way!" Okay, so I was a tad defensive. Mostly because I'd been busted. And I hated getting busted.

Lex waved me off. "Okay, okay. Just cut the guy some slack. He's a good man, and we need him."

I watched as he got up and walked away. This was ridiculous. I should have been getting a medal from the Bombays for having to be in this situation.

Lex was right. I had been distant toward Isaac. But only because I might have to kill him later. I couldn't tell Lex that, but it made sense, right?

We picked up our torches for Tribal Council. Jimmy showed up alone to film us before Julie arrived. Most members of the camera crew pretty much had given up on the whole show and were just making appearances.

Everyone was quiet as we walked through the jungle. Maybe it was because Julie hadn't ordered us to be silent. Maybe we were all feeling a little down about voting Silas off. Add that to the feelings of elation I experienced whenever I saw Lex, and you have quite a soup. I like soup. Mom used to make this stewed monkey–guava soup that was fantastic.

"Welcome to Tribal Council!" Alan stood in the middle of a basketball court. There were bleachers on both sides. Inuit sat on his left and we were seated to his right. Other shows, like *Survivor*, built really cool sets. These guys just phoned it in. I noticed that Jimmy had left, and Inuit's crew was filming this time.

"There's a new twist tonight," our host said. We all

groaned. What were we going to have to do this time? Square dance each other off?

"Instead of voting off someone from your own tribe," he informed us, "you'll be voting off someone from the other tribe."

What? We all looked at each other. What the hell were we going to do now? Granted, I could probably whisper to get everyone to vote off Kit. But we certainly couldn't control the other team. And what if I got voted off before figuring out this whole Isaac thing?

"Ottawa," Alan said, "Missi has been the clear leader in all challenges." The smug bastard looked right at me. "Missi, do you think this makes you a target?"

Shit. "Um, I don't know, Alan. The knitting thing was pretty lame. It was just luck that I knew what to do."

"Kit!" Alan turned dramatically to Inuit. "Tell me why you chose Lex and Moe to join you for the reward."

For once, Kit didn't look like she was even remotely about to cry.

"Well, Alan," she said in a singsongy voice, "I don't know if you've noticed, but Lex and I have a little romance going on." She wiggled her fingers at MY MAN!

Lex covered his face with his hands.

Alan turned back to us. "Is that true Lex? You and Kit make a cute couple."

I could feel Sami's arm on mine, as if she were trying

to stop me from jumping up and ripping Kit's throat out—which I am trained to do, by the way.

"No. I think Kit is a nice girl. But that's about it," Lex said quietly.

"So, Missi!" Alan faced me again. "Your head may be on the chopping block tonight. How do you feel about it?"

Me again? Man, this guy really hates me.

"I don't know what to say to that, Alan." And I didn't. I was getting so sick of this stupid show. The good news was meeting Lex. The bad news was that the Vic was now one of my friends and I hated the host and his malignant assistant. What's a girl to do?

"Ottawa! You vote first." Alan pointed to a clay pot on a Blanco Tigre lectern in the corner of the court. Sami got up and went over to vote.

"Kit!" I whispered loudly. "Kit's got to go!"

Sami came back and I got up, walking slowly to the podium. I wrote Kit's name in huge, black letters, folded the paper and put it in the pot.

"I'll tally the votes." Alan retrieved the pot once we were all through.

"The first vote is for Kit."

Kit chewed her lip but managed not to cry. Maybe she was getting used to the idea of being the first rejected.

"The second vote is for . . . Kit."

We got a trembly lip from the model.

"The third vote is for Moe. Two votes for Kit."

The bimbo sighed a little. One more vote and that would be it. Come oooooooooooooon!

"The third person voted off of *Survival* is Kit."

Kit burst into tears and ran the length of the court, flinging herself into Lex's arms.

"Thank you for not voting for me, Lex!"

"Kit! You have to leave the Tribal Council area immediately!" Alan shouted.

I watched in horror as she kissed Lex on the lips and ran off. Lex looked at me and shrugged.

Kit was led away, obnoxiously blowing kisses at Lex.

"Inuit! It is your turn to vote!" Alan commanded with a squeak.

We watched as the remaining four members of Inuit voted someone from our team off. It really was a crapshoot at this point. I only really knew Moe, so there was no way of knowing how anyone else would vote.

"I'll collect the votes." Alan was basically just speaking for his own sake. We were all pretty much ignoring him.

"The first vote is for"—he cast me an oily grin—"Missi. The first vote is for Missi!" Did he have to be so happy about it?

I looked across at the other team. Moe gave me the thumbs up. What did that mean?

"The second vote is for . . ." Alan frowned. "Silas. One vote for Missi, one vote for Silas."

I couldn't relax. It wasn't over yet.

"The third vote is for Silas. One vote Missi, two votes for Silas."

This could go either way, really. Lex reached for my hand. At least he didn't want me to go.

"And the fourth and final vote is for . . . Isaac. Silas, you are the fourth person voted off of *Survival*."

Silas nodded to us, then went up to Alan to have his torch snuffed out. He actually looked happy to be going. I let out a loud breath. It was over. Damn.

"You are the remaining eight," Alan said. "Tomorrow, your tribes will merge. For now, go back to camp and enjoy your evening." Alan and Julie fled toward the resort and I saw that all the cameramen were now gone.

Ottawa and Inuit just looked at each other.

"Let's just go to the guesthouse," Isaac said. The others nodded and we made our way toward our own refuge.

Chapter Twenty-two

Some people try to pick up girls and get called an asshole. This did not happen to Pablo Picasso. He could walk down the street—girls could not resist his stare. Pablo Picasso was never called an asshole.

—The Burning Sensations

A hot shower, a good dinner, two bottles of ice-cold beer and one fluffy robe later I was feeling better. Kit and Silas didn't show up, so I guessed they were pleased with their own accommodations. No one really said much. We were tired and sick of this whole mess. In fact, everyone pretty much headed off to bed early. Sami didn't call me dumbass when she said good night. Not even once.

I stepped out onto the veranda, trying to find some alone time to figure a few things out. The information the boys had given me wasn't anything concrete. A few mentions in an Interpol file was not enough to condemn the man to death. As for the sabotage, the fact they were worried about me wasn't new. They were convinced, however, that they were bulletproof. I remembered thinking that at their age. Of course, I knew better now. The death threats and sabotage were a little frightening—but really nothing compared to the punishment I'd get if I didn't take care of my Vic.

The fact I'd received a vote made this whole thing real. The Council might let me off the hook somewhat if there were extenuating circumstances. But what those circumstances were was completely beyond me.

Still, I'd made it to the final eight. Vic was still within my clutches. And Lex and I were having sex. Not bad if you look at it that way.

"I thought I'd find you out here." Lex came up behind me and wrapped his arms around me.

I pulled away. There was too much on my mind.

"Tomorrow's the merge. I think the game will wrap up soon."

I nodded. "Yeah. Ernie said there were major budget problems."

Lex lifted my chin. "Are you worried about being voted out?"

I didn't speak for a moment. Finally, I asked a question that had been bothering me since the beginning. "Why are you really here? Why agree to be on this show?" There, I'd said it.

He smiled. "Probably the same reason you're on it."

Damn. I couldn't tell him that my reason was because I come from a long line of assassins and my job was to kill Isaac. That might hurt the alliance. But I had to come up with something if I was going to get any info in return. "You know how family can be." Okay. Not a lie. Well, not completely a lie.

"Really? Why did you go through with it?" Lex asked.

"I don't know. I guess I'd been in a rut for a long time. Maybe I thought it would be an adventure." Again—not a lie.

Lex sighed and leaned on the railing. "Well, I guess it's the same for me. My family thought I needed to do something with my life other than being a bartender in a small town. I did this thinking I'd never get picked and they'd leave me alone."

"Backfired, eh?"

"Not really. I found you. I'd say that's better than twenty-five grand."

Once again, it surprised me that we hadn't had this conversation before. Something about being around Lex always translated to sex first, get-to-know-me later. Why was that? This wasn't how relationships usually started out. Then again, most relationships didn't happen on the set of a lame reality show in Costa Rica, either.

I thought about what he'd said about the twenty-five thousand dollars. It had never crossed my mind that maybe he needed the money. He couldn't have been making much as a bartender. It was something I was completely unfamiliar with. I grew up wealthy, never worrying about money. Maybe this competition meant more to him than I thought.

"How did you go from being a stuntman to a bartender?"

Lex sobered. "Actually, I was a stunt*master* out in LA. So was my wife. That's where we met."

So, Fiona had been a kick-ass stuntwoman? I liked her already.

"What happened to her?"

"There was an accident during a stunt. I was in charge—had choreographed it and everything. It was my job to make sure she was safe. But due to a technical malfunction, she died. It was my fault. So, I moved back home." His voice snagged a bit on the last few words.

I felt awful for asking. My arms went around him and we just stood there, holding each other.

"You know, that's why I'm so attracted to you," Lex said quietly.

I pulled back. "Why?" Surely he didn't know about the stunts I'd pulled for jobs. And let me tell you, there was no stuntmaster planning for my safety.

He smiled. I liked the way his eyes wrinkled in the corners. "You take risks. You try things others wouldn't. And you have a lot of compassion." Lex waved his arm around him. "You did this for the Inuit team because they were suffering. You saved Kit's life on the zip line and made sure they got across safely before going for the easy win. You remind me of Fiona. And you are more like me than she even was."

"Oh." Wow. I didn't know what to say to that. It was the nicest thing anyone has ever said to me. And I was pretty sure I didn't deserve it.

"I'd better get to bed." I kissed him and turned away. "And Lex?" He looked up attentively. "Thank you."

As I lay there in the darkness, listening to Sami's

snoring, I felt like crap. Lex had this glorified view of who I was. His job was about taking care of people, and he thought I was all about that too. Thing was, he'd change his mind about me in a minute if he saw my workshop on Santa Muerta or knew anything about who I really was.

To him, I was just Missi, a widowed mother who might be the answer to his prayers. If only I were that woman. But I couldn't pretend I was. I was a hitman—an assassin—and a damned good one. I invented ways to kill people, and based on their level of evil, I could really make them suffer if I wanted to.

And yet, I was the woman who'd worried that the rival team wasn't getting enough to eat and plunked down her own money to help them out. It's funny. Lex thought he had me all figured out. Hell. *I* didn't have me all figured out.

In fact, if it weren't for this idiotic show, I'd have been blissfully unaware back on Santa Muerta making toys from the eighties explode with enough force to kill a man. Wow. I hadn't thought of my workshop since I arrived here. In fact, I hadn't thought much about my work.

I was here for one reason only—to do a job for the Council. I was a Bombay and I had a Vic. Nothing else should have mattered.

Right?

I couldn't sleep that night. Finally, at about five A.M., I quit pretending and took a cup of coffee out onto the patio.

"What's up, Moe?" He was lounging on the deck in a robe when I stumbled upon him.

"Hey, Missi!" I liked how his face brightened when he saw me. It's always nice to feel like someone's happy to see you, and he'd earned big points by helping me out with the Kit fiasco.

I pulled up a chaise lounge and my coffee mug. It was too early for sunrise. I'd ordered breakfast but it wouldn't arrive for half an hour.

"So what's got you up so early?" I asked.

Moe shook his head. "I couldn't sleep."

I snorted. "That's funny. Most of us can't seem to get enough sleep around here." I usually chalked that up to boredom.

"Nah. I never was that lazy," Moe responded. I hid my smile. "Actually, being here has given me some ideas for when I get back."

"Really? Then you're the first one who's been able to turn this charade into something positive." Did that come out wrong?

"I've just been thinking. Sometimes getting away from home shakes you up. I needed that." He shifted in his seat.

Huh. I wondered if the same thing had happened to me since I'd been there. Well, I had a kind of boyfriend in Lex. And I'd call Sami and Moe friends. Being away from my monastic existence on Santa Muerta probably had been somewhat good for me. All the same, I still wanted to get my job done and move on.

We sat there quietly until there was a knock on the

door. Sami looked at us with some amusement when we came back into the guesthouse. The laundry was delivered with the food and I slipped off to the bedroom to change before joining everyone.

Moe's words made me think. I was getting some benefit from being here. But what did that matter in the grand scheme of things? If I had to take out Isaac, not much.

Chapter Twenty-three

Misty water-colored memories . . .
> —Hamlisch, Bergman and Bergman,
> "The Way We Were"

"As you may have guessed," Alan was saying to us poolside at the Tigre, "both Inuit and Ottawa will now merge into a tribe of eight."

I picked at the rubber sole of my shoe. Why did he always have to state the obvious? Like we didn't know there were only eight of us left?

He reached into a bag and pulled out a bright yellow bandana. "You are now all part of Team Tico."

I sighed restlessly. Well, at least he got that right. A howler monkey went off, as if to give his approval.

"And you will set up a new camp together on the site of Ottawa's old camp. Bert and Ernie will be your only camera crew."

Sami snorted beside me. I guess the merge made the budget cuts easier to deal with. I wondered what had happened to Jimmy? Maybe he got sent back to Canada.

"Today, you will spend the day getting to know your new tribe. You will not have any challenges until tomorrow. I will see you then."

I waited for Julie and Alan to leave before snagging Ernie. "What's going on?"

Ernie looked around before answering. "They're flying back home to beg more money from the network. I've got to drive them to the airport. You won't see anyone until tomorrow." He motioned to Bert and the two of them took off.

I filled Team Tico in on the latest developments. Lex and I volunteered to throw together a rudimentary shelter as subterfuge, and the others decided it would be a good day to spend at the guesthouse.

"What was your husband like?" Lex asked softly as we worked.

"What? Oh. Rudy." I thought for a moment. "He was great. You would've liked him." I hoped my insecurity wasn't showing. In all honesty, I hadn't seen Rudy in fifteen years. My memory was rusty when I tried to think of him, and that bothered me.

Living on the island, I thought about him a lot. But since I'd been here, around new people and Lex, Rudy's memory seemed to fade. Why was that?

"Are the boys like him?" Lex pressed.

"Monty is," I answered without thinking. "He's quiet . . . thoughtful. Jack is outgoing and a handful. Rudy was more like Monty." But was that true? I could barely remember.

"I always wanted kids," Lex said. "So did Fiona. It just never happened."

An aching feeling I recognized as sorrow welled up

in my throat. Lex obviously had no problem remembering his wife. How sad that they'd wanted children and never had them. My boys had been my life for nearly two decades. I couldn't imagine life without them. As they prepared for college in the fall, I was preparing for the whole empty-nest thingy. And I was not looking forward to it.

I touched his hand. "As I told you before—I bet you would've made a great dad."

Lex shook his head. "Sorry. I shouldn't have brought it up. I guess I was just feeling a little melancholy."

"Well, I'd be happy to loan you the boys anytime you want." I laughed thinking about Lex chasing after Monty and Jack.

"I'd like that. Kind of like a fun uncle or something," Lex said.

Yeah, a fun uncle who didn't teach them how to kill people. That would certainly be a novelty to them.

Once we were finished with the saddest excuse for a lean-to ever, I sent Lex back to the guesthouse and slipped away to find my boys. They'd better have something, I thought. I couldn't go on much longer with all this confusion. Back at Santa Muerta, everything was safe. The only decision I usually had to make was how much C-4 to order online.

"Mom!" Jackson's voice caught me off guard. Apparently, I'd walked right past our tree.

"Where's Monty?" I asked, always suspicious when they didn't turn up together. In my seventeen years of experience with these two, I'd learned the hard way that if one was gone, the other was likely covering for a punishable offense.

"He's in town, doing some research on the show." Jack grinned a big, toothy grin. Damn, he was a good-looking boy!

"Forget that. I need stuff on Vic." I really didn't care too much about the show.

Jackson frowned. "Well, I don't exactly have anything on him."

"What? What have you been doing?" I threw a mom tantrum. It surprised even me.

"Geez, Mom!" Jackson looked left and right. "It's okay. No big!"

I sighed and took a deep breath. He was too old for shaken baby syndrome, but I was considering it. "Jackson. My son. My youngest by two minutes. The only reason I'm here is to do a job. If I don't have a job to do, I'd just as soon not be here. Got it?" Wow. I sounded pissed. I wouldn't want to be him arguing with me.

"Did something happen with Lex?" My little boy folded his arms over his chest. When did he get so smart?

"No!" I said a little too forcefully. "No!" I said it again as if repeating it would make it true. Hey, now there's a thought! I wonder if I could do something with that in the lab? Suddenly, I felt very homesick.

"Mom, you've got that screwy look on your face. Snap out of it!"

I ran a hand through my hair. "It's nothing," I lied to my child. Truth was, it was something. Lex's words bothered me. There was no way I could live up to the memory of his dead wife. And I was pretty sure he wouldn't want me once he knew what I did for a living. I mean, he spent his career making sure people didn't die on his watch, while I made sure they did on mine.

"Look. I'm just anxious to finish the job," I lied again. And from the look on his face, I was getting good at it. "So I need to know whether to take him out or not."

As Jackson nodded his head to agree with me (or admit to himself that I finally had gone nuts), slivers of his red hair seemed to burst into flame as they hit patches of sunlight.

"I'll find out. If I don't know soon, we'll just call the whole thing off and Monty and I will get you off the show."

I hugged him before he fled. As Jackson disappeared, it hit me. How were they going to get me off the show? I shuddered in spite of the heat.

I didn't go back to the guesthouse. I told myself it was because I didn't want to get any closer to my Vic, but in all honesty, it was Lex and not Isaac I was worried about.

After buying a large sun hat and a huge pair of sunglasses in the gift shop, I ordered a pitcher of vodka tonics and sat down in the most remote corner of the pool area. Now, I know drinking doesn't solve anything. And I have the alcoholic tolerance of plankton. But being alone with my thoughts seemed to be the best option right then.

Patience may be a virtue, but it never did right by me. I've had some pretty tricky hits over the years.

The first time I used one of my inventions for a hit was, oh, about twenty-five years ago. It was 1982, something like that. I'm not that good at math. That's weird for an inventor—don't you think? Anyway, I had to take out a woman who'd engineered a major terrorist plot that killed a marketplace filled with innocent people in the seventies and was then living as a divorce attorney in Tempe. She was a real dragon-lady bitch. And she favored suits with huge shoulder pads. I could've just plugged her, leaving the cops to think it was the ex-husband of one of her clients. But I wanted to try something new . . . have a little fun with it.

At first I thought about exploding shoulder pads, but that would have been hard to rig, and what if it just blew her shoulders off? I mean—she'd look pretty silly and would probably survive. So I rigged her garage. I messed with her car's ignition so that once turned on, it wouldn't turn off. Then I built sensors for the garage door and the door to the house that would lock when it sensed CO_2. I guess they found claw marks around the doors where she'd tried to scratch her way out.

The detectives put it down to equipment failure. There was no CSI then so no one knew what to look for. From that moment on, I was hooked.

Shortly after that, I went through a James Bond phase where I experimented with everything from the deadly bowler hat Odd Job flings (for a vicious white slave trader) to the suffocating gold paint from *Goldfinger* (on a visiting nurse who murdered her senior charges once they'd put her in their wills). After about four hits, though, I got bored and wanted to get back to developing my own stuff. Besides, no one got it. I was at least hoping to terrify people with the 007 Killer—but no one figured it out.

That was followed by the time I had to take out this Vic who worked in construction and dealt crack to middle-school kids in his neighborhood (they had only a 50 percent survival rate due to his lethal blend). I rigged a nail gun to backfire via remote. The gun shot the nail out backwards, killing the bastard instantly. I switched the gun out before the body was found. It looked like he'd committed suicide. I guess I rambled a little in the suicide note I left for him, because the police spent months interviewing employees at Hostess Foods in an attempt to discover a reason for the Vic's obsession with Ding Dongs. I love Ding Dongs.

Where was I? Oh yeah. Probably my favorite job was where I invented a pair of stroke-inducing panty hose. You know how they have massaging nylons for people with poor circulation? It's kind of the same theory, really, except that as you move, my hose constrict in a way that creates blood clots in the legs. From there, it's only a matter of time before death by aneurism occurs. Of course, I had to trail the Vic for a while to make sure they worked. Boy, was he surprised. Oh, did I forget to mention the nylons were for a man? Yup. A corrupt judge with cross-dressing tendencies who liked to wear them under his robes. He'd had a weakness for mob money and was known to slap the brutal defendants in his courtroom with nothing more than community service. Two of the guys he set free later went on to murder a prominent female district attorney who posed a threat to the Cosa Nostra.

I'd looked into various means of death, but that was the only thing I could come up with. I even tricked them out with an old L'eggs egg. Remember those? They don't make them anymore, do they? I think they came out the same time as *Mork and Mindy*—maybe they were cross-promoting?

Oooh. This vodka was smooth. It seemed pretty strong but as I said before, I didn't have a lot of experience drinking.

Anyway, as I was saying, I was pretty much obsessed with inventions by then. Let's see. . . . I had the sunglasses that spray poison in your eyes; the garbage disposal and faucet rigged to electrify the sink—when the Vic washed dishes he was electrocuted; the weight belt that crushes your spine—I got the inspiration for that having my blood pressure read; the remote-controlled brick falling from a building to crush your skull (timing is really important on that one); the floor wax that looks dry but is actually slipperier than Crisco on an eel; oh yeah, and the super "Viagra."

You know, I think I really missed an opportunity there. I actually invented the stuff before anyone else knew about it. But being a Bombay means no future as a patented inventor, so what are you going to do?

Anyway, as you of course know, a vasodilator opens capillaries, which can cause a dangerous drop in blood pressure. Too much of it, your blood pressure is so low you have a heart attack because your heart is pumping harder. My little blue pill (I should've sued them for that too) was ten times stronger. So when a certain pimp of kidnapped child prostitutes from Thailand took what he thought would increase the duration of his erection, he keeled over before getting his pants off.

The coroner's report said he had an erection that lasted more than ten hours after his death (take that, Cialis!). I guess it made the news and everything.

Ahhhh . . . memories. Like a fine pitcher of vodka and tonic on a warm day. I was starting to feel better, remembering my successes. But my head was starting to feel thicker, kind of like being stuffed up. I hate that alcohol does that. My glaucoma stash doesn't have that effect—that's a whole different thing. Unfortunately, I have a very low tolerance there too.

Chapter Twenty-four

WESTLEY: *I've spent the last few years building up an immunity to iocane powder.*

—*The Princess Bride*

"Missi? What are you doing here?" Lex pulled up a chair next to me.

"Bitch is fucked-up." Sami grinned as she helped herself to my cocktails. Now if she would only stop quivering . . .

"I just needed a few mishuts." I waved my hand and stared at it as it moved. It was quivering just like Sami.

"What?" Lex looked at the almost-empty pitcher. "How long have you been out here?"

"Damn!" Sami cried out. "This is straight vodka! This dumbass should be dead!"

I shook my head and had to stop it with my hands. "No. There's tomik init." I'd asked for tonic. Maybe Sami was right. If so, was this sabotage too?

Lex frowned and sniffed the pitcher. "Dammit. Who served you?" When I didn't answer he turned to Sami.

"She could've died from alcohol poisoning." His words sounded like they were far, far awaaay. . . .

Lex began to rotate in place like a spinning wheel.

I was fascinated. How did he defy the laws of physics like that?

"Let's get you back to the guesthouse." He started to lift me out of the chair, and I walked sideways into a wall.

The next thing I remember was waking up in bed next to Sami. It was completely dark outside, so why did it feel like the sun had taken up residence in my brainpan? I shrugged on one of the fluffy robes and stumbled into the great room.

Damn. No aspirin. What kind of luxury cabana was this? I was in no shape to go rooting through my stuff to find the supply my sons had given me.

"How are you feeling?" Lex appeared next to me, no longer rotating 360 degrees. Good for him. That could be dangerous.

"Great," I lied. I was doing a lot of that lately. "I need aspirin." Now that was actually true.

"Here." He handed me a whole bottle of ibuprofen. "I picked this up in the gift shop after putting you to bed."

It took all of my strength—which at this point was not considerable—not to throw myself into his arms. Instead I swallowed four capsules on the spot.

"I thought you were only supposed to take two?"

I waved him off. "I developed a high tolerance to this stuff a while back." It was true. Back home I chugged these pretty regularly, what with all the concussions from my explosions and whatnot.

"Apparently you handle medicine much better

than you do alcohol." Lex smiled before wrapping his arms around me. Mmmmm. He smelled really good. Like soap. I love that smell. I'm sure I smelled like a distillery.

I pulled back and smiled weakly. "Well, thanks for taking care of me. I guess I overdid it a smidge."

He laughed. "A smidge? Sami had two glasses and got a buzz. She told me that back home it usually takes a case of beer for that to happen. That was strong stuff."

I would've laughed, but my whole body threatened to explode if I even giggled. Everything—and I mean everything—hurt.

"It's not funny, Missi. That could've been an attempt on your life."

Okay. I stopped laughing as I remembered that my head had been on the keg seconds before it exploded. Damn. Had Isaac figured me out and started trying to kill me first?

"So why did you disappear like that?" Lex looked concerned and I loved him for it. I loved him for it enough to lie some more.

"I just needed some time alone. You know how it is, having a camera and everybody else around twenty-four hours, seven days a week." I hoped that sounded sincere.

Lex smiled. "I can totally understand that. It's like being under a microscope. I wish I'd thought of it, actually."

I hated myself. I hated lying to him and my sons.

This job was killing me. And I had to lie to everyone here. And while Lex was being so supportive and thoughtful, I felt even worse.

"Well, good night." I kissed him lightly on the lips and practically raced back to my room.

My monastic life on the island was never like this. I didn't have to treat people badly and pretend I was someone else. I didn't really have any stress in my life. As soon as I got back, I was going to come up with some evil sort of revenge on the Council for putting me through this.

That was a comforting thought, and my last one before I fell asleep.

We were running late the next morning as the eight of us careened into each other (the fluffy robes acting as shock absorbers) while grabbing fistfuls of bacon off the cart and getting ready.

We arrived at Camp Tico looking well fed and clean. The site hadn't had any activity in almost twenty-four hours and it had been days since we'd lit a fire. Julie and Alan looked too distracted to care, but I was sure the audience would notice something wasn't right when the show aired. Oh well—not my problem.

"Well, I hope you all slept well," Alan began, sounding a little sarcastic. "Due to some . . . um, changes at the network, we will be sending two of you home today."

We looked around at each other and rolled our

eyes. Obviously the changes at the network included a healthy round of budget cuts.

"So the two slowest people in today's challenge will leave, becoming part of the jury." Alan looked tired.

"You mean we're voting two people off, right?" Moe asked, and I automatically brightened.

Julie shook her head. "We won't have time for Tribal Council tonight. So the two of you with the lowest scores will exit the show."

"If you'll just follow Julie, I'll meet you at the site of today's challenge." Alan stood there, waiting for us to leave. No doubt so he could reappear at wherever we ended up.

The eight of us on Team Tico followed Julie silently into the jungle. I don't even think she noticed how quiet we were. Man, something was really eating them.

It took almost half an hour of hiking to get to a riverbank deep inside the foliage. As we emerged from the jungle, I noticed a large crocodile laying on the bank. Crocs were native to this area and I'd seen them many times before. My teammates, however, had not. This I gathered from the screaming that followed.

"What the fuck is that?" Sami shouted down from the limbs of a nearby tree.

Everyone else pretty much said the same thing. Julie stayed a safe distance away, but tried to appear calm. Alan miraculously appeared and with a stick began to point at the crocodile.

"Alligators are native to Costa Rica," he began.

"Um, no they're not." I couldn't help it. The temptation to correct him was unbearable. I thought I saw Ernie grin from behind his camera.

Alan looked unshaken. "Yes, they are. And this is an alligator."

I stepped forward. "No. Alligators live in parts of North America. This is a crocodile. An American crocodile to be exact." He hated me already, so I thought I'd just have fun with it.

"Whatever!" An angry Alan struggled to regain his composure. "Same thing."

"Listen, dumbass!" Sami shouted down. "My friend says it's a crocodile and I believe her. The question is—what the fuck is it doing here?"

I couldn't resist giggling. Sami had my back all right.

"You will wrestle this alli . . . crocodile," Alan said, as one by one Team Tico's jaws dropped. "You will be timed to see how long it takes you to drag the gator . . . I mean croc, to shore."

"Are you fucking insane?" Sami shrieked and I could swear that dogs in the nearest village covered their ears.

"This time you've gone too far!" Isaac raised his voice—which startled me. "You can't ask us to do anything life threatening."

The rest of the group murmured their agreement and Alan just held up his hands.

"This is a challenge! Would you rather I had you wrestle a miniature dachshund? For christsake people! The name of the show is *Survival*!"

We barely had time to reply before he shrieked, "Missi! You're up first!" Why was I not surprised?

Lex put his arm out to bar me from moving. Not that I was racing for the challenge, mind you. Crocs are very dangerous. And although this one seemed to be only four feet long, that wasn't a guarantee some of us would come out in one piece. For a moment I wondered if what they had in mind for eliminating two of us was to feed us to the crocodile.

"You can't make us do this," Lex said in calm, measured tones that made all kinds of butterflies flip-flop around in my stomach. Then I thought about Fiona and realized there was more to his concern than I thought.

"If you refuse, you will be taken off the program," Alan said, and sniffed indignantly. I wanted to feed him to the croc. It wouldn't take long. We'd all just stand there on the shore, watching calmly as the croc grabbed him and pulled the smarmy host under. Soon, the thrashing would begin as the slimy reptile—Alan, not the crocodile—was spun around in the water until he drowned. Then if the croc was still hungry, we could feed him Julie.

"If you don't do it, Missi," Alan snapped, "Sami will have to go first."

I knew how much Sami needed the reward money for this show. She wouldn't refuse the challenge. At least I'd done this before (hello, I'm a Bombay!). Maybe I could buy some time or even injure the croc so it couldn't hurt anyone else. As long as I could keep its mouth closed, I'd be all right. I took a deep breath and pushed away the protective arm Lex had wrapped around my waist. I immediately missed his warmth and support, but I had to do this. "It's okay. He's a small one. Just make sure everyone watches what I do, all right?"

Lex and Isaac tried to stop me, and I believe Sami would've intervened too, had she come down from the tree. I just pushed through them and made my way to the animal.

Now, few people know this because I've never told anyone my trick when it comes to reptiles. We had a couple of freshwater crocs on the island and I'd studied them for a while to see if there was a way I could use them for work.

Besides the usual—hold them in a half nelson and get their tail tight between your legs so they don't smack you around—there's a spot where, if you apply the right amount of pressure, they just go into brain-lock. Then you can do whatever you want for about ten minutes. Humans have the same trigger. For men, it's porn. For women, it's chocolate.

As I walked up to the croc, a native Tican emerged from the jungle and quickly wrapped a leather muzzle around the croc's nose. Well, at least that was a bit of a relief. Crocodile jaws are very powerful. And if they get a grip on you and drag you into the water, you're pretty much done for.

The Tican then dragged the animal into the water

and motioned for me to go in. I was barely wading when Alan shouted for Julie to start the timer.

It really only took a minute or two to jump the poor beast from behind and lock my arms around him and my legs around his tail as I dragged him to shore. I didn't even have to use my trick. The muzzle kept him from snapping and, unless I miss my guess, the poor croc was drugged. What a lame idea.

"He's drugged and docile," I whispered to my team when I rejoined them. "Just do what I did and you should be all right."

"Sami!" Alan called, and I realized she'd gotten down and was standing next to me. "You're up!" He'd regained some of his smarmy cockiness and I hated him for it. I'd have given anything to see him turned into crocodile crap.

Sami froze for a moment. I thought she was going to give up. Not that I could blame her. The scariest thing she'd probably ever seen was the guy on the next bar stool at closing time when the lights came on.

To my amazement, she walked over to where the croc was being dragged into the water by his handler. Even more impressive was the fact that she managed it in three seconds less than me.

"Goddamned bitch gonna show me who's boss!" she swore under her breath as she strutted back to us.

"So far, Sami has the fastest time, followed by Missi. Lex, your turn."

My heart jumped a little as I feared he might get hurt. Then I remembered that the croc was muzzled and drugged and Lex was stronger than I was. Lex calmly waded into the water. I was so proud. He came back with a time that matched mine. And I liked the way his arm muscles bulged as he dragged the poor creature onto the bank.

We watched as, one by one, Isaac, Moe and Dr. Andy managed to wrestle the crocodile to shore. It seemed to be going well. Only Liliana and Brick/Norman remained. Surely the reptile was getting weaker by now.

Liliana straightened her back and walked into the water. To my surprise, she managed to grab hold of the animal and was just beginning to bring him to the bank when the muzzle sprang from his jaws and he started snapping. Liliana dropped him out of shock and the croc managed to grab hold of her clothes.

Once he got a good grip, he started spinning in the water, dragging Liliana with him. I ran into the thrashing water to save her. Isaac and Lex appeared beside me. Lex grabbed the beast by the body as Isaac held the tail. I brought my hand down as hard as I could, stabbing him between the eyes with my fingers.

It worked. The croc went slack and as the men dragged him onto the beach, I pulled Liliana from the muddy river. She said nothing as she staggered toward the rest of the group. I was seriously impressed.

"Brick!" Alan acted as though what had happened hadn't really happened. No one tried to fix the muzzle. What was going on?

"Hold on!" Isaac shouted. "We need to get another muzzle on him first!"

Looking around, I noticed that the croc's handler was nowhere to be found. What did that mean?

"We move ahead," Julie said steadily. Was she nuts? One of the safety precautions was gone!

"You know what?" Brick/Norman said in a squeaky, not-very-leading-man sort of voice. "I quit. I'm off the show, okay?"

Alan and Brick glared at each other for a few moments. Alan backed off.

"Liliana and Brick—you will go back to the Tigre."

Julie agreed with Alan and began leading the two out of the area.

"The rest of you head back to camp," Alan said, then promptly disappeared.

I made a mental note to put some scorpions in his bed later. That would be fun.

"Look at this," Lex whispered to me on the way back to camp. He held out the harness. "It's not broken."

Sure enough, I could see it was cut midway through.

Chapter Twenty-five

Nobody likes me. Everybody hates me. Guess I'll just eat worms.

—Children's song

"Why would anyone cut the muzzle?" Lex frowned at me. It was the first time he'd ever frowned at me and I decided that I didn't like it.

Isaac and Sami were quiet. We were sitting at the dinner table—the rest of Team Tico had already gone to bed. No one's heart was in this contest anymore since it appeared the host didn't care one way or another if anyone got hurt.

I picked at what was left of the turkey. "Maybe it's Alan—trying to up the ratings."

"That's fucked-up." Sami glowered.

"It's irresponsible," added Isaac.

"It's dangerous," Lex said quietly.

My stomach backflipped as I remembered that Lex's wife had died because of stuff like this. The others weren't privy to this knowledge, so I tried to change the subject.

"Oh well. It'll all be over soon enough."

Lex frowned at me again. I really hated it. "What does that mean?"

"Um, I guess I meant that the show will probably go

bankrupt before we can do another challenge any-way—then we can go home." I shrugged for emphasis.

"Man, this shit stinks." Sami shook her head. "I could've used that goddamned money."

I forgot that these people were here because twenty-five thousand dollars was a life-changing amount to them. While Brick/Norman, Dr. Andy and Kit were here to get media exposure, Moe, Sami and possibly Lex wanted the cash to turn their lives around.

Guilt is a horrible thing. I remember my mother once told me it was a useless emotion. Of course, that didn't stop her from applying it like a thick-cut slab of bacon whenever she could. But the fact of the matter was that I was here on false pretenses.

The only reason I was on this ridiculous show was to tail Isaac so I could kill him if I had to. A stab of the "useless emotion" got me in the heart when I thought of how I was throwing money around for this guesthouse. What did they possibly think of me? My guess was they wondered why I was even involved.

And let's face it—I hadn't even done my job. I never tailed Isaac or even tried to pump him for information. Hell, I hadn't even remembered to pack my truth serum. It's strawberry flavored with half the fat, so it's good and good for you!

My shoulders slumped. I'd screwed everything up. If I won the contest I would be nothing short of a jerk. Homesickness burned like Mountain Dew on acid reflux. I missed my house. I missed my kids. And I didn't know what the hell I was doing.

"I agree with Lex," Sami said. I guess I also missed an entire conversation.

"Agree with what?" I asked before I could stop myself.

My three allies scowled.

"Missi, what's wrong with you?" Isaac asked.

"Nothing." I tried to think up a lie but came up empty. "I just spaced out."

Sami sighed. "Lex thinks we should try to find out what the hell is going on so no one else gets hurt."

"Oh."

Lex's right eyebrow went up. "Oh?"

Uh oh.

"Well," I started uneasily. I couldn't dedicate myself to one more thing. I had a job to do and the Council would hand me my ovaries on a Bombay-crested plate if I didn't do it. "Don't you think we should just leave it alone? I mean, the show is still on and we should just see it out. It's probably not even sabotage—just an unfortunate series of coincidences." Okay, what I meant to say was "let's not risk one of you losing the money you seem to so desperately need." Problem was, I couldn't "invent" a way to say that so it wouldn't sound condescending. Words are much harder to put together than actual inventions. And I'm pretty sure I just proved that.

"Fuck this, I'm going to bed." Sami rose and Isaac nodded, leaving Lex and me alone in a very uncomfortable silence.

"Missi, what is wrong with you?" Lex asked after a moment.

I threw my hands up. "What? What did I say?"

"Why are you here?"

Why am I here? So I can possibly kill Isaac. Duh.

"The same reason you're here," I answered. "The money."

Lex stood and went off to bed, leaving me what to wonder what had just happened. Obviously I'd said something wrong, but what? I didn't like the way my lover was looking at me. Something had just changed in our relationship and I was pretty sure it wasn't something good.

As I got to my feet to follow him, there was a short, sharp knock at the door. Figuring it was room service here to clear the plates, I answered, only to find Ernie standing there.

"Julie and Alan will be at the campsite at six in the morning." He winked. "Thought you'd like a heads-up."

I closed the door and leaned against it. Great. My teammates now had another reason to be miserable, and I got to deliver the news.

I didn't sleep. Basically, I sat in the living room fully dressed until five A.M., when I woke the troops with the news. No matter how you looked at it, this was a bad situation. Lex was right worrying that someone could get hurt, but I didn't have any more time to devote to figuring out the mystery, Nancy Drew Club be damned.

"Are you all right?" Dr. Andy sat down next to me on the sofa. I looked around, but he was the only one there. Apparently the others were still getting ready.

"Sure," I lied. "I'm fine," I lied again. Damn, I was doing a lot of that. In spite what you might think, the Bombays aren't big on lying. Well, at least to each other and the important people in our lives. We lie to our victims all the time.

"You look like you need to talk," he said gently.

Looking around again, I found no trace of our camera crew. Maybe Dr. Andy was more than just the shallow media hog I made him out to be. That made me feel worse.

I was tempted to actually tell him my problems. He had a comforting, easygoing manner. But what would I tell him? What could I tell him?

"Lex and the others think the show is being sabotaged." I thought that too, but for some reason left it out.

He thought for a moment. "What do you think?"

"It doesn't matter what I think. I just want this mess to be over."

"I don't believe that Missi. I've seen nothing but compassion from you for everyone here. Why wouldn't you care if someone may get hurt? It's not in you to be apathetic."

I looked at him archly. For a moment, the other cast-aways paraded through my mind. How many of them did I dismiss as two-dimensional? I called Brick/Norman Brick/Norman out of spite. Some compassion.

"No," I lied yet again. "You're wrong. I just want to

win or go home." Dr. Andy was right. But if he thought that, I couldn't do my job. And what it all boiled down to was that I was getting too attached to the people on this show to do that job. If I didn't complete my mission, I had a much worse showdown waiting for me at Santa Muerta.

"I don't care about any of these people," I added. "It's only a game, after all." Tough words, but would he buy it? I folded my arms over my chest for emphasis.

"Oh."

That wasn't Dr. Andy's voice. It was Lex's. I turned slowly to find him standing behind me with a shocked look on his face. Damn.

Lex turned and walked away, but I just sat there frozen, staring after him. What had I done?

Chapter Twenty-six

RUSTY: *You'd need at least a dozen guys doing a combination of cons.*

DANNY: *Like what, do you think?*

RUSTY: *Off the top of my head, I'd say you're looking at a Boesky, a Jim Brown, a Miss Daisy, two Jethros and a Leon Spinks, not to mention the biggest Ella Fitzgerald ever!*

—*Ocean's Eleven*

Icy numbness crept over me, as if I were being slowly frozen from the top down (which is something I can do to a man, by the way—it just takes the right equipment. . . . Gah! Focus Missi!) as I walked with my five remaining teammates. No one spoke to me. I was pretty sure that was because Sami, Isaac and Moe were tired. Dr. Andy gave me a wan smile I'm sure was intended to cheer me up. Lex had a scary look of determination on his face.

"You okay?" Moe whispered from behind me.

I nodded, saying nothing.

"What's wrong?" he pressed. You know, he really was a sweet guy. I'd misjudged him too. Maybe he had a perfectly good reason for being unemployed and living with his mom. Maybe he had a rare, undetectable disease? I can make those. There's a whole shelf of them in my lab, under the bobbleheads.

I shook my bobblehead, pretty sure I would burst into tears if I spoke. I'd really blown it. Lex was probably convinced I had played him—which made me look like an evil whore. If only I hadn't opened my big, fat mouth and shoved my whole leg into it.

Alan and Julie joined us at the site shortly after we arrived. They had six men with them I didn't recognize. Locals, I'd guessed. Each one of them held what looked like a black sack.

"We are down to our final six," Alan intoned with considerably less confidence than he'd had when the show started. "Each of you will be blindfolded and taken to a remote location. You will remove your blindfold and try to find your way back here, to camp, where I will be waiting with further instructions."

Another lame event. Where were the cameramen? There were only two left—Bert and Ernie. How would they cover six people in different locations? Were they even trying anymore?

My thoughts were interrupted as a black hood was thrown over my head. Man, it was really dark in there. Black is a good color on me though. Not that anyone would see me.

"I'll see you back here soon," Alan said as someone took my arm to lead me away. He smelled like fish and onions. Super.

What were they going to do? Time us, and the last

two to make it back would be voted off? I struggled to find the point of it all. Maybe this was just another way to try and kill us. Moving through a jungle blindfolded is dicey at best.

This wouldn't be a tough challenge for me. Part of our training in the Bombay clan is to do the same thing on Santa Muerta as children. As we got older, we were taken to other remote locations in the world in an attempt to eradicate our fear of the unknown. One time, back in the early eighties, Mom left me alone in a remote area of Tibet. How was she to know the Chinese army was just on the other side of the mountain? Anyway, once I got my hood off (they didn't take them off for us—that would have been too easy) and saw several thousand Chinese heading my way, it kind of took the wind out of my sails. There's a real funny story about that and a yak herder, but that's for another time.

I started memorizing the number of steps I was taking and the direction I was being led. Sounds and smells all contributed to where I was going, which seemed to be down the beach, away from the Blanco Tigre. Sand churned beneath my feet and the gulls cried out as we moved in a straight line. How stupid was that? At least make it interesting.

After what I deduced was about ten minutes, we turned left and in fourteen steps were heading into the jungle. Leaves crunched as I stepped on them and branches pressed against my arms. Again, we moved in a straight line. How original.

Howler monkeys shrieked and I could swear I heard the word *Mom*. I smiled beneath the hood. The boys were following me. I felt a little better knowing that they loved me enough to keep an eye on me. When a mango dropped on my head, I knew it was Monty and Jack. Good boys, but enough with the mangoes already.

After a few more minutes, we stopped and the hood was pulled off. A rather bored looking man shrugged at me and then disappeared into the jungle. Apparently, his job was done.

Monty jumped down, followed by Jack. They threw their arms around me and squeezed.

"Why are you crying?" Jack asked with a look of fear.

Monty, always the more intuitive one, took me back into his arms. "It's okay, Mom. We're here. It's okay."

I sobbed for a few moments, getting it all out. Then I told my sons what had happened.

"Whoa," Jack replied. "You were harsh to Lex."

"Shut it!" Monty snapped at his brother. "Can't you see she's been through enough?"

Jack hung his head. "Sorry, Mom. I'm one half of an idiot."

Normally I would've laughed at his typical swipe at Monty, but instead I wiped my nose on my arm. "It's okay. Before you show me back to the camp, tell me you have something on Vic."

The boys looked at each other for a long time. Too long a time, actually.

"You do have something I can use, right?" I asked again.

Monty shook his head. "Not really. It's like he doesn't really exist. I can't even find anything that says he's a poker player."

Jack nodded. "Yeah. This is the weirdest assignment ever. Isaac is the invisible man. He's off the grid . . . completely."

I behaved rationally, by screaming in frustration. Birds flew to get out of my way and howler monkeys voiced their admiration.

"There's something else," Monty added in a voice that always makes a mother's insides shrivel. "We haven't heard anything back from the Council."

"What? Why would you contact them?"

Jack ran his fingers through his hair. "We thought maybe we could sweet-talk Grandma into giving up more on Vic."

"Problem is," Monty finished for his brother, "no one on Santa Muerta is returning our calls or text messages."

"That's not much, considering they don't even know what texting is." I guess I'd have to have a BlackBerry course for them when I got home. I'm talking really remedial here. "But why wouldn't they answer their phones?"

"We could go back to the island and see what's going on?" Jackson asked.

I shook my head. "No. It's too risky. If something's gone down I don't want you two involved." In our business, there was always the possibility of a raid or espionage. I was less worried about the Council than I was about my boys. I know it sounds blasé, but we've been through drills for emergencies so many times I figured my mother and the others were handling whatever it was.

"I want you two to go find Isaac and tail him." I should have been doing that all along. It was time to get this thing over with.

The boys nodded and with a quick hug were off on their new mission. I dried my eyes and turned to head back the way I came.

The long walk gave me time to think. It was easy to trace my way back, mainly because I just had to follow the footprints. Stupid show.

So, what was I going to do about Lex once the Isaac thing was sorted out? I didn't think it was possible to feel worse than I did. This man was the first I'd trusted—hell, slept with—in years. My feelings for him were overpowering. I had really fallen hard.

And now Lex thought I'd betrayed him in the worst way. That sucked. The question was, what would I do? Should I come clean and tell him I hadn't meant it? Would he even believe me? Maybe I should wash my hands of it and just let him think I was a horrible, manipulative witch. Then I could just go back to the safety of my island and forget about it.

But could I forget about it? Sure I could, I thought with no confidence whatsoever. It was just a sweet little fling. Meant to be over in a few weeks. I didn't need a man—hadn't I told my mother that when I left?

And what about the boys? No, it was too soon to

cut them loose. They still needed a full-time mother. Monty and Jack had come here to help me. They deserved my complete attention. Having a boyfriend would just complicate things.

Another justification popped into my head. My sons knew I was an assassin and they didn't care. Lex wouldn't be able to accept that. And how would he feel once he knew my inventions were actually meant to kill people?

Once I'd talked myself into the idea that Lex would change me if he could, and the fact that I couldn't change if I wanted to due to the blood oath I'd signed as a child, it didn't really matter.

In fact, I was just about to talk myself into both changing my hair color and prospecting for a "boy toy" in Venezuela, when I stumbled gracelessly into camp. I was the first one there. As long as Lex wasn't the second, I might have been all right.

Unfortunately, my luck wasn't good. Who do you think strolled in minutes after me? That's right. Lex. We sat in the sand quietly, intensely uncomfortable.

"So, I suppose you meant what you told Dr. Andy this morning?" Lex asked.

Damn him! Why couldn't he just leave it alone?

"Yes. I did. It's just a game." I tried to sound convincing. Lex looked at me as if trying to see through my head. If I'd wanted to, I could've told him I had an invention for that. But I wasn't feeling especially charitable. Mostly, I was deeply offended that he had to ask. If he really had feelings for me, he would've known I was lying to Dr. Andy. The bastard! Hey, yeah! It's his fault.

Moe joined us, sweating profusely and seriously out of breath. He doubled over to recoup as Dr. Andy joined us, followed by Alan and Julie.

Alan smirked. "I see you four made it back okay." I wondered what he'd look like with a barbecue fork sticking out of his jugular. Pretty funny, I bet.

"Sami and Isaac will be here soon," I grumbled, just to be contradictory.

Alan shook his head. "I'm afraid not. You four now have a choice to make." He paused dramatically. Julie leered. I pictured her with that same barbecue fork protruding from her forehead. That helped. *Oooh! Maybe it's a rusty fork! Then she'd get tetanus too. Wait, would it even matter, if she had a pointy piece of metal piercing her brain?*

"Isaac and Sami have been kidnapped," Alan continued. "They are hidden somewhere in the jungle. You can go and look for them and if you find them, they will stay on the show. Or you can avoid going after them, which will eliminate them from the team—making you the final four."

"Are you serious?" I asked.

Julie piped up. "Yes. The choice is yours. Do the right thing and risk yourselves or do nothing and increase your chance of winning."

Alan glared at her for taking the spotlight. Apparently, Alan didn't like sharing. He probably didn't watch *Sesame Street* as a child. You know, that would explain so much. I wonder if the Council would allow me to do a survey of our Vics—asking them just before killing them if they'd ever watched *Sesame Street*. I'd bet none of them did. Wouldn't that be revealing?

I noticed that Bert and Ernie were here to tape now.

"If you fail to find them before sundown, your choice is made for you. We will join you in the morning to see what you have decided." Alan and Julie exchanged smug grins and strolled up the beach toward the resort. I added our flaming torches shoved up their asses to my fantasy.

I snagged Ernie's ankle as he tried to walk past me. "Where are they?" I growled. Burt looked at us, then started running up the beach. Apparently he was in no mood to be challenged.

"Where are they?" I repeated.

"I don't know! They didn't tell us what they were going to do with them!" Ernie began to whine. I let him go and he took off after his little Muppet roommate. Either I scared him or the show had totally given up on us.

"Well," Moe said slowly, "I guess this solves our problem."

Dr. Andy nodded. "It seems pretty clear what to do. Or at least, not do."

I stood up. "What are you talking about? We have to go find them."

Lex didn't move or speak.

Moe stood up to face me. "I know they are your

friends, Missi, but this is how the game is played. We have an opportunity to do nothing and get closer to winning."

"I'm sure they're locked in a room at the Tigre," Dr. Andy said. "It isn't a question of ethics here—it's how the strategy works."

I realized I was behaving contrary to what I'd just told Lex, but it really bothered me that no one wanted to find Sami and Isaac.

"Lex, let's just you and me go . . . ," I started.

He looked up at me. "I don't know. I mean, I came here to win. And if they're safe at the resort, there's no reason to lose the challenge, right?" I could see Lex was struggling with this.

"But we have an alliance," I pleaded.

Lex shook his head and stood up. "Apparently not. And since when did you care about anyone in this game?"

I watched with my mouth open as the three of them walked away.

Chapter Twenty-seven

DELIVERY MAN (inventorying the items he has just brought): *Meat hooks, four lengths of chain, forty gallons of plasma, and an elephant syringe.*
                                        —*Attack of the 50 Foot Woman*

"Stupid, selfish bastards," I mumbled as I made my way into the jungle, looking for my missing teammates. "All they care about is this idiotic game. There's no way Sami would have copped out for a room at the Tigre." In case you're wondering, I do talk to myself a lot. I don't know if it's because I'm an inventor or if it's due to the fact I spend so much time alone. Isolated. On an island.

Sami and Isaac would've done the same for me. And I really wanted Sami to win. I got the distinct impression that she needed the money. If I hadn't been a giant ass this morning, Lex would probably have been with me.

I couldn't blame him for being confused. Now he figured it really was just a game and this was a chance for him to win. Lex thought I'd used him. Why should he have trusted me?

Because you slept with him, you moron! Okay, there was that. We'd shared an intimacy that made me feel like my organs had turned to goo. Images of making love to Lex spooled through my brain like an X-rated film reel.

I'd really made a mess of things. Usually I like to make a mess of things. It's how I make a lot of my discoveries. Like that time I spilled one of my chemical concoctions on Silly Putty. Wow—you should have seen what that did to comic book pictures!

But in this case, someone had been hurt. I knew trying out a relationship would end in fiasco. Hadn't I told Mom I didn't need a man? More like shouldn't have a man.

What did Lex see in me anyway? He'd just met me. We knew nothing about each other except for some moments of explosive, sexual chemistry. Damn, he was good. That thing he did with his elbow was impressive.

There was also a sense of ease I felt when I was around him. Lex made me feel completely comfortable. It was like we'd known each other forever. When you meet someone like that, it's like a sixth sense kicks in.

Great. Now I was utterly depressed. I had a great thing with a terrific guy and . . . and what? He'd overheard me saying that he meant nothing to me. Yeesh. Was I obsessing or what?

And what about the fact he wouldn't help me find Sami and Isaac? He wasn't the greatest guy, I tried to keep telling myself. In case you're wondering, it didn't work.

Several hours later (with a full-blown migraine), I still hadn't found my missing teammates. I'd scoured the jungle, the beach and even the hotel. Stopping by the guesthouse, I ordered a tuna salad sandwich and a Diet Coke. No one was around. Maybe it made them feel too guilty? It was almost three in the afternoon when I headed back out to check the remaining grounds of the Tigre.

Damn, it was getting late. It was only an hour away from dusk as I wandered onto the last hole on the resort golf course. It was then I heard what sounded like gravel swearing.

Just off the eighteenth hole was a little maintenance shack. I rounded the corner to find Sami tied up like a cocoon on the ground, swearing up a blue streak with her voice half gone. After I untied her and broke into the shack to get her something to drink, she calmed down.

"Bastards dragged me here and left me! I'm gonna kill 'em!"

I let her rant for a while because she'd earned it. I even picked up some juicy new cuss words to use on my mother when she tries to set me up in the future.

"Sami," I said, trying to calm her down at last, "where did they take Isaac?"

Sami stopped shouting and stared at me. "They took him too?"

I nodded, and she began expelling expletives that didn't even make sense. How could a jackass even have sex with a rat anyway?

She seemed okay to walk and together we made our way through the falling darkness to the guesthouse.

I stopped short of the tennis courts.

"Sami, you go check in at the campsite so you don't get disqualified. Then head to the guesthouse and tell Lex what happened. I'm going back out to find Isaac."

I thought she'd argue with me, but she was obviously exhausted.

"Roger that." She turned and vanished into the foliage.

After "borrowing" a flashlight from a drunk security guard who was napping on the putting green, I decided to check out the rest of the area.

My mood grew as dark as the night. Where was Isaac? Alan and Julie weren't this good at hiding someone. Hell, they barely managed to think straight most of the time.

I hoped Monty and Jack had found him. It occurred to me that I hadn't seen the boys all day. That gave me heart palpitations that I was sure would leave a mark. Where in the hell were they?

Of course, I started to panic. My kids were missing, and so was my Vic. My boyfriend hated me, as did everyone who worked on the show. Weathermen have the "lake effect"; *Survival* had the "Missi effect."

At least Sami appreciated me. That was some consolation. I was walking in circles and still saw no sign of Isaac, Monty or Jackson. Exhaustion descended like a wet, wool blanket in July. I needed to get back. There was the smallest hope I'd find Isaac at the campsite.

No such luck. Julie and Alan looked pissed. Moe and Dr. Andy seemed upset that their odds of making the final four weren't as good. Lex glanced at me with what I thought was curiosity. Oh, why did I have to think that? Getting my hopes up would only complicate things.

"So, you're finally back," Julie sneered. I was seriously sick of her doing that.

"Since you found Sami, she stays in the game. Isaac, however, is off." Alan seemed to be taking pleasure in my failure to find Isaac.

I was in some serious shit if I didn't find him. I'd pretty much blown my assignment from the Council—something I've never done before. Not ever.

I followed the rest of the team back to the guesthouse. Sami was the only one who talked to me. I got the feeling the others let her know they weren't too happy to see her, but she didn't care.

Dinner arrived but my heart wasn't in it. Food didn't sound good. There was no room in my stomach for it. Between worrying about Vic (that was a new one) and the boys and being treated like a leper by Dr. Andy and Moe and being loathed by Lex, I had enough action in there to last a lifetime.

"Thanks again for keeping me in the game, Missi." Sami spoke so loud there was no doubting her intentions.

"You're welcome. After all, we did have an alliance." I shot a snide look at Lex.

"Could have fooled me after what I heard this morning," Lex sniped. "You made it clear that you thought of this only as a game to be won."

"What the hell are you talking about, dumbass?" Sami gave him a look that should've melted his face.

"Why don't you tell her what you told Dr. Andy?" Lex pointed at me with his fork.

Moe didn't say anything but tried to give me a supportive smile. I felt bad that he had to witness this. It wasn't his fault I was a jerk.

"Let's just calm down and talk this through . . . ," Dr. Andy started.

"No thank you." I threw my napkin on the table and slid my chair back.

"Who cares what the bitch said? She's the only asshole who came looking for me." Sami winked at me.

"She said she didn't care for any of us. That this was a game and we didn't mean anything to her," Lex said quietly.

Damn. I'd hurt him more than I thought.

"She also acted like she didn't believe there was any sabotage. And she didn't think we should look into it," he added.

"What's that supposed to mean?" Oh, it was on.

"Well, maybe you are the one sabotaging the show." Funny. Lex didn't look like a man I wanted to kill.

"Why would I sabotage the show?" I have to admit I was pretty shocked at the accusation. I never saw this coming.

"Maybe you did it so you could guarantee a win. Although your generosity"—he waved his arms about him—"indicates that you don't need the money."

Wow. That's it. Just wow. I had nothing.

"Oh, I get it," Moe said thoughtfully. "She sabotaged it so she could play the hero."

"Uh, no. It's not me," I said numbly. "I lied to Dr. Andy. It was a stupid strategy, I'll admit. I really do care about you guys." I drew myself up to my full height. "But now that I see your true colors, Lex, I wonder how I let my feelings for you get so out of control." I slid my chair dramatically under the table and went to my room, where I pouted. All night.

Chapter Twenty-eight

That would be a good thing for them to cut on my tombstone: wherever she went, including here, it was against her better judgment.

—Dorothy Parker

Sami woke me in the morning, so I must have gotten some sleep. Apparently, I'd been crying, as was evidenced by my swollen eyes.

After soaking my face for twenty minutes with a cold washcloth, I ventured out to breakfast. In my absence, one of the other guests had ordered Danishes and coffee. Whatever. It all tasted like sawdust anyhow.

We arrived at the campsite just seconds before Julie appeared. No one seemed to care about the consequences anymore. Last night took the fight out of everyone. Moe winked at me and Sami called me dumbass and that felt like a small victory. Lex never made eye contact.

Julie chewed on her lip. Strangely enough, she didn't have her clipboard with her.

"I need all of you to follow me to the resort. I'll explain once we get there."

That was weird, but none of us really cared. I was wavering between quitting and killing everyone, so my being rational was right out.

To our dull surprise, Julie marched us into a conference room. Alan sat at a long table with what appeared to be network brass and the local police.

"I need your attention." Alan looked tired for the first time since I'd met him. "We've lost Isaac. The challenges for today are canceled and the police have some questions for you. Please cooperate with them."

My heart sank. I'd feared the worst and it had happened. Isaac was missing. I'd blown the job. The others looked around helplessly.

"What do you mean, missing? How could you lose him?" Moe asked with a catch in his throat.

Julie looked at Alan quickly, then responded. "He wasn't where we left him. We've searched everywhere." She shrugged.

A lot of thoughts went through my mind. Isaac could have become the victim of foul play by the saboteur—whoever that was. Or maybe he'd figured me out and fled. In any case, things couldn't have been worse. Either I'd screwed up or someone had done the job for me. And where were Monty and Jackson? No one could've taken all three of them. My boys were too well trained for that. Unless they were unconscious . . .

An ugly, ovary-shrinking fear filled me. It had never occurred to me that they could be in danger. If something happened to my sons, I would never forgive myself. And then I would never forgive my mother. One was mental, the other would be physical.

There was only one thing to do. I had to get to that

mango tree, and I hoped that Monty and Jack were waiting for me there. But how? The conference room was locked up tighter than brand-new Tupperware.

"I think I'm going to be sick." What? I did a little acting in college. "I need to get out of here. . . ." My body swayed and my eyes rolled back in my head as I staggered to the door. To my surprise, no one tried to stop me.

"I'll be right back," I promised with a lie. As soon as the doors closed and without looking behind me even once, I ran until I got to my meeting place with the boys.

"Monty! Jackson!" I shouted. Nothing. "Boys, it's okay! I'm alone!" Still nothing.

I imagined everything a mother imagines when her children are missing—from terrorists to ice picks to disfiguring acid. Okay, everything that a Bombay mother imagines.

Snap out of it! What were the possibilities? This line of thinking slowed my pulse a bit. After taking a few cleansing breaths, I considered what might have happened. Either Isaac met with foul play or he was on the run. The boys were either with him or still looking for him. Okay. That seemed a little more re- alistic.

Then, crazy mommy took over my brain. If they were with Isaac, they were most likely in trouble or they would have contacted me. Right?

How long had I been sitting there? It felt like hours. Somehow I managed to convince myself that doing nothing was counterproductive. I started back toward the guesthouse. Sami and Moe would help me look for Isaac. They didn't have to know that my sons were in the mix too.

"Missi?" Dr. Andy was standing outside the door to the guesthouse. He came up to me, studying my face. "You weren't sick, were you?"

"You're pretty intuitive, Doc." I paused. "Can I ask you something, professionally?"

He pulled up two plastic chairs and motioned for me to sit.

I didn't wait for him to ask. "You probably guessed that I'm worried about Isaac."

"You think you are somehow to blame. But you're not, are you?"

I shook my head. "No, I'm not the saboteur. I just feel like I didn't look out for him."

"Do you have any children?" he asked.

That got my attention. "Well, yes. Twin sons. They just turned seventeen."

He nodded. "I remembered you saying you were a widow. It's very textbook."

I squinted at him. "It is? How so?"

Dr. Andy leaned back and crossed his legs. "You have a mother-hen complex. Your husband's death left you to raise two little boys. Now they're grown and getting ready to leave the nest, right?"

Did hens have nests? "Well, yes."

"That's why you went after Sami when no one else would. That's why you've looked out for all of us on the challenges and when there was danger. And that's why you are obsessed with finding Isaac."

"Um, okay . . ."

"You are facing your future. Your sons will go off to lead their own lives and you will be all alone. The whole world has started to become your nest. But you can't save everyone, Missi. And you aren't responsible for all of us. We're adults, like you. You need to let go and move on."

I thought about what he said. There was some real insight there. I guess I'd misjudged him too.

"That's pretty good. I think you'll go far as a television psychiatrist."

Dr. Andy's face flushed a deep crimson. "Between you and me, Missi, I'm not really a doctor. I'm not even a certified therapist."

"Why are you telling me that?" I looked around but there were no cameras.

He looked to his left and his right before continuing. "I took a couple of courses online. I just wanted you to know that this talent is all natural."

So he was bragging. I did not have time for this.

"I was a follower of the late Anthony Lowe—well, before his unfortunate death in Indiana. I just wanted to see if I could do it."

"Great. I've got to go." I pushed past him into the house.

Sami and Lex turned when they saw me.

"God damn!" Sami shouted as she ran to me. "You're all right!"

I wanted to tell her she couldn't be more wrong. Lex gave me a weak grin. What the hell was that about?

"I just came back to get some food and water and head out again to look for Isaac."

"We'll go too," Lex said.

I turned to face him. "You don't have to. Dr. Andy just informed me that I have an overdeveloped need to take care of people, so it's my thing. Do whatever you want." I threw the things I needed into my tote, threw it over my shoulder and turned toward the door.

"Fuck that! We're going with you." Sami followed me out the door.

I noticed that Dr. Andy was gone. Where was he? Moe was still absent. Maybe the fake doc was counseling him now. Poor kid.

"All right, fine." I sighed. "You two take the golf course—where I found you yesterday. I'll head directly north, into the jungle. It's the only area I haven't been."

They looked like they were about to argue and I stopped them. "There is no discussion. Come and find me if you don't locate Isaac."

They agreed, which was a good thing or I would've had to kill them. And I'm somewhat serious when I say that.

Chapter Twenty-nine

CAPTAIN JACK SPARROW: *Look! An undead monkey!*
—*Pirates of the Caribbean: Dead Man's Chest*

"All right boys, Momma's coming," I said quietly as I made my way through the trees and vines. My attitude had gone from freaked-out mother to Rambonator in a matter of seconds. This transition was important or I'd never have kept my head in whatever situation I found.

This was the only area I hadn't yet searched and I stayed close to the trail. I hoped something would surface to give me a clue.

Even though I'd spent a lot of years in the lab, I still knew how to launch into stealth mode. I'd spent my whole life learning how to be silent and invisible—which was probably a lot different from growing up in other families. But if I'd had to kill someone, I could have. And if my kids were in danger, I'd take out anyone who had them, even if it was Isaac.

Thinking about that for a moment made me realize that I was finally in the Bombay zone. If Isaac wasn't dead or in danger from some mysterious stranger, he was probably holding my kids hostage. And that, I just couldn't have. Mother hen, indeed. More like deadly-ninja-angry-mother-hen thingy!

I went over various scenarios in my head, preparing for any kind of combat there might be. I've always been like that. It gives me quick reflexes and allows me to think fast and implement almost anything as a weapon. I remember this one time when I had to kill a guy with a drinking straw. That was actually funny. Because if you hold your thumb over one end of a straw, it's pretty much a deadly weapon. . . .

Sorry, got off track there. Damn, this was taking a long time. I had to keep my mind busy or I'd . . . Too late. I was thinking about Lex.

The man really had to hate me. After catching me saying I'd more or less used him to win the game, he had to be upset. Forget the fact that it was a lie. I'd hurt him and that was very bad.

Truth was, I think I was actually falling in love with him. I shook my head to clear it.

Keep moving, Missi. I willed my feet to continue even though I felt like I was dragging my heart behind me like a deflated parachute. I tried to think of something else but the idea refused to budge from my brain.

What did you expect, Missi? That after the show you and Mr. Ethics would shack up together in your condo on Santa Muerta? Maybe he could use his stunt-planning skills—the ones he used so no one got hurt—to help you kill people?

I shuddered in spite of the heat. *Forget Lex! Forget him! Focus on Isaac, Monty and Jack. Think of tough things.* I pictured scorpions, poison, laser sights, anything to take my mind off of Lex Danby.

At least Sami still liked me. And Moe and possibly the fake Dr. Andy. Hell, Isaac liked me, even if he had figured out I was sent to kill him. I didn't know if that was the case or not, but it really didn't matter.

I'm gonna harden my heart. I'm gonna swallow my tears. Oooh, a little Pat Benatar should help. Picturing the lyrics, I kept pressing farther north until the trail ended. I'd been gone about an hour. Now what? Should I go back?

Just as I was about to turn around, I thought I saw a flash of red. Jackson? *Maybe I should push on a bit farther.* I turned in the direction where I'd spotted it and followed.

"Boys!" I called out. "Monty! Jackson!" I didn't want to yell too loudly in case they were in jeopardy.

After about five minutes I spotted a clearing ahead. At the far end was a dilapidated shack. How cliché was that? I mean seriously? A ramshackle lean-to in the middle of nowhere?

Could the boys or Isaac be there? It was a little obvious, but I had to check it out. I carefully made my way around the perimeter, trying desperately to be silent, but my heart was pounding like tribal drums in anticipation.

The shack was only a few feet away. Rough-hewn planks spotted with holes where the wood had rotted away was all that stood between me and some answers. And through the holes, I could hear voices.

"Yeah, you boys almost had me." I heard Isaac's voice through the splintered wood. He laughed, and my blood ran cold. "It's a good thing I caught on, or this would've been bad for me."

Oh shit. Isaac *was* the baddie. And I'd led my boys into a trap. There was no way I was winning Mother of the Year.

"As soon as I get out of here, I'll make sure your mother is taken care of."

I heard the boys mumbling. Obviously they were bound and gagged.

"And it's a good thing you had these sandwiches on you or I'd have to resort to cannibalism," Isaac stated, as if it were all a joke.

Damn, damn, damn! No one threatens my sons.

I hoped that Isaac's monologue was distracting him as I slipped up to the door. Taking a deep breath, I flung the door open, jumping out of the way of potential gunfire.

"Mom?"

I leaned into the doorway. Isaac, Jack and Monty were sitting on the floor of the shack, eating turkey paninis.

"Mom!" Jack sprang from the floor into my arms and pulled me into the cabin. Monty closed the door.

"You're . . . you're okay?" I blinked. "All of you?" Well, this was a bit anticlimactic.

Monty cocked his head to the side—a motion he made when he thought I'd lost my mind. "Well, duh. What did you think?"

"I . . . I . . . I . . . ," was all I could manage.

Isaac stood up, grasping my shoulders in his hands. "It's okay, Missi. We're all right."

The four of us looked at each other for a moment. They were safe. All three of them. No bad guys anywhere. I relaxed. And then I blew my stack, because I was an angry-lethal-assassin-chicken, or something like that.

"Oh my God! You guys scared the crap out of me!" I stabbed a finger toward Isaac. "And the police are looking for you! They think you've been kidnapped!"

Jackson put his hand over my mouth as Monty brought his finger to his lips and peered out of one of the knotholes.

"Your boys rescued me, Missi." Isaac shrugged.

Monty gave the all-clear sign. Jackson flashed me a look that told me to shut up.

"Isaac is an officer from Interpol, Mom! Isn't that cool?" Jack feigned fascination. Obviously, Isaac had no clue who the boys and I were (which was good), so they were pretending they'd never met anyone from that agency before. As if.

I narrowed my eyes at Isaac. "Is that so?"

He flipped out his wallet and handed it to me. Yup. It was real, all right. I'd made enough forgeries of these to know the real thing when I saw it. But what was going on? The Council would never ask me to take out an Interpol agent. We just didn't kill the good guys. Maybe he was rogue?

"But I don't understand. You said you rescued him?" I pointed at Isaac as if he were a fish or a plant.

"The guys from the show had him tied up on the seventeenth hole," Monty explained. That was only one hole away from where I'd found Sami. Either these guys weren't very imaginative or they just got bored and left them next to each other.

Jackson, as usual, added his take. "We thought something was up." He left out the fact that they knew Isaac had been taken as a challenge and was actually in no danger. My kids were good at playing dumb.

Isaac started. "Some guy was leading me into the jungle and I thought I was just doing what everyone else was. Then the moron ties me up and tells me the others have to find me or I'm off the show. Your boys came along and found me and brought me here."

I looked around the shack. Crumpled and deflated bags and boxes that had once held a delirious array of junk food peppered the corners. On my left was the generator-run minifridge I'd invented for my workshop. On top of that was a *Playboy* magazine.

"You two have been living here?" I shrieked. "I thought you said you were staying at the Tigre!" All this time I thought I was the only liar. My kids trumped me! Not like it was the first time, but it still bit.

Monty shook his head. "We did have a room at the Tigre. But we also made up this place to hang out."

My eyes widened as I looked around the seedy building. "You made this?"

Jack nodded proudly. "Yup. We found some scrap wood and put it all together using paper clips."

"And my fridge?"

The boys looked at each other. "Well," Monty said, "we needed someplace to put the pop."

It took only two steps before I was able to yank open the door. If I found beer in there, they were going to suffer. Slamming the door shut and grateful that there were only two pop cans and a water bottle inside, my rage was still boiling.

"And that?" I pointed to the magazine. On the cover was a dazed-looking blonde, half-naked in a library. She looked as though she was about to say, "Oh! I didn't see you there! It was getting hot in here so I had to remove a few articles of clothing. Is that all right?"

Isaac turned away to hide a grin. Men. Monty and Jack froze. I'm not a prude, but I don't like that crap. It's hard enough raising teenage boys. And I understand their curiosity about the female body. But the thing about these rags is that they don't show real women. Blonde Librarian looked like she'd had everything done but her eyelashes. And we are not giggling idiots, either!

The boys hung their heads. "Sorry, Mom."

For a moment, I debated the idea of letting them drown in an expletive-strewn stream of feminist dogma (swear jar be damned). But then I remembered that they had Isaac and we had to get him back to the resort to call off the search party.

"We'll talk about this later," I hissed through my teeth at my young. "We need to get Isaac back before they call out the Costa Rican national whatever."

"That's just it, Mom," Jack protested. "He's in hiding right now—since the kidnapping stunt."

"That's why we brought him here instead of returning him to you," Monty answered as if Isaac were a missing lump of headcheese.

I spun around. "Why are you in hiding? Can't we just go back?"

Isaac shook his head. "Not yet. I have to make sure you guys are safe. The man I'm dealing with is very dangerous. You could get hurt just by being with me."

I held my breath to keep from laughing. Yeah, right. We needed protection from him. If Isaac had had a clue, he'd have realized the three of us Bombays were far deadlier.

"Why?" I asked.

"I'm on a case," Isaac said using the typical vernacular these guys used on civilians. "One of the castaways is an international arms dealer."

"What? Who?" Was he joking? Uh oh. The Bombays had the wrong guy! I almost killed the wrong guy! But who was the right guy?

At that instant, the door crashed open and in walked my friend Moe, carrying a submachine gun. Huh, Moe wasn't really the washed-up loser he'd led us all to believe he was. I guess I'd really, *really* misjudged him.

Moe grinned, this time a sickly leer. "Thanks for the lead, Missi. I never would've found him if not for you."

"You followed me? How?" How had I missed a three-hundred-pound man behind me? I had to work on my skills.

He reached over and plucked a ladybug off of my tote bag. At least I thought it was a bug.

"Tracked you. I knew you'd find him."

Ah. The old ladybug-that-wasn't-a-ladybug trick. How did I fall for that one? I make them to look like flies. Far more believable than a pansy ladybug.

Moe punched Isaac with the butt of his gun, causing him to double over. "I've been trying to lose this son of a bitch for two years."

He turned the gun toward Isaac. "Tie him up," he told me. Moe kicked a length of rope toward me. "Then tie up your brats."

Well, that was just great. I hate it when someone throws rope at me and tells me to tie up my own sons. Isaac sat down in front of me, demonstrating compliance, and I tied his hands behind him. I was still in shock. Moe? Seriously?

Moe shoved Jackson toward me and Monty sat next to him. "Pretty clever—having your sons infiltrate the show. You probably could've won with a strategy like that."

I said nothing as I tied first Jackson, then Monty, hoping my silence would encourage him to talk. Of course, he didn't know I was using a special knot I'd invented when I was ten. It looked like a real nasty mess, but in truth it fell away when you pulled the left tail. Monty and Jack gave me the thumbs up behind their backs, indicating they knew what I'd done.

"I didn't want you to get hurt, Missi," Moe continued,

but not saying what I wanted him to. "I thought I could just lay low here for a while. Of course, if I knew this bastard was who he was from the beginning, I'd have killed him and moved on. Once my contacts at the Blanco Tigre told me he was Interpol, I put it all together."

"Uh, if you knew someone was tailing you for two years, how come you didn't know who he was?" Isaac asked. Maybe that was a tad impertinent.

Moe sneered and turned the gun on him. "I knew it was *someone*, dude—not you in particular. And I don't have to explain myself to you!" Moe was starting to get a bit panicky.

"Don't kill him," I said slowly, stalling for time. "Just leave us here and run." Then I almost laughed picturing a man as big as him running. I didn't really expect him to take my advice. It was just something to say.

Moe shook his head. "Too late. I tried laying booby traps but nothing worked. That damned zip line was beautiful. I had the wrong team on the right line, but those are just details. And then you screwed it all up."

"You are the saboteur?" I couldn't believe it. Big, clumsy doofus Moe.

He paused and stared at me for a moment. "You thought I was a nobody, didn't you?" He seemed surprised. "I must've done a good job fooling everyone."

"No, I wasn't fooled." Yes, I was. He did a great job.

"It doesn't matter anyway because now I have too

many witnesses." Moe leveled the gun at my head. Nasty way to die—having your skull split by machine-gun fire. A bit overly dramatic if I do say so.

"Knock it off. Kill me but leave Missi and the boys alone." Isaac was dead calm.

I rolled my eyes. "Puhleese! Don't give us that alpha-male-macho, save-the-women-and-children-first schtick!" I pointed at the magazine. "You know, both of you, it's hard enough to raise two boys without all the chauvinistic messages out there! Do you guys even think before you speak?"

Isaac and Moe looked at each other. They didn't appear to have the same mind-reading skills my boys did.

"Missi," Isaac started, "this isn't the best time to . . ."

"Oh, and I suppose it's okay to act like a gorilla when a woman is in danger. Is that it? Because I can take care of myself."

Monty and Jack were looking at each other as if to say, "Mental note—Mom needs Midol."

"And you two!" I turned toward my whelps. "Women don't want to be rescued! We're not airheads and we don't wear garters and stockings anymore!" Okay, even I wasn't sure where this was going.

"Enough!" Moe screamed. "What the hell is wrong with you?" He pointed at me. "I have a gun! That means I'm in charge and I don't need a feminist-bullshit lecture from you!"

I crossed my arms and said, "Fine! The floor is yours, Moe. If that's your real name."

"Um, no. What kind of international criminal mastermind would I be if I used my own name? Not a very good one, I can tell you that."

Isaac growled. "His name is Brad Underwood. A real, first-class asshole."

Oh boy. Here we go again. I could just picture the two of them in puffy shirts and breeks, slashing at each other with fencing foils.

Moe raised an eyebrow. "You knew more than you let on. How nice."

"And he's responsible for supplying terrorists of fifteen third-world countries with all the weapons they need to kill innocent people."

Great. Just great. The Council had given me the wrong guy.

I watched as the boys gently tugged at the knots in unison. Man, they did everything in perfect sync. Now that I thought about it, it was kind of weird. But then, this wasn't really your average situation.

Chapter Thirty

MCMANUS: *Old MacDonald had a farm, ee-i-ee-i-o.
And on that farm he shot some guys. . . .*
                                        —*The Usual Suspects*

Moe leveled his gun at Isaac, but for some reason didn't pull the trigger.

"Just shut up," Moe snapped. He was silent as he weighed his options. Unfortunately, I was convinced that each of those options included four lifeless bodies. And I couldn't allow that.

Moe held the submachine gun in a solid grip about midtorso. Rushing him wouldn't be a good idea because he could mow us down in seconds. Usually, the old adage, "rush a gun, run from a knife," is reliable. In this case it was too risky. I had to do something and fast.

"I can't believe I fell for that whole useless-fat-guy-who-is-really-an-evil-genius ploy!" I shouted dramatically. "You really had me going, thinking you lived in your mom's basement and were unemployed and ignorant!"

Monty shot me a look that said, "Um, Mom, what are you doing?" I ignored him.

"Wow. You really had me and everyone else fooled!" I slapped my forehead with cartoonish exaggeration

251

but tried to keep sarcasm out of my voice. Moe looked at me quizzically, uncomprehending. At least he took the gun off of Isaac.

"Although you must admit, you were pretty convincing," I added loudly. "I mean look at you! Who lets themself go like that in order to go underground? That must have taken some real willpower on your part. Pretty impressive!"

Moe looked at me as if I were nuts, as if he couldn't figure out whether I was insulting or complimenting him. And that's what I wanted. It was time for Crazy Missi to take over.

"I mean you really had to work at putting on all that weight and acting that stupid. How much did you have to eat to get so fat?"

"Um, what are you getting at?" Moe asked cautiously.

"Oh! Am I stealing your thunder by monologuing for you? It's just that I've never met an international criminal and I never ever would've guessed you were one. Good job!"

Moe's eyes went back and forth like a computer that couldn't make something compute. Like in *War Games*. Remember that movie? Where Matthew Broderick asked the superenormous computer to play tic-tac-toe until it wins—shutting it down in the process? I love that film.

"I always thought people like you were tall, dark and gorgeous, with a devious mind and nerves like steel. You sure had us all fooled." I was starting to worry that I was going too far.

"Listen, bitch!" Moe sputtered. "Shut up before I kill you first!"

"That's interesting! Keep us all guessing about who would be more valuable to kill first. You should write a book!" I sounded completely sincere, which confused him. *Confuse-A-Criminal*—maybe I'll trademark that phrase.

What was my strategy? Well, Lex and Sami were heading in this direction now that they hadn't found Isaac on the golf course—since, obviously, he was right here. Talking loudly might get their attention, I thought. Talking like a madwoman was just to buy time. And for fun. In spite of the danger, it *was* a little fun.

I watched as Monty and Jack each slipped the loose ropes into his grip. Smart boys.

A twig cracked outside, and Moe spun toward it, firing wildly. Taking advantage of the distraction, Monty and Jack sprang from the floor and tackled him. The big man went down like a sack of potatoes.

The door opened very slowly and I ran to it. To my horror, Sami staggered in, bleeding heavily from the shoulder.

"Dumbass!" was all she said as she slipped to the floor, unconscious.

Lex rushed into the room as I pulled Isaac's knot loose behind him. Lex kicked Moe in the head as Isaac removed the gun from his grip.

It was over. And we'd all survived it. A moan from the floor caught my attention, and I knelt beside Sami. A quick examination showed that, while no internal organs were hit, she was bleeding fast. Too fast. The boys were busy making sure Moe was tied up securely and Isaac had his gun trained on the man.

"Lex," I said and he turned to face me. "I need your belt and shirt." Lex didn't hesitate to pull off his clothes. I folded up the T-shirt to cover the wound and tied it on tightly with his belt. It wasn't that good a tourniquet but it was all I had.

"We have to move her," I said, even though I knew we shouldn't. It was very dangerous. But she was more likely to get medical help back at the resort than here in the middle of nowhere.

At my direction, Lex tore several planks of wood off the shack walls (shirtless and looking sooooo hot as he did so), and using the leftover rope, we managed to stabilize Sami. Using the invention as a makeshift cot, Lex and I carefully moved toward the trail. Isaac pushed Moe ahead of him while Jackson held one end of his bonds. Monty, my lean and lithe boy, ran like hell to the Blanco Tigre to try to advance the assistance.

Isaac, Jack and their prisoner moved faster than we did, but I wasn't pushing it. Sami had lost a lot of blood. Lex walked in front, with me in the back. She remained unconscious for a while, then started coming to, babbling incoherently about the unlikely sexual relationship between a chicken and a dog. Finally she passed out again.

Lex's naked back distracted me to no end. The man had an awesome back—muscular in all the right places, but not overly so. I shook my head to clear it.

"Why did you come looking for me?" I asked.

He said nothing for a moment. "I had to make sure you were all right."

"I'm sorry I was such a jerk," I admitted. "I really didn't mean those things I said to Dr. Andy. Especially not about you."

Lex spoke slowly. "No, I'm an asshole. I should never have accused you of destroying the show."

Neither of us said much else for the rest of the way. We simply focused on getting Sami back safely. It was a tough trip. In spite of Sami's lean physique, my arms ached as I carried my half of the litter.

We were met at the end of the trail by two paramedics, who took over carrying Sami to the ambulance. Lex and I walked through the staring resort dwellers (we probably looked pretty weird, covered in blood and Lex without a shirt) up to the conference center, where Julie ushered us into the room we'd been in earlier.

I looked around the conference room, which was full of television producers, policemen and what I assumed were network attorneys (they were wearing lawyerly shoes—dead giveaway). No one seemed to notice Lex, me or the boys. All the focus was on Isaac and Moe.

Monty and Jack hugged me, then went over to watch the chaos. I turned to Lex, and his muscular, naked chest.

"I'm sorry about your shirt and belt," I offered.

Lex smiled. "You can have the pants too, if you want."

That was all it took for me to dive into his arms. Lex kissed the top of my head. Whatever happened next didn't really matter, as long as this moment lasted forever.

Chapter Thirty-one

PLANKTON: *Hey, where'd you get that piano?*
— *SpongeBob SquarePants*

It took hours for us to sort things out. The boys disappeared, returning twenty minutes later with a Blanco Tigre shirt for Lex. He laughed as he took it from them.

"Dude, seriously, put a shirt on before Mom goes crazy," Monty said, grinning. I smacked him.

Lex pulled the shirt over his head. "No more mangoes?" he asked the boys. I guess he'd figured it out.

Jack laughed. "No more mangoes. We promise."

The police were just hauling off Moe, taking the last few bits of Isaac's statement. In the opposite corner, a red-faced Alan and worn-out Julie were being grilled by the network execs. I wondered how they'd got here so fast?

Ernie joined us, pressing cups of coffee into our hands. "They flew down yesterday to check the show out. Brought a whole team of accountants with them to investigate what was going on."

"They find anything?" Isaac asked as he joined us.

Bert shrugged beside Ernie. "About one hundred grand used for all kinds of deviant behavior."

Ernie nodded. "They even found receipts for an in-room donkey show."

Ick. I didn't even want to think about that.

"So what happens now with the contest?" I asked, thinking about Dr. Andy, Lex and Sami.

Both cameramen shook their heads. "It's over. The accountants have locked up the prize money."

"That's not fair! You dragged us all here and after what we've gone through, you aren't going to even award the prize money?"

Bert backed off. "Don't blame us! We have nothing to do with it."

"Will the show even air?" Lex asked.

"Afraid not. The attorneys are too afraid of litigation. No one will ever see this footage." Then Bert and Ernie walked away.

I looked at Lex and Isaac. Well, this was fucked-up, as Sami would say if she were here.

"Look," Lex said, "it doesn't matter. Isaac got his man and I got you. It's okay."

While I was all choked up over Lex's words, I was mad as hell about Sami. What did she get besides a bullet?

"Missi!"

That's weird. I could swear I heard California Bombay. Judging by the look on my sons' faces, I guessed my mother was standing right behind me.

"Mom? What are you doing here?" I asked as I dragged her off to an empty corner. Monty and Jack were suddenly very busy studying their hangnails. Cowards.

"I'm sorry I didn't get back to you sooner," she said,

patting my arm. "I had no idea all of this drama was happening, and we were dealing with a slight cartel invasion."

I didn't even ask. In my family, this kind of thing happened. "Mom, you sent me here to tail a Vic." I nodded toward Isaac. "A Vic who turned out to be an Interpol agent."

Cali's eyes grew wide. "Really? Well isn't that exciting!"

I crossed my arms over my chest. "You didn't know that? How could you not know that? And why would you send me after one of the good guys? It's against Bombay policy!"

Mom shifted from one foot to the other. "Let's go someplace where we can talk privately. I have a room on this floor." Then she turned and walked away as if she knew I would follow.

I stopped and told Lex to meet me at the guest-house later, then followed my mother to her room.

"So what was this really about?" I asked before the door fully closed.

"Well, dear, it was a setup." Mom fiddled nervously with a bracelet. Upon closer inspection I realized it was one of my bracelets. Did she get rid of me so she could pilfer my closet?

"A setup? What does that mean?" My mood was darkening quickly, but I'd let her finish before I "accidentally" shoved her out her window.

"The whole thing was a ploy to get you out of your office, off the island and into a social setting."

I couldn't believe what I was hearing. "Wouldn't it have just been easier to sign me up for a speed-dating seminar or something?" My nails were digging into my palms.

My beloved (and soon to be dead) mother cocked her head to one side. "It was my idea. A way to force you into a situation where you couldn't leave. I thought maybe you'd meet a man. And you did!" She clapped her hands with glee.

"You sent me on a bogus mission to kill an innocent man *just so you could force me to date*? Are you insane?"

Cali tut-tutted like I was a moron. "That's why I sent the boys, dear. To make sure you didn't kill Isaac."

I'm such an idiot. My mom set me up on this nightmare and the boys were in on it from the beginning. How could she get two minors involved? The wrong guy could've died!

The room started to spin and make flashing, popping thingies. The last thing I remembered before I hit the floor was that my mom was wearing my most expensive pair of shoes.

Chapter Thirty-two

KLYTUS: *Most effective, Your Majesty. Will you destroy this Earth?*

THE EMPEROR MING: *Later. I like to play with things awhile before annihilation.*

—*Flash Gordon*

I came to in the guesthouse, not really caring how I got there. I was just grateful that it wasn't a jail cell or a room with my mother's rotting corpse.

"You okay?" Lex's face swam into view over mine.

"I think so. Physically at least. I'm not going to promise you anything on the mental right now."

He kissed my forehead. "I'll take that."

I sat up and looked around. This was the room I shared with Sami. My stomach lurched.

"How's Sami?"

"She's just fine. It was a clean shot. She's being released as we speak. Isaac is bringing her back here."

"And my sons?" I asked, blood on my mind.

"They told me to tell you they were going home with your mom. She's nice, by the way."

"What? You met Mom?" Knowing Cali Bombay, she'd probably already proposed to Lex for me. And knowing my boys, they would be hiding on the ropes course on Santa Muerta for months waiting for me to cool down. Bile started a perilous journey up my throat and I sat up to accommodate the fury. Actually, I was beginning to embrace the fury.

Lex pushed me back down. "You need to get some sleep." He lay down next to me, holding me in his arms.

I leaned back against his chest. As much as I wanted to be part of the welcoming committee for Sami, sleep sounded like a good idea.

And it took very little time to fall into dreamland.

"Good morning, dumbass!" Sami stood in the doorway of my room, her right arm in a sling. She looked pale (which was remarkable, considering her deep tan) and thinner (which was scary, since she was thin to begin with). The superconfident-take-no-prisoners Sami was small and frail.

"Sami!" I got up to hug her, very gently. "Are you okay?"

She shrugged. "I can't work for a couple of months, but at least I'm alive! Thank you."

"Sami! You didn't swear once!" I laughed.

"Well, maybe I'm turning over a goddamned new leaf!"

I hadn't realized how late it was until I saw that Isaac and Lex were eating lunch on the veranda. Sami and I joined them, eating as if it were our last meal on earth.

What a mess I almost made out of things—screwing up with Lex, almost killing Isaac, almost losing Sami.

And yet I was so unbelievably angry at my mother and sons. That rage would have to be dealt with, and soon.

Isaac cleared his voice. "We're going to have visitors this afternoon."

I looked up, a forkful of salad en route to my open mouth. "Who?"

Lex answered. "The network. They called an hour ago to tell us."

"What do those fucktards want?" Sami asked.

"My guess is that they want to give us bad news," Isaac replied.

"Really?" I said once my mouth was empty. "How much worse could it get?"

Mr. Smith and Mr. Brown (if those were their real names) slid four sheets of watermarked, vellum paper toward us. Smith and Brown were attorneys for the CAB network. As they explained, we needed to sign legal documents absolving the network of liability for any wrongdoing. None of this was, of course, CAB's fault and we should be grateful they allowed us out of the show.

I slid the forms back toward them. "Shove it up your ass," I said politely.

Lex, Sami and Isaac said nothing. They had my back.

Mr. Smith (who wouldn't tell me his first name—which pissed me off) slid them back to us. "Ms. Bombay, you signed a release when the program commenced agreeing to whatever terms the corporation determines necessary."

"Billy," I replied, assigning him a random name since the bastard wouldn't give me his, "we're not signing anything. In fact, our attorney is on her way down from New York right now to look into suing your network for ten million dollars."

"My name is not Billy," Smith answered tensely.

"Since you wouldn't give me your name, I made one up," I said. "You didn't have me sign anything saying I couldn't do that, did you?" I waited as he nodded. "So, Billy, my attorney has reviewed the documents we signed and says we have a 99.7 percent chance of winning."

All right, so I made that up too. I just wanted to watch them squirm. I didn't have Mother or the boys to punish, so these two suits would have to do. In all honesty, the Bombays have the best law firm in the world representing them. I was pretty sure we could at least score twenty million if we tried.

Smith looked at Brown, whom I didn't have a name for yet. Brown shrugged, which was good because I was thinking of calling him Seymour.

"What do you suggest, Ms. Bombay?" A vein on Smith's neck twitched.

"I want you to award the twenty-five-thousand-dollar prize money to Ms. Sami Lee. I also insist that you pay her medical bills and pay full transportation home for her. Then I, Mr. Danby and Mr. Beckett will sign your forms."

Smith's eyebrows went up. "And Ms. Lee? She signs too, right?"

"Wrong. She doesn't sign anything and you walk away hoping she doesn't change her mind and come after the network." I leaned back and crossed my arms. I had considered making them wrestle crocodiles too—without muzzles. But the others thought that might be a smidge over the top. *Sigh.*

Smith shook his head. "I'm afraid that's unacceptable."

I sighed because it looked dramatic and, using the remote, clicked on the TV. There, on the screen, was footage of Alan snorting cocaine off a donkey's ass. In the corner of the screen was a little CAB logo. Alan then began to spill the dirty little secrets of seven of the twelve members of the network's board of directors. Talk about sexually repressed. Ernie had given me the tape for free. I tipped him five grand for the favor.

Brown leaned forward, pushing forms toward only me, Lex and Isaac. "I think we have a deal, Ms. Bombay."

The men returned with a check within the hour and the hospital confirmed that the bill had been paid. I let them have the tape. I had two more in my suitcase. A girl needs all the blackmail material she can get.

Chapter Thirty-three

SAM TREADWELL: *The man is a psychopathic killer.*
GINGER: *Don't impose your values on me, Sam.*
—Cherry 2000

After helping Sami and Isaac into the car that would take them to the airport, Lex and I strolled back to the now-empty El Conquistador guesthouse.

"I'm sorry, but there's something rude I must ask you." Lex said this while nuzzling my ear on the veranda after some explosive sex.

"Hmmmm?"

"How can you afford this place? The accountants didn't mention a guesthouse on CAB's bill, so unless you're deeply involved in identity theft, you are paying for it."

I stared into his lovely eyes for a moment. There was no way I could lie to him anymore. I'd jumped the shark on that one too many times. It was time to tell him the truth, and maybe face the fact that he'd run screaming out the door. Taking his hand, I led him into the house to the dining room where I opened a bottle of ridiculously expensive wine.

"Do you really want to know the truth?" I asked as I handed him a glass.

He nodded. "I really want to know."

We sat down and I didn't speak at first. I mean, how do you tell the man you love that you are an assassin and come from a long line of assassins?

"I'm an assassin and I come from a long line of assassins." Oooooookay. Not exactly poetic, but there it was.

Lex nodded indicating he wanted me to continue. So I did. I started with the whole history of how a young Greek woman in 2000 BCE with a name I found totally unpronounceable decided that she wanted to be an assassin. After that, I wound my way through history, leaving out the names of our victims of course, and ended up with my story. How Rudy died, how I retreated to Santa Muerta and blew things up for fun. I didn't tell him about the bobblehead doll collection. I'm not a total git.

As I sat back in my chair and swallowed the last of the five bottles we'd gone through, I could see he was working through everything I'd told him.

I failed to mention that if the Bombays knew I'd told him before he legally became a Bombay, he'd end up one of my assignments, but there's only so much you should tell your date the first time.

The sun was rising, indicating we'd been up all night with this. How long would he need before he said anything?

And what would that be, "Sorry, Missi. It's against everything I believe in to even know you. We'll always have Costa Rica"?

"Missi?" Lex said for what I realized was the third or fourth time.

"Uh, yes?"

"You didn't explain the money part."

"I didn't? Oh. Um, we all have huge trust funds. I'm independently wealthy." That was easy. Hopefully all of his other questions would be like that.

"So Monty and Jackson are killers too?"

Okay, that's a bit tougher than I'd hoped. Maybe I could come up with something really profound to explain this.

"Yes. I've been training them since they were five."

Lex sighed. "You only kill bad guys, right?"

That sounded like a good sign. "Absolutely! Which was why I was so angry that the Council had sicced me on an Interpol agent."

He looked out the window, then back at me. "I love you. I knew it that first night out there on the patio."

I reached for his hand. "I love you too. I know this is pretty hard to accept and I understand that."

Lex shook his head. "It's not that. It's just that I don't know if I can handle it if my girlfriend has more money than I do."

"Does . . . does that mean it's okay?" Did it? I really didn't expect him to accept it so easily.

"I don't know if it will ever be okay, but this is a package deal. If I want you, I have to realize who you are."

"Um, okay. Does that mean you still want me?"

"I do. But we need to work on our relationship for a while until I get used to it. Is that all right?"

I nodded. Then I dragged him into the bedroom for some scorching-hot howler monkey sex.

"Where are we going?" Lex asked as we stood on the tarmac in San Jose. He looked really good in his white linen shirt and new sunglasses.

"I thought we needed a little time away, just the two of us." I spotted the Bombay jet and picked up my bag. Lex followed.

"We need to spend some time getting to know each other," I added.

Lex's eyebrows went up as we climbed aboard and the pilot greeted us. I was really impressed that he didn't say anything about money.

We taxied down the runway and I leaned against him. Lex smelled like coconut and cocoa butter. That's a good smell.

"You sure you can take more time off of work?" I asked him as the plane lifted into the air.

"Oh, I think I can swing it." He leaned to kiss my hair and I sighed. This was only the beginning. We had two weeks ahead of us to explore the attraction that held us together. For now, we would take it slowly, getting to know one another.

But I had a good idea that everything was going to turn out just fine in the end.

Epilogue

Let the others make statues of Apollo and Mercury and Hercules. . . . You're the man I want to chisel.
—Gracie Allen

It only took a few months and a lot of sex for Lex (hey, that rhymes) to decide I was more important than what the Bombays do. It took a lot of talking to draw it out, but somehow he chose me. I can't imagine how hard it must be for outsiders to marry into the Bombays. Men have to take the family name as their own and become part of a secret that has made many men lose their minds. The women seem to have no problem with it, though. I wonder why that is?

After a quick trip to the mainland to get married and a two-week honeymoon in Mongolia, my new husband moved into the condo on Santa Muerta.

By this time, the boys were visiting colleges in the States nearly every weekend and I'd accepted that. Lex took to my workshop with bizarre zeal and together we've blown up a lot of stuff.

Of course, that meant he eventually found my B-list bobbleheads, and after some counseling I think our marriage will survive it.

Actually, Lex's talents as a stuntmaster have improved my game. He's been able to look at my inventions in a whole new way. This is largely because before, he had to stop people from getting hurt whereas now, death is the desired result.

Mom threw a huge reception on the island when we returned from our honeymoon and the whole Bombay clan attended. Mostly this was because my relatives wanted to see what kind of man the goofy inventor would choose. Yes, I know what they all think of me. It's never really mattered and they don't care, especially when I can whip up cell phones that shoot lasers and can still hold five thousand songs.

It was wonderful to see everyone. Gin, Diego and Romi flew in with Dak, Leonie, Louis and Sofia. Liv and Todd and their kids were there. Coney gave me a beautiful felted bag he picked up during his travels. The wool had had been dyed into the shades of a Caribbean sunset and I loved it.

In the end, it all worked out. Moe was tried and convicted and sentenced to a lifetime in prison. Duh. Sami started her own business, teaming up with a female plumber and carpenter. The company slogan is "If you want it done right the first time, hire a woman." She's doing very well. I sent her the swear jar. She mailed back a note saying, "Fuck you." I had it framed.

As for Alan, he ended up a porn star in Thailand. I heard he's pretty popular with the sex tourism trade there. I know, you're thinking, "how predictable." I guess the network launched a huge lawsuit so he fled the country to avoid paying. Maybe I'll get a contract on him someday. His stage name is Dick Dangleballs and he does this really weird thing with mayonnaise and rope you have to see to believe. What? It's on YouTube.

Julie became a cruise activities director for a shipping line in Finland. She did okay for a while, until the entire boat—passengers and crew—mutinied, marooning her on an uncharted island near Kiribati, known to be populated with cannibals. No one has seen her since.

As for the others? Let's see, Dr. Andy had a talk-radio show in Mobile, Alabama. He had a pretty good run too. If only he hadn't dared that suicide caller to actually take those pills. Now he works at the Department of Transportation asking people how their driver's license photos make them feel. One woman stabbed him in the shoulder with a pencil. He's doing better now.

In happier news, Silas achieved his ultimate fantasy when he was killed accidentally by a canon misfire during a recreation of the Battle of Gettysburg. (I'll bet he was ecstatic—he actually died at Gettysburg.)

To everyone's surprise, Kit made it as a model. She's the poster girl for the Society to Prevent Anal Leakage. I've seen her commercials and constipated-looking countenance everywhere.

Lilianna has actually started creating art. No longer does she just think about it. Lex and I went to a show she had in a small town in northern Montana. It was pretty interesting to see busts of famous Montanans carved out of patchouli-scented mashed bananas.

I heard that Brick/Norman was doing a one-man

show in LA about his experience on *Survival*. Of course, no one even knows what that is since the show never aired, but oh well.

Bob the politician finally ran out of political positions to run for in his hometown of Leavenworth, Kansas. After a disastrous, yet inspired campaign for county coroner (on a platform that included the ability to slay zombies should the dead ever rise in the morgue), he decided to launch a bid for president of the United States. He's counting on being a write-in. I guess Kit endorsed him, so he may have the incontinence vote sewn up.

Turns out Cricket and Jimmy the cameraman were screwing around during the show and she was keeping his hotel-room key hidden in her pockets while with us. In the aftermath, they got Bert and Ernie to help them set up a filmmaking camp for blind kids in Banff. I'm pretty sure the irony is lost on them.

So everything worked out okay. Lex even has some great ideas for using stunts with my inventions on assignments. (I just loooooove the human catapult he came up with.) Who knew I would really enjoy having a man in my life? Well, okay, my mother did. And after I've had my fill of tormenting her by spiking her tea with my severe, intestinal gas–producing and sleep-inducing powder (laxatives are sooooo juvenile and she's a hit at Council meetings), I might just agree with her.

A beautiful young blonde was so depressed she decided
to end her life by throwing herself into the ocean. But
just before she could throw herself from the docks, a
handsome young sailor stopped her.

"You have so much to live for," said the sailor. "Look,
I'm off to Europe tomorrow and I can stow you away
on my ship. I'll take care of you, bring you food every
day, and keep you happy."

With nothing to lose, combined with the fact that
she had always wanted to go to Europe, the blonde
accepted. That night the sailor brought her aboard
and hid her in a lifeboat. From then on every night he
would bring her three sandwiches and make love to
her until dawn.

Three weeks later she was discovered by the captain
during a routine inspection.

"What are you doing here?" asked the captain.

"I had an arrangement with one of the sailors," the
blonde replied. "He brings me food, and I get a free
trip to Europe. Plus, he's screwing me."

"He certainly is," replied the captain. "This is the Staten Island Ferry."

This particular blonde stood pier-side and cast a land-lubber's eye on the huge, bright white cruise ship docked to receive passengers at the Port of Galveston.

I found myself experiencing a similar sense of *caveat emptor*. You know. *Let the buyer beware.*

Okay, okay, so *I* wasn't actually the buyer of record here. My passage had been bought and paid for by my grandma and her hubby of less than seventy-two hours. Still that totally insignificant, piddling little detail didn't exempt this virgin sailor from feelings of nervousness and a nagging sense of unease that so didn't bode well for one's maiden voyage.

How do you say *Titanic*? Gulp.

I watched the few remaining stragglers as they prepared to board the vessel ahead of us. They chatted and laughed while they waited to have their paperwork and identification cleared. I gnawed away at a newly polished nail.

"Something wrong, girlie?" asked my seventy-something-year-old "new" step-granddaddy, Joe Townsend. "Afraid you won't have sea legs?" he asked.

More like fear of design flaws, inferior steel, and too few lifeboats.

"Legs like that"—I gave 'Grampa Joe's' scrawny, chicken legs a nod—"and you're worried about *my* sea legs?" I shrugged off my uncharacteristic anxiety issues. "Give me a break. And you should have warned us you were planning to put on shorts. You know. So we could don protective eyewear," I said. "The reflection from those white legs is brutal."

When Joe Townsend failed to fire back with one of his trademark, take-no-prisoners responses, I frowned.

"Aren't you going to respond to that?" I asked. "You know. Make a remark about how it's a wonder anyone can see you at all with my thunder thighs blocking the view. Maybe take this opportunity to remind me about the blonde pirate who walked around with the paper towel on top of her head because she had a *Bounty* on her head?"

He shook his head.

"Nothing?" I asked and blinked. "You got nothing?"

Joe shrugged.

"This is so not like you," I said and put a hand to his forehead. "Are you sick? Too much connubial bliss, maybe? Or are you suffering from constipation? Not enough fiber in your diet?"

He slapped my hand away. "No!" he said. "But I'm your stepgrandpa now. I have to set an example. Act like a mature adult. Be a role model."

That one got my attention. Role model? Who was he kidding? The old guy had been known to maintain surveillance logs on his neighbors' comings and goings, pack unregistered heat (he considered the Colt Python a collector's item and, therefore, exempt), and was probably on a government watch list somewhere from frequenting websites that featured terms such as *mercenary, covert, commando*, and *assassin* in their domain names.

I admit I've pimped his predilections for senior snooping in the past but always for the greater good, I assure you. Joe helped me get the down-home dirt on some prime crime stories that not only saved my cowgirl cookies but also resuscitated a "code blue" newspaper reporting career a year or so back.

Our crime-fighting collaboration makes the *Rush Hour* duo look as tame as Holmes and Watson in comparison. A cantankerous crime-fighter wannabe with NRA and AARP memberships who fantasizes about black masks and dark capes paired with a blonde, frizzy-haired, aspiring reporter working two dead-end part-time jobs and hauling around a history of chronic misadventure and long-term self-esteem issues related to a nickname that sums it all up: *Calamity Jayne*. Uh, yup. That's me. Tressa Jayne Turner, aka Calamity Jayne. Grandville, Iowa's answer to extreme boredom.

The totally misplaced moniker was bestowed courtesy of my new grampa's grandson and my new stepcousin, Ranger Rick Townsend—yet another Townsend male who wreaks havoc with my psyche. Oh, and with certain unmentionable parts of my anatomy that will go . . . unmentioned.

Rick Townsend is a uniformed officer with the Iowa Division of Natural Resources (I love a man in uniform, don't you?) and he gives a new meaning to the term "kissin' cousins." Oh, and "keeping it in the family."

Hubba hubba.

I shook my head to get myself back on topic and away from naughty nautical girl thoughts.

"Excuse me, but did you just say you were a role model, Joe?" I asked. "Role model? As in what? The neighborhood watch commander? A Green Hornet groupie?" (Joe's deceased first wife had been particularly enamored the TV comic crime-fighter in the sixties.) "A geriatric GI Joe, maybe?" I suggested, hoping to get a rise out of Joe. Or, at the very least, a rise in his blood pressure. Something. Anything. Joe's born-again, turn-the-other-cheek attitude was giving me a pain in a couple of my cheeks (the gluteus maximus ones) and making me more leery—and suspicious—by the minute.

"Role model as in your basic, loving, caring grandparent, of course," Joe replied. "What else?"

*Oo*kay. This was getting downright scary.

"Ain't that boat somethin'?" My gammy snapped a picture with the digital camera my folks had gifted the newly married couple with to use on their honeymoon cruise.

"I think this vessel qualifies as a ship, Hannah," Ranger Rick Townsend, boat aficionado, and stickler for proper sailing terms it appeared, corrected. "And it is something," he added. "Would you like me to take a picture of the happy couple as you embark on your very own honeymoon loveboat?" Townsend offered, reaching out to take the camera. "Smile and say bon voyage!" Ranger Rick snapped the picture. He looked at it. "Perfect!"

"You sure it's not overexposed?" I asked. "You know. From the glare bouncing off Joe's legs there?" I snorted. I crack me up sometimes.

"We can't all carry off the oh-so attractive farmer tan like you do, girlie," Joe said. "Those cowboy boot lines are particularly fetching."

I searched for my customary snarky comeback but was too relieved the cantankerous Joe I was used to had returned and things were back to normal to lob one back at him. Well, whatever passes as normal with a Townsend, that is.

"You'll get rid of those tan lines in no time," Ranger Rick said with a lift to his dark brows. "By sunbathing as God intended," he explained, flashing me a smile hot enough to send tiny rivulets of sweat trickling between my size-B boobs.

"Maybe I'll do just that," I said, adding a challenging lift of my own brow. "Care to join me?"

"I'm in!" My wrinkled, shriveling, shrunken grandmother stuck her hand up faster than she had when she volunteered me as Mort the Mystic's guinea pig for the hypnosis portion of the evening's entertainment at the State Fair several years ago. And just so you know, I was the most realistic chicken on that stage. Okay, so I was a little handicapped in the breast department. But I kicked tail feathers with my deeply evocative strut and cluck.

"I don't plan on missin' out on anything," my gammy continued. "You never know if this will be my first and last cruise, so I'm goin' for the gusto. What about you, Joe? You gonna let it all hang out?" she asked her new husband.

I winced. The very thought of anything physically attached to Mr. or Mrs. Joseph Townsend, Esquire naked and hanging out made my innards revolt. And I wasn't even aboard the ship yet.

"You never know what this old salt'll be up to," Joe responded, his eyes on me. "One thing I know for sure. It's going to be a whale of a sail. 'Don't rock the boat, baby.'" He started to sing and I looked at Townsend, Jr.

"Remind me again why I agreed to come on this shipwreck lookin' for a place to happen," I said.

He put an arm around my shoulders.

"Don't you remember? You signed on as my own personal purser," he reminded me. He squeezed my arm. "You jumped at the opportunity once you saw my benefit package. Remember?"

If possible I grew even hotter. I needed a drink. Bad. One of those exotic fruity ones with the cute little umbrella stuck in it. At the rate I was heating up, I'd have to stick the tiny umbrella upside down in my cleavage to catch the river of perspiration running between my breasts. Rick Townsend knew just how to turn up my internal thermometer while the roguish ranger didn't even appear to break a sweat. So not fair.

"As I recall, I was promised one sweet sign-on bonus," I reminded Townsend. "When can I expect to see it?"

"How about when you come to turn down my bed and plump my pillows?" he asked.

"I see. So when hell freezes over then," I told him.

"I have a stateroom all to myself, you know," Townsend reminded me, lowering his head to put on his hangdog look. "All alone. A romantic cruise ship. Couples everywhere. Don't you feel some sympathy for me?"

I might. If I didn't know that Rick Townsend was about as likely to be a lonely sailor as I was to strip down to my altogether and stretch out on the lounger next to my au naturelle granny and volunteer to apply her tanning oil. Eeoww.

I patted Townsend's tanned cheek.

"Poor baby," I said. "But I hear these cruises are filled with tons of single women searching for romance on the high seas. Maybe you'll get lucky and meet the perfect one. One who is comfortable caring for the slithering residents of Ranger Rick's reptile ranch while you're off on some hunting or fishing expedition or another, who carries her very own impressive rack, and lives only to please her man. Isn't that what most randy ranger types look for in a woman?"

"You know me better than that, Tressa," Townsend said. "But you're right about one thing. If what I've heard about cruises is right, there's usually an abundance of young, willing flesh to keep a sailor company on a long, lonesome voyage. But remember, my cabin door is always open to you."

"Uh, that's stateroom door, ye scurvy, ignorant wretch," I corrected in my best pirate lingo. "Arrrggh, it's the plank for you matey!"

"You're not going to keep that up the entire cruise, are you?" Joe Townsend cut in.

"What? Keep what up?" I asked.

"All the sea-faring speak and pirate prattle," he elaborated.

I looked at him. "I don't know. Does it bother you?"

"It irritates the hell out of me," Joe said.

"Good to know, Gilligan," I said. "Good to know. And pardon me for getting into the seafaring spirit of things. Jeesch."

We made our way to the front of the line and showed our tickets and government-issued I.D. cards to the uniformed crew and went through security procedures before we were permitted aboard. Once officially checked in, strapping young porters took our carry-on luggage and secured our stateroom assignments.

Our accommodations were located on the veranda deck—arranged to permit the newly "blended family" an opportunity to blend, according to my gammy. With the exception of my sister, Taylor, and yours truly, everyone else had upgraded to exterior staterooms or suites with ocean views or balconies. Taylor and I would share an interior stateroom. How do you say claustrophobic?

Still, beggars couldn't be choosers, I thought.

Townsend nudged my arm as he followed his folks down the narrow hall to their accommodations.

"You might regret not taking me up on my offer," Townsend said. "Your sister got air sick on the plane coming here and car sick on the shuttle from the airport. I can't even begin to imagine what sea swells will do to her. Better keep the barf bags handy, mate," he said and grinned and saluted me before moving on down the hall.

I shook my head. Just set foot on the ship and already he thought he was the friggin' lounge act.

"Here we are, ladies." The fit, blonde cabin boy with short-cropped hair, highlighted tips, and cute knees slipped the computerized keycard in the slot. "Your luggage should already be in your stateroom," he said, opening the door to our cabin. Once we entered, he handed a card to me and one to Taylor. His look lingered on Taylor, his fingertips slow to release her card when she reached for it.

"Are you by any chance a personal trainer?" he asked Taylor and she shook her head.

"Aerobics instructor, maybe?"

I smirked. Oh, buddy. Did this guy need help on his pickup lines or what?

Taylor smiled at him, her face still pale and wan from the shuttle transport. "No. I just like to keep in shape," she said.

"Oh. Right." I thought he looked a tad bewildered.

"Right." He glanced over at me and gave me one of those up and down body looks.

I shrugged. "I just like to eat," I said.

"I see," he said.

"From what I hear, this is the place for me," I commented, thinking of the stories I'd heard about cruises' breakfast buffets, the dessert buffets, the all-night buffets. A tiny droplet of drool escaped the corner of my mouth.

"You're right there," he said. "Well, I'll leave you to unpack." Taylor handed him a tip and he nodded as he backed out of the room. "If there's anything you need, don't hesitate to let me know." He pointed at his name plate on his shirt. "Just ask for Denny."

"You aren't by any chance affiliated with the restaurant by the same name, are you?" I joked. "Because their sausage and hash brown skillet with a side of cakes is to die for," I added, already looking forward to indulging my Midwestern appreciation for good—and abundant—food.

He looked at Taylor.

"Good luck," he said and left.

I frowned.

"Good luck? What did he mean by that?" I asked.

"I have no idea," my sister said and dropped to the bunk farthest from the door and nearest the john. "I'll take this bed," she said.

"Okay," I agreed, noting the sweat beads popping out on her upper lip like tiny blisters. Her pallid complexion. The long, drawn-out moan. And we hadn't even raised anchor yet.

Ohmigawd. The puke pails! Where were the puke pails?

"Denny!" I opened the stateroom door and barreled out of the room. "Oh, Denny! Ooompf!" I plowed into something rock-hard. Like a brick wall. Or one of those long, heavy punching bags like Rocky Balboa beat up on when he was trying to whoop Apollo Creed. And Apollo Creed Part II. And Mr. T. And that big, tall Russian who looked like RoboCop.

Only this impenetrable object had a heartbeat. And respiration. And body heat that caused my own temperature to rise quicker than the fur on my gammy's cat, Hermoine, when my two golden labs, Butch and Sundance, invaded her space.

I found my fingers tracing the outlines of abs that seemed chiseled in stone. I looked up and spotted pecs that strained the limits of the black T-shirt covering them. My eyes traveled to an arm so large it was bigger around than my thigh. (Hey, now. Be nice.) My heated gaze came to rest on a tattoo I'd seen before. A very distinctive tattoo. A tattoo that could belong to only one person.

The time it had taken for drool to collect in my mouth as I'd pondered all-you-can-eat breakfasts and all-night-long buffets, my saliva dried up in half that time once reality set in.

I didn't need to examine the thick, corded neck; the rugged, stubbled jaw; or the full, sensuous lips for positive identification. I didn't need to note the ear-ring in a finely shaped lobe or study the arrogant contour of the nose to make sure. I didn't need to lock gazes with irises so dark against the white of the pupils they appeared jet black for positive identification.

But I did it all just the same.

My belly did a flip flop that had nothing to do with moving water beneath my feet when hot breath seared my face.

"Ahoy, Barbie."

Okay, I admit it. I dribbled in my drawers here. Nothing significant. And I was wearing white so who knew?

"Ahoy back," was all I could think of to say. I was in shock. Or maybe denial. This was the very last person in the world I expected to run into outside my stateroom on the Custom Cruise Ship, *The Epiphany*. The bad-boy biker I'd first met at a smoky bowling alley bar and later bailed out of jail for fighting. A guy I next encountered in a makeshift cell on the Iowa State Fairgrounds. A specimen whose size made me feel like Tinkerbell in comparison. Okay, okay, more like Peter Pan.

Yet here he stood. All six foot three of him.

Manny DeMarco/Dishman/da name du jour.

My super-sized, super sexy, super-secret, so-faux "fiancé."

How do you say *abandon ship*!

What's a blonde pirate always looking for, even
though it's right behind her?
Her booty.

ANCHORS AWEIGH

Ahoy, mateys! With her grandma wedded and bedded
(eeow!) Tressa Jayne Turner is looking forward to the
weeklong cruise that follows. Good food. Warm beaches.
Romantic sunsets. A swashbuckling ranger-type, Rick
Townsend, who shivers her timbers. Nothing can take the
wind out of Tressa's sails this time.

Nothing except this *Love Boat*'s the *Titanic*. For one thing,
it's a lo-cal cruise. And Tressa's barely got her sea legs before a dastardly murder plot bobs to the surface. Add one
whale of a Bermuda love triangle, and Tressa knows just
how Captain Jack Sparrow feels when the rum is gone.

Kathleen Bacus

ISBN 13: 978-0-505-52735-6

To order a book or to request a catalog call:
1-800-481-9191
This book is also available at your local bookstore, or you can
check out our Web site **www.dorchesterpub.com** where you
can look up your favorite authors, read excerpts, or glance at
our discussion forum to see what people have to say about
your favorite books.

> "Carpe Scrotum. *Seize Life by the Testicles.*"
> —*Electra-Djerroldina*

Knight's Fork

The Queen Consort of the Volnoth needs a sperm donor, and only one green-eyed god has the right stuff. Little does she know she has pinned all her hopes on the crown jewels of the fabled Royal Saurian Djinn. Not only is he the son of her greatest enemy, but he has taken a vow of chastity.

The Saurian Knight is caught between a problem father who has all the moral integrity of a Mafia Don, and a married Princess who would stop at nothing to have his seed in her belly. No matter which way he turns, he's "forked."

Taking the wrong lover…in the wrong place, at the wrong time…is dangerous. And when the High and Mighty intervene, it can be fatal. Can true love and a pure White Knight's virtue triumph, when society loves a right royal scandal?

Rowena Cherry

ISBN 13: 978-0-505-52740-0

It's never a good day when an ancient demon shows up on your toilet.

ANGIE FOX

For Lizzie Brown, that's just the beginning. Soon her hyperactive terrier starts talking, and her long-lost biker-witch grandma is hurling Smucker's jars filled with magic. Just when she thinks she's seen it all, Lizzie learns she's a demon slayer—and all hell is after her.

The Accidental Demon Slayer

That's not the only thing after her. Dimitri Kallinikos needs Lizzie to slay a demon of his own. But how do you talk a girl you've never met into going straight to the underworld? Lie. And if that doesn't work, how dangerous could a little seduction be…?

ISBN 13: 978-0-505-52769-1

To order a book or to request a catalog call:
1-800-481-9191
This book is also available at your local bookstore, or you can check out our Web site **www.dorchesterpub.com** where you can look up your favorite authors, read excerpts, or glance at our discussion forum to see what people have to say about your favorite books.

The Druid Made Me Do It

NATALE STENZEL

For centuries he's worked his magic, seducing and pleasuring women as befits his puca nature. But Kane made one big mistake—punishing his brother for a crime he did not commit.

Oh yeah, he also left Dr. Janelle Corrington after the most amazing night of her life.

She thought she'd made a once-in-a-lifetime soul connection, but he was simply having sex. Why else would he have disappeared without a word?

That's why the Druid Council's punishment for Kane's other crime is so delicious: for him to be Janelle's ward, to make amends to all he harmed, to take responsibility for his actions. Finally, Kane would have to take things seriously. And only true love would be rewarded.

Sometimes, it's good to be guilty.

ISBN 13: 978-0-505-52777-6

Award-Winning Author

Minda Webber

The Daughters Grimm

In eighteenth-century Cornwall, life as a Grimm sister could be...well, grim. But when an aunt invited the self-proclaimed beauty Rae, and Greta, her literary-minded sister, to the Black Forest, things started to shape up. With all the paranormal oddities cropping up, life in this forest was better than being two Corny hens, and the hairier their situations got, the clearer it was to both sisters that, like Little Red Riding Hood, they'd stumbled onto a couple of wolves...and would love every minute of it.

ISBN 13: 978-0-505-52771-4

☐ YES!

Sign me up for the Love Spell Book Club and send my
FREE BOOKS! If I choose to stay in the club, I will pay only
$8.50* each month, a savings of $6.48!

NAME: _____

ADDRESS: _____

TELEPHONE: _____

EMAIL: _____

☐ I want to pay by credit card.

☐ VISA   ☐ MasterCard.   ☐ DISCOVER

ACCOUNT #: _____

EXPIRATION DATE: _____

SIGNATURE: _____

Mail this page along with $2.00 shipping and handling to:
Love Spell Book Club
PO Box 6640
Wayne, PA 19087
Or fax (must include credit card information) to:
610-995-9274

You can also sign up online at **www.dorchesterpub.com**.

*Plus $2.00 for shipping. Offer open to residents of the U.S. and Canada only. Canadian
residents please call 1-800-481-9191 for pricing information.

If under 18, a parent or guardian must sign. Terms, prices and conditions subject to
change. Subscription subject to acceptance. Dorchester Publishing reserves the right to
reject any order or cancel any subscription.